NAMED BEST BOOK OF THE YEAR BY THE SOUTHWESTERN BOOKSELLERS ASSOCIATION

"Meredith is an artist with words. Her well-rounded characters are vivid, her presentation of idiomatic language makes for realistic dialogue, and the almost unknown geographical area seems more than a spot on a large-scale map."
Murder Ad Lib

"Meredith has another winner."
The El Paso Times

Also by D.R. Meredith
Published by Ballantine Books:

MURDER BY IMPULSE
MURDER BY DECEPTION
MURDER BY MASQUERADE
MURDER BY REFERENCE
THE SHERIFF AND THE PANHANDLE MURDERS

THE
SHERIFF
AND THE
BRANDING
IRON
MURDERS

D.R. Meredith

BALLANTINE BOOKS • NEW YORK

Copyright © 1985 by D.R. Meredith

All rights reserved under International and Pan-American Copyright Conventions. Published in the United States of America by Ballantine Books, a division of Random House, Inc., New York, and simultaneously in Canada by Random House of Canada Limited, Toronto. Originally published by Walker Publishing Company, Inc. in 1985.

Library of Congress Catalog Card Number: 91-93143

ISBN 0-345-36950-5

Manufactured in the United States of America

First Ballantine Books Edition: September 1992

In memory of my brother,
Jim Moser,
who always cared

ACKNOWLEDGMENTS

David Hawkins;
Mary and Tommy Hodnett, Sneed Ranch, Moore County, Texas; P. J. Pronger, The Lost Camp Ranch, Sherman County, Texas; Ollie Phillips, Weymouth Ranch, Moore and Potter Counties, Texas; Cathy and Harley Kiser, formerly of the Weymouth Ranch; Bert Clifton, curator of the Moore County Museum; Phoebe Strother and the staff of Killgore Memorial Library; Carolyn Stallwitz, who kept me from making critical errors when describing Willie's sketches; and John Erickson, my very favorite modern cowboy

The Texas Panhandle exists, the plazas did exist, but the characters, places, and events in this story will exist only if the reader believes in them.

PREFACE

For every writer there is a special book, one that is more than images projected on the blank screen of the creative mind and translated into words, but a sensory and emotional experience. The writer does not merely create the story; she lives it in some inexplicable way. For me, *The Sheriff and the Branding Iron Murders* is that book. It is the story of a people little understood and much misunderstood, whose past is (as Meenie says) "if not yesterday, at least late last week." It is a story of cowboys and culture, and neither is a myth. But most of all, it is a story with a sense of place: the Texas Panhandle. The events, the motives, the characters, all are influenced by the environment, that vast, treeless, waterless expanse of land and of empty sky that men seek to control, and failing that, to coexist with.

It is that sense of place, its influence, and the characters' reaction to it that provide most of the material in this revised edition. *The Sheriff and the Branding Iron Murders* has not been rewritten as much as it has been restored. The 1985 edition was shorn of certain characters, much of its sense of place, and had its subplot shortened in order to fit within a set number of pages. Economic needs dictated the form of its publication. But nothing lasts forever, and economic needs gave way to artistic needs as both critics and industry recognized that a specific regional setting lent strength and vitality to a mystery novel. As a result, that very special book whose story and characters I loved so well has been restored to its original length.

CHAPTER

1

HE'D LIVED TOO LONG IN THE TEXAS PANHANDLE to be scared by a twister. Respectful, yes. A man who didn't respect that whirling funnel of wind was a damn fool, and Willie Russell wasn't a fool. But he wasn't fixing to bolt for a cellar every time some TV weatherman hollered ''Storm!'' either. Hell, if a man did that, half of Texas would live underground during the spring. Crawford County's being under a tornado watch wasn't going to change his plans. If one did strike, he'd be safe. Red Barn Cave had sheltered bootleggers from the revenuers during the Thirties; it ought to keep one broken-down cowboy artist safe from the weather.

And he was damn sure broken-down, he thought as he dismounted, grimacing as pain shot through his back. A bad disk, the doc said. Not that he was going to let somebody cut him open to fix it. Hell, every cowboy had back trouble. You couldn't ride a horse for hours every day, not to mention getting throwed every now and then, without ending up with a bad back. He was just getting old, too old to be climbing on horseback to chase cattle out of the Canadian River. And certainly too damn old to be working twelve to fourteen hours a day when the winter wind blew out of the north and cut through you like a knife.

He grinned to himself as he reached in his breast pocket for his chewing tobacco. Not that the summers were much better—the winds were hot, and dried a man out instead of

1

freezing him solid. Plus, you had the dust and flies. And dumb cattle. Cowboying might be all right if you didn't have to work with cattle. If a fellow could just practice his riding and roping, instead of fixing fence and trying to round up the dumb brutes, there'd be more cowboys than ranches to hire them.

He held his horse's reins and looked toward the southwest at the boiling gray clouds. Those weathermen just might be right for a change. Those clouds were bad, all dark with lightning stabbing through them. He sighed and unfastened the cinch strap of his saddle. If a twister hit, it hit. There was nothing he could do to stop it.

Stripping off his saddle and saddlebags, he faced a more immediate danger. If he didn't hobble his horse, the damn animal would head back toward the ranch and he'd be stuck on foot. And, in spite of what greenhorn Yankees might think, boots were made for riding horseback, not for walking. The heels were too high and the soles too slick. He'd slip and bust himself on the grass a hundred times before he made it back to headquarters.

If he hobbled his horse and a twister did hit, the poor dumb animal would have no chance to get away. Hell of a situation for a man to be in, having to decide between two evils. Putting his saddle on the ground, he glanced up at the clouds and shrugged his shoulders. Unbuckling a short piece of leather from around the horse's neck, he looped it around the animal hocks just above the hoofs, slipped the two ends through O-rings to make a figure eight, and buckled the remaining end. A tornado was a maybe, but his horse running off was a damn sure thing.

Tossing the bridle and saddlebags over his left shoulder, he picked up his saddle, tucking the saddle horn under his armpit, and grabbed hold of the cantle, resting the weight on his left hip. He started up the side of the canyon toward the cave, the pointed toes of his boots digging into the packed dirt, his eyes focused on the gnarled mesquite tree by the entrance. He was suddenly anxious to get inside the cave, to take out his sketch pad, arrange his paints, and begin. This would be his best work; he could feel it. No one had ever really painted the region's past as he intended. There were plenty of paintings of cowboys and horses, Indians and buffalo, windmills and decaying old ranch buildings, and God knows he'd done enough of them himself, but no one had ever done the history of the Texas Panhandle on canvas.

He bent over and entered the cave, unconsciously thankful to be out of the dust and wind. He shivered in the noticeably cooler air, and glanced around at the caliche walls and low ceiling. The cave was no more than four feet high and maybe ten feet square. He'd always wondered if the cave was natural, or if the bootleggers had dug it out of the canyon walls. Maybe it was older than that. Maybe some Comanche brave had sheltered here. He didn't know. Probably nobody knew. There was a lot about the Panhandle that was a mystery. A man could stumble onto almost anything in some of its arroyos.

Walking hunched over, he moved to the back wall, and carefully, almost reverently, unwrapped his treasure, the mystery he had stumbled across. He held it up, shocked again by its incredible weight. How could something less than three feet long be so heavy?

He stroked the object lovingly, frowning a little at the gaudy jewels that marred its smooth surface, then placed it against the caliche wall and lit the kerosene lamp he'd brought the week before. He needed more light, but he couldn't risk taking the object back to his small house at the ranch. Someone might see it, and the secret would be out. They would claim it and might not allow him to paint it. And he had to paint it.

Crawling over to the opposite wall, he pulled a sketch pad, a pan of watercolors, and a collapsible tin cup out of his saddlebags. He lifted a canteen from around his saddlehorn, unscrewed it, and poured a small amount of water into the cup. Opening the sketch pad, he propped it on his knees. Damn good thing he wasn't one of those artists who had to paint standing up. Not that he had much opportunity to do that. Too often he had to make a quick drawing in a pocket-sized spiral notebook while sitting on horseback. Not too many artists had to do that. But he had the whole weekend. He could do several watercolors of his subject, taking his time, making sure it was absolutely right.

He studied the first sketch in the dim light, a frown drawing his bushy brows together. Was the background too dark? He shook his head. No, it wasn't. Were the men's expressions too fearful? No, they weren't. They knew they would die, and they were afraid.

Opening his paints, he dipped his brush in the tin cup and painted in the object being held aloft by the man. It dominated the painting, but its very shape led the eye downward to the faces, and from the faces to the woman crouched by the fire, her face a study in horror. When he transferred his sketch to canvas, using acrylics to give the picture the luminous quality he wanted, it would be perfect.

Tearing the sheet off and laying it to one side to dry, he began another sketch. He must paint the object as it was now, propped against the dark caliche wall of the cave. He bent his head over the paper, the delicate brush almost disappearing in his large hand. He needed several sketches of the object from several different angles. He knew the end of its story now, and he intended to paint it, and for that he needed more than a frontal view.

He stopped to flex his fingers and wondered if any other artist ever had hands like his. He rubbed the burn mark that ran across his palm. Damn fool thing for a cowboy to have done, roping without his gloves on. He was lucky to have just a rope burn. He could have lost some fingers. He examined his large hands. No doubt about it, a cowboy's hands purely looked like hell. Calluses on the fingers, across the top of the palms, and the thick, yellow ones just under the second joints of his fingers caused by lifting bales of hay. He ought to do a self-portrait of his hands. But, hell, nobody'd buy it.

He folded the dry sketches and tucked them carefully in his saddlebags. Might as well put things up as they dried. Picking up his drawing pad, he settled back against the wall, propping the pad against his knees. He jerked upright at a furtive, scraping sound. He tilted his head, cursing his bad left ear. No sound at all, except the silence, and sometimes silence was loud. Like now. He ought to be hearing the wind whistling around the cave entrance, and the rustling, creeking sound of the mesquite tree just outside.

Laying his sketch pad aside, he started to the entrance, but stopped suddenly. He turned his head to look at object against the further wall. If someone was outside, he couldn't let them see it. He couldn't lose it now, not when he was so close to being through with his sketches.

He crawled over to the opposite wall and grabbed the object, clutching it to his chest as he looked about the cave for a hiding place. Nothing but caliche walls met his eyes. and he groaned. Why hadn't he figured out a hiding place before? Half the county knew he came up to Red Barn Cave to paint. Why the hell had he let himself get caught with his pants down? But he had, and he'd better make the best of it.

Wrapping the object in a blanket, he threw his saddlebags over it. It wasn't much, but it'd have to do, he thought as he crawled over to the entrance and peered out.

Stillness lay over the canyon like a blanket, thick, suffocating, dangerous. Clumps of buffalo grass and the rough, gray trunk of a dead cottonwood tree stood out with startling clarity, almost as if they were outlined in black like an object in a child's coloring book. His last thought was that the

weatherman was right for a change. There was definitely
going to be a tornado. A split second later, he had ceased to
worry about tornadoes for all time as the branding iron de-
scended in a short arc to open his skull, the dull sound of the
blow disturbing the stillness.

A gloved hand reached under the body and pulled a small
spiral notebook out of Willie's pocket. A satisfied release of
breath whispered through parted lips as the notebook was
slipped into another pocket. The figure stood over the body,
then reached down to dislodge the branding iron. As his
hands closed over it, a faint rumble to the southwest drew
him upright to stare at the twisting, tortured clouds. He wasn't
a fearful person, but the obscene funnel dipping and swaying
from the clouds dried his mouth and cramped his belly. He
dragged Willie's body from the cave entrance and crawled
inside, his body trembling with delaying reaction. Damn
Willie for being so stubborn, for leaving him with no choice
but murder.

The man sat down, leaning back against the wall, and
picked up the discarded sketch pad. His eyes narrowed and
he glanced around the cave, focusing on the carelessly
wrapped object. Crawling over, he tossed aside the saddlebags and unwrapped it. He grinned and touched the golden
object.

"Good hiding place, Willie, but not quite good enough,"
he murmured, folding the blanket around the object again.

Crawling back, he tore off Willie's sketches, folding them
up and sticking them in his pocket. No one would know
about it now. He glanced around the cave again. He could
safely leave everything else as it was. It would be assumed
the cowboy artist has taken shelter against the tornado. Of
course, there was no way to hide his murder, unless he buried
the body—and there was no way to do that. He didn't have a

shovel and you sure as hell couldn't dig through the packed dirt in this country without one.

He rubbed his gloved hand over his forehead. No point in dragging the body back in the cave either. Everybody knew Willie spent time at Red Barn Cave. It would be the first place checked when he didn't show up Monday morning.

He lifted his head at the rising sound of the wind. If the wind was blowing again, it meant the danger of tornado was over, at least temporarily. Now he could figure out what the hell he was going to do.

Crawling back out of the cave, he studied Willie's crumpled body. He'd tear hell out of the man's skull when he dislodged that branding iron. No one would believe Willie was killed accidentally unless he could arrange for a stampede. And whatever he did, the sheriff was going to swoop down on the ranch like a hawk on a jackrabbit. But there was no point in making him a gift of any evidence either.

Planting his foot on Willie's shoulder, the man grasped the branding iron and yanked, his face paling at the sharp cracking as the iron came free of the old cowboy's skull. He straightened, a smile stretching his lips. No one would notice blood and hair on a branding iron, and after being heated in a mesquite fire, all the evidence would be gone. Not a bad afternoon's work after all.

CHAPTER

2

SHERIFF CHARLES TIMOTHY MATTHEWS PACED REST-
lessly, his boots making a clicking sound against the bare
tiles of the squad room. He ran his fingers through his
tobacco-colored hair and leaned impatiently over the dispatcher's desk.

"Miss Poole, check with everyone again, please."

The elderly lady with her iron-gray hair twisted into a knot
at the back of her head glanced up. "Sheriff, they'll call if
they see a tornado. I just made a fresh pot of coffee. Pour
yourself a cup and relax."

Charles' stomach was still burning from the last cup. It
might be possible for someone's coffee to be stronger than
Miss Poole's, but he didn't think so. "No thanks, I'm trying
to cut down."

Miss Poole opened her mouth, and Charles braced himself
for her lecture on the benefits of coffee in general, and her
coffee in particular, when the decrepit radio equipment
squealed into life, causing the sheriff to grit his teeth. Damn
it, he was going to talk the County Commission into buying
a new communication system.

"Twenty-two, come in."

Charles grabbed the microphone and flipped the switch.
"Meenie, what's happening?"

Meenie Higgins's voice was sharp and irascible. "I'm
fixin' to tell you, Sheriff, if you'll give me a chance. We got

a twister on the ground about a mile away, heading northeast. Looks like it's going to miss Carroll, but you better sound the sirens anyway. Never can tell about these damn things."

"Where are you exactly, Meenie?" Charles asked.

There was a moment's silence and Charles started to repeat his question, when Meenie's voice interrupted. "I'm on one of the ranch roads on J.T. Brentwood's place. But that twister ain't anywhere near the headquarters, Sheriff. I reckon it touched down in a pasture. You don't need to worry."

"I'll meet you at the headquarters, Meenie." Charles dropped the microphone. "Keep a close check, Miss Poole, and call the Civil Defense people. Tell them to sound the sirens. I'll be at the Branding Iron Ranch."

Miss Poole grabbed his coat. After thirty years of teaching school, three weeks' stay in the hospital as a victim of an attempted murder, and nine months as dispatcher in the Crawford County Sheriff's Department, very little frightened her, certainly not Charles Timothy Matthews, Crawford County Sheriff.

"Sheriff, you can't leave; if there is an emergency, you'll be needed here. That nincompoop in charge of Civil Defense couldn't direct traffic, much less rescue efforts in a major catastrophe." Miss Poole was a uncompromising judge of Crawford County residents and never hesitated in making her judgments public.

Charles jerked his coat free of her clutches. "Angie's at the Branding Iron."

Miss Poole's face softened. "Perhaps I can manage things if worse comes to worst. I'm certainly more competent than the head of Civil Defense. Go on Sheriff. Mrs. Lassiter might need you."

Miss Poole sat gazing at the sheriff's departing figure. If she were thirty years younger, she'd be after Charles Timothy Matthews herself. "Damn Angie Lassiter," she said aloud, then stiffened in shock. My goodness, what would people

say if they knew Miss Megan Elizabeth Poole was even
thinking profanity, much less saying it?

Miss Poole contemplated her lapse of decorum. She was
losing patience with Angie—and with the sheriff, for that
matter. It was time Angie Lassiter woke up and realized the
sheriff was in love with her. It was time to quit mourning
that worthless first husband.

She chided herself. Of course, Angie didn't know about
L.D. Lassiter, and certainly no one was going to tell her.
The elderly dispatcher shook her head in disgust. Life should
be faced, even when it was unpleasant. Angie Lassiter needed
to know the true story about her dead husband. Otherwise,
the sheriff would never have a chance. It was very difficult
to fight a ghost, particularly one who has been elevated to
sainthood. And a less likely candidate for sainthood than
L.D. Lassiter, Miss Poole couldn't imagine.

Charles bypassed the elevator in favor of the stairs. He
needed physical action. He needed to know that every step
was taking him closer to Angie, and standing still in an elevator didn't give him that feeling. Besides, he ran the risk of
getting caught between floors. The elevator's dependability
had been erratic the last few weeks, to say the least.

He never remembered the three flights of stairs; his first
conscious action was unlocking his patrol car and cursing the
first few dust-laden drops of rain beginning to pelt across his
shoulders. He slipped the key in the ignition and flipped on
the siren at the same time.

He took the highway south out of Carroll, ignoring the
danger of wet, slick highways and visibility obscured by
blowing rain. All the while a kaleidoscope of images shifted
through his mind: Angie fixing supper while he and L.D.
talked; Angie holding her baby daughter and laughing; Angie
crying when he told her of L.D.'s death.

Other images took shape in front of his eyes: a spiraling

column of smoke; the sun's glint on twisted metal. His stomach cramped in its familiar way, and he slammed on his brakes and slumped back in the seat, drawing deep breaths to calm his nausea. Shakily he wiped his forehead, feeling the chill sweat against his fingertips.

If ever a man had deserved to die, it had been L.D. Lassiter. Not only had he gotten young Maria Martinez pregnant, he had murdered her when she had refused to have an abortion. When Maria's brother had killed L.D., Miss Poole called it poetic justice.

Certainly justice had been served, at least in the biblical sense of an eye for an eye. Arresting Maria's brother, exposing the whole sordid story in open court, watching Angie suffer the humiliation of being a murderer's wife, would have accomplished nothing. So he had used his power as sheriff to hide the truth. L.D. Lassiter had died in a freak plane crash, and Maria had been murdered by a person or persons unknown. It was a story everyone could live with.

Everyone but him.

By hiding the truth, he had broken his sworn oath, violated his personal code of honor, and become an accessory to murder. Now he wanted L.D.'s wife and felt guilty as hell about it.

He moved his foot to the gas pedal and attempted to blank his mind of memories and concentrate on his driving. There were so many corners of his mind with Do Not Disturb signs, he wondered sometimes how he could still function. He gripped the wheel harder and increased his speed. Life in the country was supposed to be peaceful. How in the hell did his manage to end up in such a complicated, tangled mess?

He turned off the road, the patrol car fishtailing on the gravel, and drove through the huge red gates of the Branding Iron Ranch. He'd passed the ranch road a hundred times since moving to Crawford County four years ago and had never been more than mildly curious. Until he discovered that Angie was J.T. Brentwood's daughter. Then his curiosity became a raging fever. He wondered if most men were so desperate to know everything about the women they loved.

Topping a small hill, relief flooded through him, leaving a residue of cold sweat. The headquarters of the Branding Iron Ranch, in all its white-plastered, red-roofed, adobe glory, was undamaged. Wooden stables and barns, painted deep red with matching red roofs, hugged the banks on a small creek. Tall cottonwoods and bois d'arc trees surrounded the house, creating a miniature forest. They also served another function, as did the thick adobe walls of the main house: they kept the intense Panhandle heat at bay. The location of the house, at the foot of the small hill, protected it from the fierce winter winds. The early ranchers had made use of the natural formations of the land to soften the effects of the harsh environment.

Charles eased up on the accelerator and switched off the siren. He parked in front of the red-painted wooden fence and climbed out, feeling like a knight who'd come to rescue the fair princess, only to find she'd tamed the dragon.

A bowlegged deputy of some indeterminate age between thirty-five and fifty, dressed in the Western-cut brown slacks and shirt, met Charles at the gate. Meenie Higgins lifted his hat, ran gnarled fingers through his hair, shifted a wad of tobacco from one cheek to the other, and stuck his thumbs inside his belt.

"Sheriff, everybody's safe. Hell, it didn't even rain out here, the wind just blew. I woulda called you on the radio, but I figured you'd want to see for yourself." Meenie turned his head and aimed a stream of tobacco juice at a dandelion five feet away. Charles didn't need to look to know his deputy had hit it dead center.

Charles knew by *everybody* Meenie meant Angie. His deputy knew exactly how he felt about Angie, as did several other people in the sheriff's department, but no one ever mentioned it, and for that he was eternally grateful. Angie was just as unreachable as she had ever been—and he couldn't tolerate any good-natured kidding about her.

"Thanks, Meenie," he said, confident his deputy knew the thank-you wasn't for information.

Charles reached for his hat to straighten it, only to find he'd left it behind, and immediately felt at a disadvantage. He must be more acclimated to the Panhandle than he realized to feel undressed without a hat.

He walked to the group standing on the long covered porch, his hands outstretched to grasp Angie's.

"Angie, girl, are you all right?" he asked, feeling his throat tighten at the sight of the painful shadows in the depths of her hazel eyes.

Angie smiled, a slow parting of her lips, as if she had just learned how and wasn't sure she was doing it right. "Charles, you didn't need to drive all the way out here. The tornado missed the house by miles. Dad thinks it may have hit the branding pens in the north pasture."

A tall, broad-shouldered man dressed in faded Levi's and a Western shirt, laid his hand possessively on Angie's shoulder. "We appreciate your coming out, Sheriff." He waved an arm at the house and outbuildings.

"But as you can see, we're fine. Mr. Brentwood and I certainly don't intend to let anything happen to Angie and the girls."

Charles met the other man's blue-gray eyes, aware his own were as black, cold, and deadly looking as any rattlesnake. If the bastard didn't get his damn hand off Angie, he just might end up with a bloody stump.

The man smiled easily, acknowledging Charles's look and ignoring it. He held out his hand. "I'm Kurt Reynolds, manager of the Branding Iron Ranch. I don't believe we've met before."

Reluctantly Charles shook his hand, feeling the work-roughened calluses against his own smoother palm. Suddenly he felt weak and soft. "I know who you are," he replied.

Kurt Reynolds nodded toward an older man. "This is Mr. Brentwood, Angie's father."

"I know Mr. Brentwood," Charles answered. "J.T., how are you?"

Angie's father, a stocky, grizzled man in his late fifties, shook the outstretched hand. "I see you're still wearing a suit," he said. J.T. Brentwood wore suits of Western cut, and those (or so Charles had heard him brag) only to see someone married or buried.

Charles knew he didn't fit anyone's idea of a Panhandle sheriff and ordinarily it didn't bother him. But this was Angie's father, and if he couldn't win the tough old rancher's approval, he at least wanted a declaration of neutrality. "You know how it is, J.T. I'm not a Panhandle native, so there's no point in dressing to fit that image."

Brentwood snorted. "Image! You sound just like some damn citified politician. That's what we get for electing sheriffs instead of appointin' them."

Charles' jaw clenched. "I may be elected, but I'm not a politician."

Angie stepped to Charles's side and slipped her arm around his waist. "Don't call Charles a politician, Dad. He doesn't like it and neither do I."

"Now, Angie, I'm sure the sheriff doesn't need to hide behind your skirts."

Charles didn't know which stung more: Kurt Reynolds's words or the condescending note in his masculine drawl. Either way, the ranch manager was asking for a verbal punch in the mouth. "Angie always defends someone's she's fond of."

J.T. Brentwood slapped his thigh and hooted. "Better

watch it, Kurt. The sheriff used to be a lawyer. You just can't beat them with words.''

Kurt flushed, then he smiled, revealing a dimple in his left cheek. He held out his hand again. ''Sheriff, I'm sorry. You just don't look like I expected you to. And we do appreciate your being concerned enough about your best friend's wife and family to drive all the way out here. L.D. was lucky to have a friend like you.''

Charles felt the color drain from his face. His friendship with L.D. Lassiter had nothing to do with why he was here, and he sensed that Reynolds knew it.

With some distant part of his mind he observed Angie's stricken look and wanted to choke Kurt Reynolds for mentioning L.D.'s name. Ignoring the man's hand offered in friendship, he folded his arms around Angie and stared over her head at Reynolds. ''No offense taken, Mr. Reynolds. Now, if you'll excuse us, I'm going to beg a cup of coffee from Angie, and maybe see the girls if they're not asleep.''

Charles led Angie across the porch to the house, carrying on an innocuous conversation to allow her time to regain her composure. ''You know, Angie, I've heard about the Branding Iron Ranch ever since I came to the Panhandle. I'm glad to make it out here finally. I hope you don't mind my inviting myself, but I haven't had a decent cup of coffee since I was elected sheriff. First it was Slim, now it's Miss Poole. Both of them think I eat it with a spoon.''

Angie opened the door and led him through the house. ''After that scene on the porch, a cup of coffee is the least the Brentwoods can do. I'm sorry, Charles. I apologize for Dad and Kurt. And I didn't make it any better by getting upset when Kurt mentioned L.D., but the last two months have been''—she hesitated a moment—''unsettling. Dad's been snapping at everyone, so I guess he didn't pick you out for special attention. And Kurt—well, Kurt's been acting more high-handed and possessive than usual. Something's wrong, but no one will tell me what. I've been scared. And I've missed you."

Charles cautioned himself against feeling ecstatic, and Angie's next words demonstrated how right he'd been.

"You were always such a good friend, and you always made me laugh." Angie poured his coffee and sat down across from him. "I'm going to sell my house," she said abruptly.

"You mean you'll move to the ranch permanently?"

He had hoped his tone had merely conveyed curiosity, but Angie's puzzled look told him he was revealed more than that.

"No, Charles, I couldn't live at the ranch again. Not that I don't love it. But Dad forgets I'm a grown woman and Johnny resents what he calls my mother complex. He thinks I'm butting into his life."

Charles could well imagine. Johnny Brentwood, Angie's brother, was everybody's idea of a spoiled brat, except this particular brat happened to be twenty-five years old. He seemed to think the rules were for others, not for him. The sheriff's department had arrested him several times on various charges, primarily drunk and disorderly, and Charles was sure Angie had said a few things to her little brother.

"You know how brothers are, Angie. They don't like older sisters telling them what to do."

"Someone has to, if they don't have sense enough to know how to act," she snapped, then looked guilty. "I'm sorry, Charles. I don't want to take out frustration on you."

He reached over and took her hand, threading his fingers between hers. "It's all right, Angie, girl; I can take it. Just don't move away from Carroll."

She stiffened slightly, and he saw awareness dawning in her eyes. He felt sick. Damn it, where was his famous poker face when he needed it? She had buried her husband a few months ago. She needed a friend, not a lover making emotional demands. Or demands of another kind, he reminded himself as he acknowledged how close to the edge of physical arousal he was.

He forced himself to smile. "Where else am I going to get decent coffee?"

Angie looked at him as if really seeing him for the first time, then stared at their clasped hands. "I'm not leaving Carroll, Charles—just buying a different house. I want one with no memories." She looked up again, her eyes searching his.

Charles patted her hand like a brother, although God knew he didn't feel like one. "When you get ready to move, just call. I'll be glad to help."

Angie looked at him, then away. When the question came it was hesitant. "Charles, will you do something for me? I mean something besides helping me move?" She pulled her hand away and wrapped one of her auburn curls around her finger. Charles had seen her do the same thing every time she was nervous.

"What do you want, Angie?"

Angie raised her head and looked at him, her eyes open and vulnerable. "Go with me to the cemetery on Memorial Day."

CHAPTER

3

CHARLES HAD FAINTED ONCE IN HIS LIFE, AND THAT was after being shot in the belly in Vietnam. He felt very much the same way now: his vision narrowed to a pinpoint; his stomach burned; and when he spoke, his voice sounded disembodied, as if it belonged to someone else. "Why me, Angie?"

"Because you were his friend."

He always knew that sometime, somehow, he would pay for covering L.D.'s death. Philosophically, he supposed being trapped in a lie of his own devising was a fitting punishment. Realistically, it hurt like hell.

"I'll take you, Angie," he said, pushing himself to his feet. He carried his cup to the sink, surprised he could still function.

"Thanks for the coffee." He stopped, feeling suddenly awkward. "I better get back to town. I left Miss Poole in charge."

Angie smiled, a more carefree smile than he had seen before. "You don't think Miss Poole could handle any emergency?"

Charles grinned. "I think Miss Poole could handle the devil himself. She'd probably have him shoveling coal into his own furnace. It's the rest of town I'm worried about."

"Sheriff! You better get out here!" Meenie appeared in

the doorway, his usually calm, emotionless face pale and shaken.

Charles jerked around, observing Meenie catch Angie at the shoulders. "No, ma'am, you don't need to go out there."

Angie pushed Meenie's hands away. "What's happened? Is Johnny hurt? This is my ranch. You can't stop me from going wherever I want."

"One of the cowboys has had an accident, ma'am. It ain't pretty, and there ain't nothin' you can do." Meenie looked helplessly at the sheriff. Handling woman he classified as *ladies* wasn't something Meenie did well.

Charles's arm circled Angie's shoulder. "Angie, please wait here. If Meenie says there's nothing you can do, you can believe him. And I can't do my job if I'm worried about you."

Angie looked at him, her head tilted at a slight angle as if she were seeing him out of focus. "All right, I won't go out there, but only because I might disturb you, not because I need protecting."

Charles kissed her forehead. "Thanks, Angie, girl." He headed for the front door at a run, skirting furniture and his deputy. He slammed open the screen door, pausing a moment while he scanned the yard.

"Back by the barn, Sheriff," said Meenie from behind him. "Johnny Brentwood brought him in. That kid's a damn fool if I ever saw one. Shoulda left him where he was."

Charles didn't waste his breath asking questions. He vaulted the waist-high wooden fence and ran toward the group of men clustered around a mounted cowboy leading a saddleless horse. His eyes focused on the horse's burden: one very dead man draped over its back just like every bad Western ever filmed.

"Meenie, call Miss Poole and have her send the J.P. out here. Then better have her send out the Parker brothers," ordered Charles as he examined the body without touching it. He wanted pictures taken before moving it.

"Those undertakers'll charge the county an arm and leg for coming out here," Meenie grumbled.

Charles thought again how much he wished he knew the reason for the enmity between Meenie and the local morticians. "Meenie," he called after his deputy. "Call Raul. He's got the field camera."

Meenie turned around. "You know, Sheriff, you ought to rotate the photography duty. That body will put Raul off his feed for a week."

Charles hoped he lived to see the day Meenie followed an order without throwing in some advice of his own. But he was right about one thing: that body would spoil anyone's appetite. The back of the skull was smashed and mangled almost beyond belief.

"Who was he?" Charles asked, looking at J.T. Brentwood.

The older man's normal ruddy color was gone, leaving his complexion gray. "Willie Russell," he answered, and wiped his hand over his face as if wiping out the scene in front of him.

Charles looked at Johnny Brentwood for the first time. Angie's brother was pale, his face covered with a film of sweat. He sat completely still, the knuckles of the hand holding the lead rope bloodless. Muffling a curse, Charles pried the boy's fingers loose and led the horse to the corral fence and tied it up. "You," he said, motioning to Kurt Reynolds, "help me get him down, then take him to the house, give him some hot coffee laced with brandy, and wrap him up in a blanket. He's in shock."

He grasped the boy's arm. "Johnny, can you get down?" He waited a moment, but there was no indication Johnny had heard.

Sighing, Charles pulled his arm, catching the younger

man's weight as he slid off the horse. He steadied him until Johnny seemed able to stand, then silently let Kurt lead him to the house. There was no point asking him where he'd found the body. That would have to wait until the boy was even aware of where he was.

"Raul and the Justice of the Peace will be right out," Meenie said, stepping up to the sheriff. "This is Mrs. Jenkins's precinct. She ain't gonna like looking at that body."

"I don't like looking at it myself," Charles snapped. "She knew when she ran for office she'd also have to serve as coroner. There are a lot of women J.P.'s in Texas. If they can handle something like this, so can she." He hadn't supported Mrs. Jenkins in her bid for election. She was more concerned in making a statement about women's rights than in doing her job. She was just another politician, female variety, and he didn't care for politicians.

He turned to J.T. Brentwood. "Who and what was Willie Russell?"

Brentwood turned away from the mangled body. "Can't we take him off that damn horse? Cover him up? A man shouldn't be treated like that."

Charles shook his head. "Not until my deputy takes some pictures, and the J.P. pronounces him dead."

"Dead! We don't need to wait for anybody to tell us he's dead! Hell, you don't think he's alive with his head all bashed in?"

"That's the law; no one is officially dead until the J.P. says so," Charles replied. "J.T., I need to know everything about the victim. I can't figure out a motive without knowing the victim."

Brentwood doubled up his fist and shook it in Charles's face. "Motive! Are you crazy? You're talking like someone killed Willie. A man gets thrown by his horse and hits his head, or bumps into something kinda hard, and you start acting like someone killed him. This isn't Dallas or Houston; it's Crawford County! No one had any reason to kill Willie!''

Charles grabbed Brentwood's wrist. Angie's father or not, no man was going to threaten him. ''That's enough, J.T.! Getting angry at me, or the J.P., or the State of Texas, isn't going to change anything. Willie didn't hit himself in the back of the head, and I've seen enough murder victims to recognize one. I could be wrong, and I hope I am, but I don't think so. Willie Russell is dead, and I need your help to catch the murderer. Now calm down and talk to me!''

J.T. Brentwood stared at him as if startled both by the sheriff's surprisingly strong grip and the anger and impatience Charles knew his eyes revealed. ''Sorry, Sheriff. I didn't mean to go off half-cocked. But damn it all! Murder!''

Charles released the man's wrist, satisfied Brentwood was more in control of himself. He rubbed his hand across his forehead in an effort to ease the throbbing ache anger always caused. ''Let's hope I'm the one going off half-cocked, J.T. I don't want another murder in Crawford County any more than you do, but pretending it didn't happen won't catch the killer.''

Brentwood rubbed his wrist. ''But I meant what I said. Nobody had any reason to kill Willie; he never hurt anybody in his life. And I ought to know. He's worked for the Branding Iron for over twenty-five years. Him and me were green kids together. Hell, everybody liked Willie. Only thing he ever did that was a little different was his painting.''

Charles raised an eyebrow. ''Painting?''

J.T. Brentwood looked disgusted. ''Might of figured somebody from Dallas wouldn't know anything about Western art.''

Charles felt a twinge of irritation. ''Are you telling me Willie Russell is Wilson Russell, the cowboy artist?''

Angie's father grinned, then immediately looked guilty, as

if suddenly remembering humor was out of place around murder. "He's the same."

"And he worked for you as a cowboy?" Charles asked.

Brentwood snorted. "How the hell do you think he knew how to paint cowboys? Willie painted cowboys better than anybody around because he *was* one."

"Where was he today? I mean, what was he supposed to be doing?"

Brentwood lifted his hat and scratched his head. "Well, you see, Sheriff, sometimes Willie would ask for a weekend off to paint. He never said where he was going. He'd just load up his saddlebags, tie his bedroll on the back of his saddle, and ride off. Come Sunday night he'd ride back in. He asked for this weekend off. I didn't really want to let him go, it's branding time, and I need every hand, but Willie never asked for any favors, so I gave him time off."

Brentwood stopped suddenly and pulled a bandanna out of his pocket and wiped at his nose. Charles discreetly turned his back and studied a large cottonwood tree. He had heard the tremor in Brentwood's voice and knew the older man was fighting tears. He waited until the raspy voice pulled him around.

"Damn it, Sheriff, you got to be wrong. You're young, anxious to try out your spurs, but you're fixing to make a mountain out of a mole hill."

Charles clenched his fists and took a step forward. "I've seen more bodies killed in more ways than you've ever imagined. What Vietnam didn't show me, the Dallas district attorney's office did. And you can stop visualizing me as some young kid out to make a name for himself. I'd be satisfied to serve out my term doing nothing more than arresting a few drunks on Saturday night, but I'll be damned if I'll ignore a murder. Now if you can think of any reason why Willie was killed, you better tell me. Because if I find out you knew something and didn't tell me, I'll run you in for obstructing justice, and the fact you're Angie's father won't stop me.''

For a moment the peaceful ranch receded and he was back in Dallas, leaning over a desk and arguing with another stubborn, opinioned man. He drew a shuddering breath. That was different; that man had been deliberately hiding something. He glanced at J.T. Brentwood in time to catch an expression of grudging respect.

''You don't take to being pushed, do you, Sheriff? That's good; I don't myself. A real man has to cast a shadow, and that means he's got to stand firm.''

Charles heard the backhanded compliment in the older man's words and brushed it away. J.T. Brentwood couldn't know the cracks and fissures in his life, or he wouldn't be impressed. Thankfully he heard the siren that announced Raul's arrival.

He walked a few steps to greet his deputy. ''Raul, bring your camera; the body's on that horse tied to the corral.''

The slim, olive-skinned deputy glanced toward the silent tableau of horse and body, and grimaced. ''*Madre de Dios!* I don't think I'll ever get used to this.''

Charles glanced at the gray undertone to his deputy's olive skin. ''If you ever do, Raul, I'll fire you.''

Raul lifted the camera out of the patrol car and walked reluctantly toward Willie's body. ''You're sure it's murder?''

Charles swore in disgust. ''I'm already trying to persuade J.T. Brentwood this is murder, not a simple case of being thrown from a horse. Don't you start in.''

He stepped close to the body and gestured toward the skull. ''Whatever hit him not only crushed the skull but also splintered it. If he had simply fallen on a rock, we would have a depressed wound with the bone embedded in the tissue. But there is a section of the skull actually missing. And we don't have the traditional blunt instrument being used either. It was something sharp. I may not be a pathologist, but I have seen murder victims before, and, damn it, this is murder.''

Raul examined the dead cowboy's skull, then stepped back and began taking photographs. "I'm sorry, Sheriff. I just don't want to believe anyone could do that to another human being.''

Charles eyed him curiously. "You've been a deputy long enough to see what human beings are capable of doing to one another. Why is this more shocking?''

Raul stood holding the camera as if it held the answer. "I think because whoever did it was a coward.''

Charles frowned. "Why do you say that?''

"Because he hit him in the back of the head.''

CHAPTER

4

"THAT'S RIGHT, SHERIFF." MEENIE SHIFTED HIS TO-bacco and took aim at a horsefly on the corral fence. "It's one thing to kill a man face-to-face, but to sneak up on him, that's something else. A man like that is lower than dirt."

"I suppose you'd rather men still met in the middle of the street at high noon to settle their arguments with a gun," Charles snapped.

Meenie looked at the sheriff with an expression akin to sympathy. "Hell, Sheriff; that didn't happen most of the time. Most men couldn't hit the broad side of a barn with them handguns. They used shotguns and made sure they got the drop on whoever they was plannin' to kill. The only people who made heroes out of killers like Billy the Kid and Jesse James was Yankees who wrote books about them. A lot of their neighbors never thought too highly of them."

Charles shook in head. He knew Meenie was trying to make a point, but he couldn't figure out what. "Front or back, murder is murder."

"That ain't quite true, Sheriff," Meenie said with the air of an oracle delivering a prophecy. "You see, if the killer had hit Willie Russell from the front, the jury'd want to know why. But because he sneaked up on him from behind, the jury ain't gonna care why; they're just goin' to send the killer to death row. It ain't right to kill a man, and it especially ain't right to kill a man who's lookin' the other way."

Charles looked at his deputy. "More cracker-barrel philosophy to educate your greenhorn sheriff?"

Meenie turned his head to send a stream of tobacco juice at an unsuspecting black beetle. "Hell, Sheriff, you're always usin' them big words. I'm just tryin' to tell you this is a mean one."

"You mean I'm going to have to watch my back?"

Meenie looked at Charles, his face expressionless. "No, I'm gonna do that for you."

The sheriff wondered how a man as imperfect as himself could command such uncompromising loyalty. He glanced at the leathery, sun-darkened face of his deputy and decided that whatever he had done to earn Meenie's respect, he was damn glad he did it.

He clasped his deputy's shoulder in a quick gesture of affection. "In that case, keep your powder dry," he said, and turned as the sound of a motor in need of tuning announced the arrival of a nondescript blue Ford. "Who is that?"

"I believe that's our new Justice of the Peace, Sheriff," Raul said dryly.

Charles started toward the car. "Well, I better get this over with. I only hope she doesn't faint."

"It'll take all of us to catch her if she does," Meenie said. "She's a little on the hefty side."

Just then a woman as wide as she was tall climbed out of the old Ford. Mrs. Viola Jenkins straightened the skirt of her sensible shirtwaist dress, then addressed Charles in a booming voice. "Sheriff, let's see that body."

Charles arched an eyebrow at her. "Right over here, Mrs. Jenkins."

Mrs. Jenkins uttered a single expletive, and Charles revised his opinion of the woman. He might have been wrong in not supporting her campaign.

"My God, what hit him?"

"We don't know," Charles admitted.

Mrs. Jenkins took a closer look, gulped audibly, and whirled quickly away. "Well, he's certainly dead."

"Hell's bells! Any idiot could see that. Just do whatever you're supposed to do so I can cover him." J.T. Brentwood's voice was sharp with disgust.

"Now you just hush up, J.T. Brentwood. I'm the J.P. here, and I know what to do."

Satisfied she'd disposed of the rancher, Mrs. Jenkins turned back to Charles. "Sheriff, I believe that an autopsy is in order. The state of Texas will want to know exactly what the cause of death was."

"Good God, Viola; he's dead because half his skull is gone." J.T. Brentwood wasn't easy to hush.

The J.P. placed her hands on her ample hips and glared at the rancher. "When I'm conducting official business, the name is Mrs. Jenkins. And I don't know why a man always thinks he has to stick his two cents in when half the time he doesn't know what he's talking about. Now you just stand over there and keep quiet until the sheriff and I finish our business."

Charles was treated to the sight of J.T. Brentwood being backed up against the corral fence by a very irritated Viola Jenkins, and he decided that whatever office the woman chose to run for, she would have his support in the future. Anyone who could back down J.T., could handle anything.

Mrs. Jenkins literally dusted her hands off, marched over to the body with a heavy step, examined it closely, and turned back to Charles. "I'll take care of the paperwork, Sheriff." She hesitated a moment. "I hear you always carry a flask of brandy around with you. Is that true?"

Charles blinked. "Yes."

Mrs. Jenkins held out her hand. "If I could have a swallow, I'd appreciate it; dead bodies always make me a little faint."

Charles pulled out his flask and offered it to her. She unscrewed the top, threw her head back, and considerably lowered the level of liquor. Dabbing her mouth with a ridiculously tiny, lace-trimmed handkerchief, she handed the flask back.

Reaching up, she patted Charles on the cheek. "Not quite what you expected, was I?" she asked.

His stern features relaxed in a smile that admitted his preconceived prejudice. "No, Mrs. Jenkins, you weren't what I expected."

"Neither were you, Sheriff," she said softly, then shook her head, her voice becoming brisk. "There come the Parker brothers in their best black hearse. They must be trying to impress J.T. You know they'll charge the county for a wash and wax job after having to drive over the dusty road?"

With that parting comment Mrs. Jenkins charged back to her car, and Charles watched with a bemused expression. The Texas Panhandle bred a unique brand of woman, and the short, plump woman reversing her car with a screech of gears was a good example.

He dismissed Mrs. Jenkins from his mind and turned back to watch the Parker brothers reverently lift Willie Russell's body off the horse. He spared a moment's reflection on the morticians' ability to ignore the gaping wound in Willie's skull, and his undignified posture, and act as if he had died peacefully in his bed. Even Meenie would have to admit their demeanor couldn't be faulted.

Meenie admitted no such thing. He stalked over to Charles muttering under his breath. "Damn undertakers. They just tapped Mr. Brentwood for the funeral bill."

Charles grinned. He knew Meenie would find something to criticize. "That was the generous act of a friend."

Meenie spit at a lone weed struggling for existence in the hard earth. "He don't know how generous until he gets the bill."

Charles motioned at the Parkers. "We need to search the body," he said, and watched the two brothers carefully lower the stretcher to the ground. Sucking in a quick breath, he knelt and began checking Willie's pockets. He would never get used to searching a body. The feeling of violating the privacy of the dead clung to the edges of his mind no matter how objective he tried to be. Raul and Meenie had joined in the search, and he sensed their distaste behind the carefully blank faces.

He saw J.T. Brentwood approaching, the look of a pole-axed steer on his face. Dusting off his hands, Charles rose.

"I've known that woman for thirty years; in fact, I nearly married her. And what does she do? Informs me I have to call her Mrs. Jenkins. Mrs Jenkins, for God's sake!" Then the rancher blinked. "What the hell are they doing, Sheriff?"

"We're searching the body for anything unusual, and to collect his personal effects."

Brentwood leaned over Raul's shoulder, peering at the few articles the deputy was placing in an envelope from the evidence kit. "Just a minute, Sheriff. Where's his tally book?"

"There wasn't no tally book, Mr. Brentwood," interrupted Meenie, shifting his tobacco, and spitting to one side.

"What's a tally book?" Charles asked, nodding at the Parker brothers to load the body into the hearse.

"It's a damn book that a cowboy carries and keeps a daily count of the cattle in. Hell, Sheriff, I don't know how many calves I need to brand without that book."

"Well, it isn't here," Charles snapped. "You'll have to get by without it. Now get out of the way and give the morticians room to pick up the stretcher." He watched while Brentwood reluctantly moved back. Damn the man! One of his cowboys gets killed, and all he can worry about is how many cattle he has to brand.

Jamming his fist into his pocket instead of J.T. Brentwood's mouth, Charles turned back to his deputies. "Did you tell them to deliver the body to the pathologist in Amarillo?" he asked Meenie.

Meenie spit again. "Yeah. They told me they'd send the bill for mileage to the county. They just ain't got no sense of public duty."

Charles arched one eyebrow, and Meenie changed the subject. "What now, Sheriff? You goin' to ask Brentwood some more questions?"

"No. I'm going to question Johnny Brentwood. He's had time to get over his shock. I want to know where he found the body. In fact, I want him to take us there."

"Do you want me to stay, Sheriff?" Raul broke into the conversation, his lilting voice the only reminder that Spanish, not English, had been his language of birth.

"Since you can write more legibly than Meenie here, I want you to take notes. The last time I had to read one of his reports it took an hour a page just to decipher his spelling."

Meenie shrugged his skinny shoulders. "I never claimed to be no speller. Never thought being a deputy would mean writin' reports." He shifted his tobacco and spit in disgust, for once not picking a specific target.

Charles grinned at his deputy and walked over to the corral fence where J.T. Brentwood was leaning, a mutinous, angry expression on his face. "I need to talk to your son, J.T.," Charles said without any polite preliminaries.

The rancher jerked upright. "Now, don't you go leaning on that boy, Sheriff. He doesn't know anything."

"I never said he did, but I have to know where he found the body. And I don't lean on people," he added, wanting to say it was time someone did so before Johnny Brentwood ended up in serious trouble.

"All right, but I'm staying in the room," the rancher said, leading the way to the back door of the house.

"While you're in the room, I'd appreciate it if you would

make a list of all your employees and call them in. I want to talk to everyone who works on this ranch.''

J.T. Brentwood turned around so quickly he bumped into Charles. ''Are you crazy, Sheriff? We just had a tornado. I've got men spread out all over a hundred sections of land checking cattle. Just how the hell do you think I'm going to call them in? Stand on the back porch and holler? I don't even know where they all are. You'll have to talk to my foreman. Maybe, he'll know. Of course, you'll have to find him first. He's somewhere around the ranch.''

Charles felt the flush heat his skin. If he lived in Crawford County the rest of his life, perhaps he would stop making mistakes that made him sound like an idiot. Then again, perhaps not. After having grown up in Dallas, his mind was accustomed to thinking in terms of city blocks, not sections of 640 acres each.

''Sorry, J.T., I didn't think of the difficulties.'' He saw the disgruntled expression on the rancher's face and knew he had slipped another rung in the man's estimation.

Charles followed Brentwood through the door, with Meenie and Raul behind him. Angie stood by the sink watching her brother, anger tracing twin furrows between her brows. Kurt Reynolds leaned against the counter top, arms crossed against his broad chest, blond hair attractively ruffled. Charles wished he could find something physically distasteful about the man, a hairlip perhaps.

Johnny Brentwood sat at the kitchen table wrapped in a blanket and clutching a water glass of whiskey. Charles hoped it was the young man's first drink. He wanted him relaxed, not drunk.

''Johnny, I'm Sheriff Matthews. I don't believe we've ever been formally introduced,'' Charles said, extending his hand. Technically that was true; booking a prisoner for a drunk and disorderly charge hardly counted as a formal introduction.

Johnny Brentwood looked up, his face flushed under his

tan, his blue eyes sullen. The shocked, vacant expression had been replaced by an arrogant defensiveness. "I know who you are."

Charles felt an almost uncontrollable urge to slap Johnny Brentwood's sneering face.

"Johnny, the sheriff is a good friend of mine," Angie said sharply, jerking the glass of whiskey out of her brother's hand.

"Hey, give that back," he protested, swinging around to grab his sister's arm.

Charles moved before he thought, not even hearing the muffled exclamations from Meenie and Raul. Grabbing Johnny's arm in a hard grip with one hand, he slammed the other in the younger man's chest. "You've had enough! And don't ever grab at your sister like that again."

"Charles, it's all right." Angie's hands, wet from whiskey that had sloshed from the glass, clutched his arm.

"Damn it, Sheriff!" J.T. Brentwood roared. "Let go of my boy!"

Charles stared into Johnny Brentwood's shocked eyes. "Remember what I said." He dropped the man's arm and straightened, turning to Angie and clasping her wet hands in his own larger ones. He cringed at her beseeching eyes. "I'm sorry, Angie, girl."

"You damn well ought to be." J.T. Brentwood's voice grated over Charles' nerves like a nail file.

He heard a shuffling sound behind him and knew Meenie and Raul had moved closer to back him up. He released Angie's hands and waved his two deputies back.

"J.T., I need to talk to your son, and I need him sober. Now if you want to stay in the room, keep quiet. Otherwise, leave."

"Just a minute, Sheriff. This is my house. You have no right walking in here and giving everyone orders."

Charles inclined in head. "You're right, of course. Johnny, get up. I'm taking you back to town." He stared over the boy's head at J.T. Brentwood and caught again that grudging look of admiration.

J.T. Brentwood raised his hand in resignation, and pulling out a chair, straddled it, resting his forearms on the back. "Go ahead, Sheriff. Johnny, tell the man what happened."

The young man raked his fingers through his hair and looked up at Charles. He looked younger than his twenty-five years, his hazel eyes so like his sister's that Charles felt a sense of pity. Sitting down across the table from Johnny, he motioned to Raul to take notes. Seeing the deputy seat himself at the end of the table, he began the questioning in a quiet voice.

"Where did you find the body?"

Johnny's eyes widened and seemed to lose their focus. His voice, when he spoke, cracked with nervousness. "In front of Red Barn Cave." Something seemed to give way, and the words poured out in an endless torrent. "He was lying there on his belly in the dirt. Just all crumbled up like he didn't have any bones. And the back of his head was gone, just gone. And the flies were buzzing around him. I know I should have left him there and gone for help. But I couldn't, Sheriff, I couldn't do it."

The young man stopped and wiped his nose on his shirt-sleeve. Charles knew he should have started with more routine questions. He hooked his arm over the back of the chair and leaned back, his relaxed posture at variance with his watchful eyes. "Now, Johnny," he began conversationally. "Tell me about your day. When did you leave the house?"

The young man wrapped his fingers around his arms as if seeking stability in a suddenly nightmarish world. "About noon," he said finally. He squinted one eye. "Yeah, that's right. Weather bureau put the county under a tornado watch about then, and Dad told me to go tell the men to let the cattle out of the branding pens in the north pasture. If a twister hit, he didn't want the cattle all bunched up where we'd lose a lot.''

"How long did it take you to get there?" Charles asked.

"About ten minutes." Johnny lifted his cup and took a swallow of coffee. "Course, that's in the pickup. Takes a lot longer by horseback. Anyway, I found Conrad and gave him Dad's orders and then went back to the house."

Charles interrupted. "Who's Conrad?"

"My foreman," J.T. Brentwood said.

Charles nodded at Brentwood without looking at him. "Then what did you do, Johnny?"

"I got my horse." He looked up at Charles earnestly. "I was worried about the cattle. I couldn't just come back to the house. I rode back toward the pens."

"Wasn't that dangerous?" Charles asked.

Johnny grinned slowly. "I rode down the creek as far as I could, then down a couple of arroyos. I'm not stupid. I didn't want to get caught on flat ground if a twister hit. When the wind fell and I saw the funnel, I tied up my horse and flattened up against the side of the draw. When it was over, I rode over to the branding pens." He stopped and glanced down the table toward his father. "They're all torn to hell, Dad; lost a couple of calves, too. Guess their mamas panicked and ran off."

J.T. Brentwood wiped his hand over his face. "Could've been worse. I'll have one of the hands pick up the calves and take them to the locker to be cut up. No point in wasting good meat."

"Where did you go next?" interrupted Charles. It was all very interesting to learn about ranch operations, but that wasn't the kind of information he needed.

"I could hear some cows bawling, so I headed toward the creek. I figured they'd holed up there. I rode down the creek, found a few strays, then I saw Willie's horse."

"What time was this?" Charles asked.

Johnny shrugged his shoulders. "Who knows? I never look at my watch when I'm checking cattle. It was maybe mid-afternoon, three o'clock or around there."

Charles made a mental note to check with the weather bureau on the exact time the tornado touched down. "So you saw Willie's horse and saw the body?"

Johnny shook his head. "No. I found the body maybe thirty minutes later. Willie's horse was hobbled, but it must have been scared as hell. It traveled about a mile with that hobble on. I roped it and started backtracking in the direction it had come from. When I got to Red Barn Cave, I saw Willie. I thought maybe he was hurt, and I hollered at him. He didn't answer, and I went up to check. That's when I saw he was dead." He spread his hands in a helpless gesture. "You know the rest. I loaded him on his horse and brought him back."

"Did you see anyone, meet anyone on the way to the cave?" Charles asked.

"No, but I rode up the creek. Anyone could've been at the top of the cliff and I wouldn't have seen them."

"Did you see any weapon?"

Johnny's clenched his teeth together and swallowed. "No, I didn't see anything but Willie's body. And I didn't stay around to look either. It was scary out there by myself with just Willie's body. You don't know what it was like."

He fell silent then, his lips compressed into a straight line, and Charles could imagine his fear. He was too young to have been in Vietnam, so he had no experience with violent death, no resources to call upon, only his own inborn strength. Charles felt a growing admiration. It took courage to lift a body onto a horse, never knowing if someone was behind you, ready to murder again.

Meenie's trip to the back door to expectorate yet another stream of tobacco broke the silence. Charles cleared his throat and stood up. "Johnny, I want you to take me out there."

Johnny looked up, clearly reluctant to revisit that particular spot. "Now?" he asked.

"Yes, now." He turned to Brentwood. "J.T., can you loan us three horses?"

J.T. Brentwood's mouth dropped open. "You're going to ride a horse?"

"Yes," Charles said irritably. "I do know how. I don't think you'll have to tie me on."

"You're not exactly dressed for it," Brentwood said.

"I'll manage," Charles said.

CHAPTER

5

MEENIE REINED HIS HORSE. "HOW YOU DOIN', Sheriff?"

Charles shifted uncomfortably. The polyester material of his slacks was not designed to grip a saddle; consequently, he was sliding all over the saddle. He also suspected he was going to be two inches shorter. He had to be. No one could have their spine compressed each time the horse took a step without being shorter. And he wasn't even going to think about the bruises forming on more delicate portions of his anatomy. He hadn't done a lot of riding; young boys growing up in Dallas seldom did, but he had ridden some, and by God, he didn't remember it being this miserable.

"I'm fine," he lied, and moved his shoulders as another trickle of sweat ran down his back. He looked over toward Kurt Reynolds. It didn't help that the range manager rode as if he were part of the horse, rolling easily with the gait of the animal. Damn, wasn't the man incompetent at anything?

Charles loosened his stranglehold on the saddle horn. A second later he clutched it like a lifeline as his horse side-stepped a prairie dog hole with a little dancing step. He revised his loss of height to three inches as he came down in the saddle with an audible slapping sound as his horse followed up his dance with a stiff-legged hop.

"You all right, Sheriff?" J.T. Brentwood asked. Charles wasn't impressed with his show of concern.

"I'm fine, J.T.," he said, and glared at Meenie's look of disbelief. "How much further, Johnny?" he asked, looking over at Angie's brother.

Johnny gestured toward a group of cowboys milling around what looked like a pile of lumber. "Not much further, Sheriff. There are the branding pens."

"Damnation!" J.T. Brentwood's voice held equal measures of disbelief and anger. "Look at the mess that damn twister made." He spurred his horse into a gallop and rode ahead.

Charles debated kicking his horse into a gallop but concluded the animal would arrive several lengths ahead of him if he did. His confidence in his ability to stay on a galloping horse was nil. "How far from the branding pens, Johnny?"

"About a mile, Sheriff." The young man reined in and pointed south. "We'll follow the creek bed from here to Red Barn Cave."

Charles shifted again and hoped he'd make it another mile. He envied Raul, who by now was safely back in the sheriff's office, seated in a comfortable chair that didn't sway, typing up his notes.

He saw that Johnny and Meenie had reined in by the pens. Kurt had dismounted gracefully and was talking to J.T. Brentwood and a tall, slender man with swarthy skin.

Charles dismounted, thankful his legs still worked, and led his mare to the small group of men. J.T. Brentwood's voice was loud, raspy, and angry. His arms made large cutting motions in the air.

"Damn it, Rodriquez, I want this pen put back together, and I want it done by tomorrow evening. Damn snows made us late branding this year anyway. We're going to have yearling calves before we ever get them branded. Get a couple of the boys to round up the cattle again and get them back in this pasture. Bring out some hay if we have to, but just get them here and ready to go the minute the pen is fixed."

The swarthy man calmly lit a cigarette, cupping his hands around the match to shield it from the ever present Panhandle wind. "It can't be done, Mr. Brentwood. Even if I used every hand and we worked all night, it wouldn't be finished in time. We just now got all the boards separated, and we're going to need new lumber."

"Perhaps you're not organized well enough, Rodriquez," Reynolds said, one hand holding his reins, his other resting on his hip.

Startlingly blue eyes slanted toward the ranch manager. The face was undeniably Spanish, Charles thought, not a mixture of Spanish and Indian familiarly called Mexican. The nose was aquiline, the lips thin and well formed, the face long and olive tinted. Men with faces like that conquered Mexico and South America; men with arrogance and self-confidence. He wondered what a man like Rodriguez was doing working on a Panhandle ranch.

"I'm organized," Rodriguez replied, "but I can't do the impossible."

"That's enough, Kurt," Brentwood said. "Send some men for more lumber."

Rodriquez inclined his head toward Brentwood, and Charles thought of a conquistador accepting tribune from the defeated Aztecs. He consciously held himself still when the man's blue eyes focused on him. They were filled with watchful intelligence and curiosity.

Charles held out his hand. "Sheriff Matthews from Carroll," he said.

Brentwood reluctantly made the introduction. "Sheriff, this is my foreman, Conrad Rodriguez."

The man's slender hand held a wiry strength. "Sheriff, did you come to check on the damage?"

"No, he didn't. Willie Russell got himself killed," interrupted Brentwood.

The foreman's head swung quickly toward Brentwood. "How?" he asked.

Brentwood made a gesture. "Don't know for sure. The sheriff here thinks someone killed him."

Those blue eyes came back to rest on Charles. "Murder?"

"Yes," Charles answered.

Rodriquez never blinked, but Charles sensed that a shutter had slammed shut somewhere in the foreman's mind, and his blue eyes became devoid of expression. "Willie was a good man."

"Someone didn't think so." Charles turned abruptly to the Brentwoods. "Let's go. You can worry about your pens later."

"Later? Did you say later?" Brentwood seemed almost apoplectic. "For God's sake, Sheriff, I got to get these calves branded before it gets much later in the year."

"Then I suggest you get on with it. Johnny can show me the cave."

"No sir! I'm coming along." He mounted his horse.

"I'm coming, too," Rodriquez said suddenly, and gathering his reins, vaulted into the saddle.

"I think you need to stay here," Reynolds said, not bothering to hide his dislike of the foreman. "You're hired to be a foreman. Don't you think you need to do your job for a change?"

Rodriquez shrugged off the comment. "Willie was one of my men. When anything happens to one of my men, I want to know all about it."

Meenie let loose with a stream of tobacco juice. His target was seemingly a bug. The fact that the bug was near one of Reynolds's highly polished boots didn't deter Meenie. Reynolds whirled around to glare at the skinny, wiry deputy. "Watch what the hell you're doing."

Meenie shifted his wad from one cheek to the other. "I was watchin'. If I hadn't been, I'd a hit you."

Charles sucked in his cheeks for a second. He shouldn't wish Meenie's aim had been less than perfect. "That's enough, Meenie. Let's go. I want to look for tracks before the wind blows them away."

He turned and climbed on his mare, hearing joints crack that had always been soundless. He settled himself in the saddle, wondering if there was a more comfortable position he didn't know about. He tensed his legs to kick his mare when a cowboy stopped him.

"Sheriff, I heard you talking. What happened to Willie?"

Charles looked at the cowboy. He was probably middle to late thirties, although it was hard to tell. His skin was leather brown with white creases around the eyes from squinting at the sun. He was dressed like the others: Levi's, boots, and Western shirt. The only thing different about him was an elaborate trophy belt buckle. Charles didn't know much about cowboys, but he did know that buckle had been won, not bought. No working cowboy would buy a trophy belt buckle. It would be a violation of their code.

"Are you a friend of his?" he asked.

The cowboy looked at the ground for a moment. "Everybody was Willie's friend."

Charles watched the cowboy closely. "Someone wasn't his friend. Willie was murdered."

The cowboy's head jerked up, and he looked at the mounted riders, his face graying under its leathery tan. His gray eyes were cold with fear for a moment, and Charles looked quickly at the other men. No face revealed more than curiosity, and in the case of J.T. Brentwood, impatience. Charles mentally kicked himself for watching the cowboy so closely that he missed whatever threatening glance or gesture had frightened him.

He leaned over the cowboy, his voice a low whisper that didn't carry to the listening men. "If you know anything, you'd better tell me."

The cowboy licked his lips, and dug in his breast pocket for a twist of chewing tobacco. "I don't know anything, Sheriff."

"What's your name?" Charles demanded.

"Skinny Jordan."

"I'll want to talk to you later, Mr. Jordan," Charles said, and finally kicked his horse into a slow walk.

Meenie fell in beside Charles. "What'd he want, Sheriff?" he asked in a low voice, his faded eyes, surrounded by their own white creases, fixed on the riders ahead.

Charles was studying the men of the Branding Iron Ranch: the Brentwoods, father and son; Kurt Reynolds; and Conrad Rodriquez. "He wanted to know what happened. When I told him, he looked at one of those four men and turned white. Were you watching them?"

Meenie leaned over in his saddle and spit at the white bloom of a yucca plant. "No, I was watchin' you and that cowboy. I couldn't even see his face, just the back of his head. Who do you think he was lookin' at?"

Charles shook his head. "I don't know, Meenie. Until we can figure out a motive, we might as well suspect the man in the moon. We've got a crime committed outdoors in the middle of a tornado, when everybody was hiding from the storm. Unless we find out someone was hiding in Red Barn Cave with Willie, we're not going to have any eye witnesses. And the murder weapon, if we knew what it was, could be anywhere in the county. Damn it, we've got to find a motive."

"Sheriff, you want us to slow our horses?" J.T. Brentwood called, pulling up his horse. "We don't want to lose you."

Charles wished again that Brentwood wasn't Angie's father because he was beginning to heartily dislike the man. His eyes shifted to Kurt Reynolds and caught the condescending smile directed at him. His dislike of the ranch manager was rapidly solidifying to hatred. "No, Meenie and I were just discussing what to do when we reached the murder scene. We'll speed up."

"We speed up too much and you'll fall off that damn horse," muttered his deputy.

The riding wasn't any easier along the creek bed. The horses' hooves kicked up the packed sand, and the wind sent it whirling into the riders' eyes. Stoically Charles endured, his eyes focused on the thin ribbon of water in the middle of the creek. He straightened from his slumped position when he heard Johnny Brentwood's voice.

"There it is, Sheriff: Red Barn Cave."

Charles looked up and saw the cave entrance high on the canyon wall, about six feet from the rim itself. "Where exactly was the body?"

"On that ledge just in front of the cave," the younger man answered. "Can you see it?"

Charles shaded his eyes and could distinguish the small shelf that jutted out in front of the cave. Why didn't the murderer drag the body inside the cave instead of leaving it outside in full view? And how did the killer get to the ledge without being seen from the cave? He measured the distance from the rim of the canyon and decided it must be a ten foot drop to the little ledge in front of the cave. A very dangerous drop. A man could miss the ledge altogether and roll down the embankment. And there would be no way to do it soundlessly.

He examined the wall of the canyon on either side of the cave. The gnarled mesquite tree by the cave entrance towered a good three feet above the canyon wall. Or, at least half of it did. The other half lay in a tangle of branches and split trunk on the other side of the cave. If anyone climbed down that tree, they risked a bad fall. The only alternative was to walk up to the cave.

Charles dismounted and stood holding the reins, while examining the ground. There were hoof prints in several places, and he didn't want to add more. He looked around. The only vegetation on the canyon floor was a dead cottonwood and a salt cedar tree further down the creek. He looked at the group with him. "Rodriquez, would you tie everyone's horse to that salt cedar?" he asked, pointing to the wizened tree.

"What the hell for, Sheriff?" Brentwood asked. "These are trained cow ponies. You can ground-hitch them; they ain't going to run off."

Flushing, Charles swung his head toward Angie's father. "All right, but ground-hitch them over by the salt cedar." He tossed his reins into Rodriquez's waiting hands and turned back toward the cave. He might not know a great deal about horses and ranches, but Brentwood didn't have to rub his nose in it.

He hunkered down, feeling every muscle in his body protest, and studied the double line of footprints that were still visible in the hard, packed dirt. Hearing the jangling of spurs that announced the men were behind him, Charles spoke without looking up. "Johnny, you said you found Willie's horse?"

Johnny knelt down by Charles. "That's right, but that was back by the branding pens."

"What did you do with the saddle?"

"The horse didn't have a saddle on, or a bridle either. I had to loop a rope around its neck to lead it in."

Charles looked toward the cave entrance. "There are three sets of footprints: two leading to the cave, and one away from it. Which sets are yours?"

Johnny lifted his hat and smoothed his hair nervously. "I'm not sure which ones are mine going up, but these are mine coming down. See that scuffed place?" he asked, pointing at an area halfway up the canyon wall. "I fell when

I was carrying Willie's body down.'' His voice broke, and he swallowed.

Charles glanced around the canyon, imagining the scene. Isolated, with the wind blowing eerily down its walls, and a scared young man falling under the weight of a dead body. Most men would have looked worse than Johnny Brentwood after such an experience. "Okay, Johnny, stand up and let's see which of the footprints going up are yours.''

Johnny glanced at his father, then stood up, placing his feet next to the set of footprints. Charles didn't give Brentwood a chance to protest. "Meenie, get a camera out of the evidence kit.''

Meenie untied a small kit the size of a medical bag from around the saddle horn, opened it, and pulled the field camera. "Got it, Sheriff.''

Charles stepped away. "I want pictures of the footprints.''

Brentwood's reaction was immediate. "Just a damn minute, Sheriff. You aren't taking any pictures with my boy in them. Johnny, you get away from there.''

"Stand still, Johnny!'' Charles said, moving between the young man and his father. Meenie, moving faster than Charles was aware he could, snapped several pictures before the effect of the sheriff's whiplash voice wore off.

Meenie lowered the camera and spit. "Got 'em, Sheriff.''

"You'll never get to use those pictures, Sheriff. My lawyer will have your hide first. You coerced my son.''

Reynolds's voice interrupted. "Sheriff, aren't you exceeding your authority?''

Charles was hot, tired, sore from riding that damn horse, and not in the mood to put up with any comments from Kurt Reynolds. The man didn't even look dusty. "You are strictly an observer, Reynolds. I tolerated your coming along. Don't push your luck.''

He turned back to face Johnny, brows still drawn together

in a frown. "What did you do after you brought Willie's body down?"

"I tied him on his horse and rode back to the ranch."

"Show me," Charles said. "Where was your horse? Where was his horse? Were they tied up?"

Johnny looked dazed, his earlier belligerence gone. "Over here." He pointed to the dead cottonwood. "I tied my horse and Willie's here. I laid Willie's body on the back of his horse, and . . ." He stopped, and swallowed. "Then I realized he'd fall off, his body, I mean, so I got my tie rope and looped it around his feet and hands—" His voice broke. "Well, you saw how he was tied."

"Okay, son, that's enough," Charles said. He jerked his head at Meenie to follow, then walked to dead tree. He crouched down and studied the ground. "Can you tell how many horses have been here by the tracks, Meenie?" he asked, his voice low.

Meenie set the evidence kit down, pushed his hat back, and peered at him. "What are you thinkin'?"

"I don't like what I'm thinking, that's why I want to know how many horses have been tied to this tree."

"Well, 'course, we got prints of Willie's horse kinda ranging around here. Easy to tell that one because it was hobbled."

"Then Johnny was telling the truth about finding Willie's horse?"

"Well, I saw some tracks of a hobbled horse as we was riding down here; some horses learn to hop wearin' a hobble. Why? You figure Johnny is lyin'?"

"I don't know yet. Look at the tracks and tell me how many horses we have to match up with how many people."

Meenie stood and walked around the tree, stopping occasionally to examine the sandy ground. He ran his fingers along the rough, gray bark of the tree, a frown adding lines to those already creasing his forehead. He shifted his wad of tobacco and spit, neatly missing all the hoofprints.

"Hell, Sheriff, the ground's so sandy, and the damn wind's always blowing, and the ground all chewed up, I just can't tell. Coulda been two, coulda been three, coulda been a whole damn herd. It looks like they all been shod recently, so ain't nothin' special about any of the prints, no loose horseshoes or nails. And you can't get a real clear print in this sandy ground. Sand kinda filters back in the print. On different soil, a cowboy that knows the horses on this ranch could tell you how many, and probably which particular horse made a print."

"How could he do that?"

Meenie shifted his tobacco from one cheek to another. "Well, you see, Sheriff, every hoof is different, like feet. That's why you got to have horseshoes fitted to each individual hoof. But I can tell you one thing: one of them horses was spooked." He knelt down and pointed. "See them prints that are deeper than the others, and these that are kind of gouged out?"

Charles nodded. "What does that tell us?"

"It tells us either there were two or three horses, or just one horse that something scared. Them gouged out places means the horse was pawin' the ground like a dog tryin' to dig a hole. Now a horse don't do that unless he's spooked. If I was guessin', and mind you, it's a guess, I'd say there was three horses, or maybe one horse tied up at three different times. Bark on the trunk's been worked over pretty good in one place. Probably the spooked horse tryin' to get loose."

"Any tracks leading away from the tree and back down the creek?"

"Yeah, two sets. I figure they're Johnny's and Willie's." Meenie spit again. "But hell, Sheriff, a man could ride down the middle of the creek and you wouldn't find no tracks. Ain't much water there, but it won't take much to hide tracks if a man's careful.''

Charles shook his head. "Then why aren't there tracks leading to the creek?''

Meenie gave him a pitying look. "Ain't you ever seen any cowboy movies, Sheriff? On sandy soil like this, and with the wind blowing, you can brush away tracks with a tree branch, or a coiled rope, or your hat for that matter. I ain't no Indian tracker, so I can't tell you anymore.''

Charles grinned. "Know any Indians, Meenie?''

The deputy snorted. "We chased Quanah Parker and his Comanches out of the Panhandle more than a hundred years ago. Ain't been no Indians around here since then. There's probably somebody around who can read tracks better than me, but I don't know who. And if it took him more than a couple hours to get here, he couldn't help anyhow. Damn wind'll blow these tracks away by dark.''

Charles took off his suit coat and slung it over his shoulder. He could feel his shirt sticking to his torso in great, sweaty patches. Maybe the wind that was busily blowing away his evidence would cool him off. "Take some pictures of the hoofprints and of the trunk with the rope burn. If we ever get to trial, the jury will want to see pictures. I'm going to talk to J.T. about horseshoes.''

Meenie's low-voiced comment stopped him. "Sheriff, I just found one set of bootprints around the tree.''

"I could see that, and Johnny Brentwood's boots fit them.''

CHAPTER

6

CHARLES COULD FEEL THE ANIMOSITY FROM TEN feet away. J.T. Brentwood would rope and tie him and drag him through a yucca-studded pasture given the least opportunity. He walked up to the rancher, ignoring the other men. "J.T., when did you have your horses shod?"

He heard someone inhale sharply and stepped back to include the other men in his range of vision. Johnny's dazed look had been replaced by his more customary sullen expression. Kurt Reynolds looked at him with dislike and suspicion. Only Rodriquez seemed outside the pale as he stood calmly smoking a cigarette, his eyes watchful. Charles cursed himself for being so intent on one man, that he failed to watch the others. Someone had reacted to his question and he had no idea who.

"What in the hell does that have to do with anything?" Brentwood demanded.

"I think you'd better explain yourself, Sheriff," Reynolds said.

Charles took a deep breath and exhaled slowly before he spoke. "Whoever killed Willie Russell rode a horse—and probably tied it to that dead cottonwood. Meenie tells me the hoofprints indicate the horses had been shod recently. Now tell me when your horses were last shod."

Brentwood came charging back into the conversation.

''Now just a damn minute, Sheriff. Are you accusing some-one on this ranch of murdering Willie?''

''I'm not accusing anyone of anything yet. I'm only col-lecting facts,'' Charles snapped.

''You go collect facts somewhere else. Nobody on this ranch is going to answer any more questions.'' He whirled around to glare at his son and two employees. ''Did you hear that, boys? No one talks to the sheriff.''

Meenie cleared his throat and spit. ''You want me to go back to town and get the deputies, Sheriff? I figure we can round up all the cowboys before dark. Probably take a couple of days to question them. 'Course that might put the brandin' a little behind schedule, and Mr. Brentwood pushin' hot weather now—'' Meenie was interrupted by Brentwood's in-dignant roar.

''What the hell are you trying to pull, Higgins? You know I'm going to have trouble with flies causing infection as it is. If I have to wait any longer, I'm going to have more sick calves than I can handle.''

Charles hadn't the faintest idea what Meenie and Brent-wood were talking about, but his deputy had the stubborn rancher on the run, and that's all that mattered. ''I hate to do that, Meenie, but it seems we have no choice.''

Brentwood rubbed his hand over his face and capitulated. ''Kurt, when were the horses last shod?''

Rodriguez threw his cigarette down and carefully ground it out. ''Three weeks ago, Sheriff,'' he said, his voice deep and totally unaccented.

Kurt Reynolds frowned. ''I believe I can answer the sher-iff's questions, Rodriquez.'' The foreman shrugged his shoulders and was silent.

''Not all of them, Sheriff.'' Meenie's voice interrupted before Reynolds could answer. ''That mare you're ridin' wasn't shod no three weeks ago, and neither was my horse.''

Reynolds inclined his head. ''Still a cowboy, aren't you,

Meenie? You're right, of course. Davis only shoed about eight horses. We had a problem with horses throwing their shoes. I haven't found out why, but I intend to.''

"Davis is your blacksmith?''

"I hardly think you could call him a blacksmith. Any cowboy worth his salt can shoe a horse, but Davis seems to enjoy doing it, so most of the other cowboys let him.''

"Whose horses did he shoe?'' Charles asked.

Reynolds considered, long, calloused fingers rubbing his square jaw. "Mine, J.T.'s, Johnny's, Rodriquez's, and Willie's.'' He stopped. "I'm sorry, I can't remember the others. Just some of the remuda, I think.''

"What do you mean by remuda?''

"Ranch stock, horses anyone can ride. They don't belong to any one particular person.''

Charles wanted to grind his teeth in frustration. "You mean anyone on this ranch could saddle up one of those horses?''

J.T. Brentwood grinned. "That's about the size of it, Sheriff.''

"And how many men on this ranch?''

J.T. glanced at Reynolds. "Ten men, Sheriff, plus the four of us. But knowin' that isn't going to help you.''

Charles felt his stomach beginning to burn. "Why not?''

The rancher's eyes were triumphant, like a poker player who has been losing, then suddenly draws a royal flush. "Because nobody on this ranch would kill Willie even if they had a reason to, and you'll never prove otherwise.''

Charles had a sudden mental picture of himself: hot, tired, sore, out of his element, unfamiliar with the environment, a city boy in the country, facing men at ease in the dusty, windswept land. But J.T. had pinpointed the central issue: character. And its corollary: motive. Motive was tied to character, and he'd seen too much of the dark side of men's souls to be easily fooled. He had met many people with a motive to murder, but only a few of those had the character, or lack of it, to commit one.

Charles turned to face the cave, feeling for the first time since he'd arrived at the Branding Iron Ranch that he was in control again.

He jerked his head at his deputy. "Meenie, let's check out the cave." He caught a movement from Brentwood and half turned to face the rancher. "I'm investigating a crime scene, J.T., and that means I'm in charge no matter who actually owns the property. You and your men stay here."

Brentwood heard the sharp authority in Charles's voice and nodded unhappily. "All right, Sheriff."

Kurt Reynolds either didn't have as sharp an ear, or failed to recognize that Charles, hot and dusty in slacks and sweat-splotched shirt, was no more to be challenged than a coiled rattlesnake in downtown Dallas. Both would bite, however out of place they might look.

"I'm not sure you can legally keep us out of the cave," Reynolds began.

Charles was several steps away, but Meenie swore afterward that the sheriff moved so fast he was a blur. Certainly the manager didn't have a chance to move before Charles had gathered a fistful of shirt and jerked Reynolds to within a few inches of his face. "Shut up, Reynolds, or I'll stuff that bandanna you're wearing down your throat!"

Brentwood jumped into the fray, at least verbally, his voice holding its own note of authority. "Kurt! That's enough. Back off!"

Charles loosened his fingers, turned on his heel, and stalked up the slope toward the cave, his heart sending waves of adrenaline through his veins. He could feel the sweat on his brow and upper lip, and he knew it was not from the heat but an almost uncontrollable anger. What he didn't know was how much of that anger was caused by Reynolds's supercilious attitude, and how much was caused by his sheer dislike of the man. Either way, he had reacted violently, and it sickened him. Even Meenie's well-meant observation grated.

"Been waitin' all day for you to blow. Shoulda done it earlier. Man like Reynolds pushes until someone pushes back."

"Drop it, Meenie. I had no business losing my temper."

"Why? Is it against the law?"

Charles turned on his deputy. "For a sheriff, yes. And none of your homespun philosophy, either."

Meenie held up his hands. "All right, I ain't about to waste my breath tryin' to talk to someone who's got a burr under his saddle. They ain't gonna listen anyhow."

Unwillingly, Charles grinned. Something else was a waste of breath, and that was trying to silence his deputy.

He slapped the scrawny man on the back. "Thanks, Meenie."

The deputy shifted his tobacco to swell out his other cheek. "What for, Sheriff?"

"For being such an irascible, disrespectable, constant in my life."

Meenie spit in disgust. "That's what I get for asking. I still don't understand what the hell I did."

"It doesn't matter," Charles said as he gained the tiny ledge and stepped carefully to one side. He knelt down and pointed to the ground. "I would say this is where the murder was committed."

Meenie knelt down next to Charles and stared at the discolored patches of soil. "You want me to take a sample to see if it's blood?"

Wearily Charles pushed himself up, a familiar acid taste in his mouth. If he lived a thousand years, violent death would still sicken him. "Yes, and take a picture of the footprints, too."

Meenie opened the evidence kit and took out a plastic bag. "I don't see but one set, Sheriff."

"I know it, and there ought to be at least two. Otherwise, we have to assume Willie just stood here without moving, waiting to be hit in the back of the head."

Meenie sealed the evidence bag, labeled it, and tucked it back in the kit. He pulled out the camera, checked its setting, and took several pictures. Putting the camera back, he remained couched by the evidence kit, his face a study of cynicism. "Either someone was mighty smart to erase their footprints, or mighty dumb to leave just one set."

Charles stepped to the cave entrance and glanced back at his deputy. "Or we're talking about two different people." He stooped and entered the cave.

His first feeling was one of thankfulness to be out of the wind and heat, his second, one of unease. He felt he was entering a tomb. The ceiling was too low, and he could almost feel it press against him. Gradually his eyes adjusted, and the dead man's possessions seemed to come floating out of the gloom that the yellow light of the lantern only emphasized: the saddle, saddlebags, a tin cup lying on its side, a pan of watercolors, and a discarded sketch pad, open to a clean page. It looked as if Willie had stepped out for a minute, expecting to return.

Charles held out his hand. "Give me a flashlight," and grasped the slim tube of metal Meenie took from the evidence kit. He flicked it on, and methodically swung its beam back and forth across the cave's dusty floor, lighting up the corners not touched by the rays of the lantern.

"No footprints, Meenie. Somebody was very careful."

Meenie couched down and duck-walked to the saddlebags. "I wonder if we're goin' to find anything, Sheriff."

Charles followed him, and thankfully sank to the floor. First a horse, and then a cave with a four-foot ceiling. He only hoped he could live through the day without his back being permanently damaged. "Hand me those saddlebags and let's see what we've got."

What they had wasn't much: a can opener, small skillet, a spoon and fork (both worn and scratched) several cans of beans and fruit, and a generous supply of commercially packaged beef jerky. Some folded sketches were haphazardly packed with the food. Charles sat looking at the cache. "Not a very exciting diet to live on for a weekend."

Meenie juggled a can of peaches. "He sure wasn't fixin' to waste any time cookin'. And if some sneak thief killed him, they sure as hell didn't take nothin'. Even his saddle's still here."

Charles picked up one of the sketches and unfolded it. "My God!" The words burst out without his being aware of it, and he feverishly grabbed the other sketches.

Meenie's expletive was much shorter and more profane, a word, Charles noted vaguely, that his deputy seldom used. He also noted that Meenie's hand was shaking as he grabbed the first sketch. "It's the Santiago Crucifix, Sheriff!" Meenie's eyes darted around the cave. "And he leaned it against that wall and painted a picture of it. Holy Hell! Willie Russell found the Santiago Crucifix!"

Charles spread the sketches out on the cave floor. "Look, Meenie," he said, pointing to a terrified woman's face. "This is Angie holding the baby, and the older man by the priest is J.T."

Meenie squinted his farsighted eyes to focus on the painting. "The priest is Rodriquez, and the young shepherd in the corner is Johnny."

"What's the painting telling us, Meenie? What is the Santiago Crucifix, and more importantly, where is it now?"

"Juan Santiago was a sheepherder along the Canadian River back around 1878 or thereabouts. I don't know all the story, or even half of it, but most of us old-timers have heard the legend of the lost crucifix of gold. It was supposed to have been buried by Santiago just before he and his family was killed, but nobody ever knew where. It's just one of those stories you hear and don't know whether you ought to believe or not. Lots of stories like it in the Panhandle.''

"Who knows more, Meenie?" Charles asked urgently.

Meenie screwed up his face in a painful expression of thought. "Old Judge Nourse probably would know. He's older than dirt and knows more tales than anyone around here. He lives in Carroll with an old spinster daughter. Old man must be past ninety, but he's still sharper than a tack. Ask him, Sheriff, about the crucifix if you think it'll help. 'Course I don't see how knowin' about it is goin' catch no murderer.''

Charles didn't see either, but he was holding the motive for the murder in his hand, or rather a picture of it, and he felt an almost superstitious interest in it. He folded the sketches. He felt uneasy trying to explain his unformed thoughts to his practical deputy, so he didn't try. How could he explain a silent oath not to allow the symbol of ultimate unselfish sacrifice to remain in the hands of one who committed the ultimate selfish act: murder.

"Dust the saddlebags and saddle. I should have had you do that before we touched anything. Riding that horse must have damaged my brain as well as my back. Then let's get back to town. I need some thinking time before I do anything else.''

Meenie obediently got the fingerprint kit out and began dusting the saddlebags. "Ain't nothin' here but yours, mine, and probably Willie's. Bunch of smudges from gloves.''

"You mean our murderer wore gloves?''

"If he was ridin' a horse to get here, and I don't see any other easy way to get here, he was wearin' gloves. And you're goin' wish you hada been, too, by tomorrow,'' he added darkly.

Charles flexed his sore hands and grimaced. "I think I'm goin' to wish I'd never seen a horse by tomorrow.

Meenie grinned as he industriously brushed fingerprint

powder on the saddle. "How long's it been since you rode a horse?"

"About twenty years or so. Horses weren't exactly common in Dallas."

"I think I'm goin' take patrol duty tomorrow. You're gonna be sore as hell, twice as snappish, and not fit company for anybody. I think I'll let Raul and Miss Poole put up with you. Ain't nothin' on this saddle either," he added.

Charles shoveled the food and sketch pad and paints in the saddle bags, and grabbed them and the lantern. "No, you're not. You're bringing our four friends waiting at the bottom of the canyon to town to make statements. And just for trying to evade my presence, you can haul that saddle down the slope."

Meenie grabbed the saddle. " 'Evade my presence' the man said; hell, half the time I don't know what he's talking about." He crawled to the cave entrance after Charles, dragging the heavy saddle behind him. "How come I get to bring them in? Why not Raul?"

Charles crawled outside and stood up, blinking at the brilliant sunlight. His body felt stiff and rubbery at the same time, and he hoped he could make it down the slope without falling. "Because you aren't impressed by anybody, Meenie. If I told you to arrest the president, you'd do it. Besides, you speak J.T. Brentwood's language, and I don't."

Meenie stood up by him, carrying the saddle in unknown imitation of Willie, the saddle horn tucked under his armpit, and the weight resting on his skinny hip. "Well, I worked for Mr. Brentwood back in the days when I was cowboyin'. I know which bush to shake to get him to move. And if Brentwood moves, Johnny and Reynolds ain't far behind. Rodriquez I ain't sure about. Somethin' funny about him."

J.T. Brentwood started up the slope before Charles's surprise at learning about Meenie's employer wore off. "Sheriff, did you find the tally book?"

"I didn't find any tally book, J.T., and even if I did, I couldn't turn it over to you. All personal effects will be impounded until the investigation is over," Charles said. He was a little tired of hearing about that tally book.

Brentwood took off his hat and wiped his arm across his forehead. "Sheriff, if you find that book, I got to have it. You just don't understand what's involved."

Charles' fury carried him past the rancher and over to his mare. He slammed the saddlebags over the horse's back, gathered the reins in one hand, and grabbed the saddle horn with the other.

Then he swung himself into the saddle, his face draining of color as his sore posterior made contact with the hard leather. He exhaled sharply as pain jolted its way up his spine and down each thigh.

"Someone murdered one of your cowboys, J.T., one of your friends to hear you talk about him, and you're more concerned about slapping a hot branding iron against some calf's rear than about catching a coldblooded killer. Do me a favor, J.T. Don't ever claim me as a friend."

Brentwood's eyes chilled, and he looked not ashamed but insulted; Charles felt a shiver of unease. "Did anybody ever tell you not to shoot your mouth off when you didn't have any ammunition, Sheriff? Willie Russell was my friend, and you'll never find his killer because you're too damn citified to know where to look or what questions to ask. Now ride that horse back to headquarters, then get the hell off my ranch. And don't set foot on my property again without a warrant."

Charles felt disgusted with his own loss of self-control. He'd let his own personal repugnance color his attitude toward a witness, and as a result, J.T. Brentwood had drawn a figurative line and dared him to step over it. The damnable thing was, he was going to have to do just that. The murdered victim, the murder scene, and, without doubt, the murderer, were all connected with the Branding Iron Ranch. He would be coming back whether Brentwood agreed or not.

"Meenie will be out in the morning to pick up the four of you, or, if you prefer, you can drive yourselves in. Be at my office at nine o'clock."

"The hell you say," Brentwood said flatly.

Charles crossed his hands over the saddle horn. "Shall I get warrants, J.T., or will you come without them?"

Brentwood spread his legs and crossed his arms over his chest. He jerked his head toward his son and the other two men. Reynolds stepped quickly to his side, a faint smile curling his lips. Johnny followed but stood slightly behind his father and Reynolds, looking at the ground. Rodriquez stood apart, one foot resting on a rock, smoking a cigarette. His face was expressionless, but his eyes were trained on Brentwood. J.T. frowned at his foreman, then looked at Charles. "Do what you want, Sheriff. No one at the Branding Iron leaves."

Charles caught a movement out of the corner of his eyes and swung his head. Meenie was mounted on his horse, his revolver drawn and resting on the saddle horn. Nausea cramped his stomach. Guns and violence, pride and stubbornness; the ingredients of any bad Western novel. Even the fair damsel was represented. He shivered in spite of the heat and wiped the icy sweat off his forehead. He couldn't walk away from this power struggle even for Angie.

He shifted in the saddle to face J.T. Brentwood and hoped his face didn't reflect the agony he felt, because his next words would alienate the Brentwoods, and Angie was a Brentwood. "J.T., once I'm forced to get a warrant, then I may legally use all any means necessary to serve it. Are you willing to go to jail to protect a murderer?" He lowered his voice and held Brentwood's eyes with his own. "Are you willing to shoot me, because that's the only way to stop me."

Charles held himself straight and stiff, his pent-up breath

tight in his chest, and watched Brentwood struggle with his conflict. The man stared endlessly into Charles's eyes before looking away, his face suddenly haggard. "You win, Sheriff. We'll be there."

Charles watched Brentwood and the other men mount their horses and let his shoulders slump. "You're wrong, J.T.," he whispered under his breath. "I lost." Angie would never forgive him for threatening her father.

CHAPTER

7

"SHERIFF! WHAT THE HELL HAPPENED TO YOUR EYE?"

Slim's voice grated along the sheriff's spine like a fingernail on a blackboard. He paused with his hand on his office door. There was no way to avoid questions, no way he could sneak into his office without answering them. He might as well get it over with now.

He turned and tilted his head back slightly so he could see through the swollen slit that constituted his right eye. "I hit it on something," he said flatly.

Raul stared first at the swollen purple flesh around Charles's eye, then at the crimson sunburned skin on the rest of his face. "Sheriff, what happened?"

"It's a long story, and we have more important things to worry about than that, like who murdered Willie Russell out on the Branding Iron Ranch."

"Did you have a run-in with the murderer, Sheriff? Is that why you look so beat up?"

Charles glared at Slim, thinking the young, freckled-faced boy might never reach twenty-five unless he learned when to drop a subject. "No, I didn't have a run-in with the murderer, and I'm not beat up. Just a little sunburned and my eye hurts."

"Sheriff, you're filthy." Miss Poole's voice was censorious; in her opinion, gentlemen did not come to work in soiled clothes.

Charles whirled around, but the quick motion caused a throbbing in his eye. He clapped his hand over it and attempted to stare Miss Poole into silence. However, Miss Poole had nearly forty years of character development over Slim, and she ignored his fierce look.

"Now, Sheriff, are you going to tell us what happened, or shall I ask Meenie?" Miss Poole sat at her dispatcher's desk, every iron-gray hair in place, and all the moral authority of an ex-schoolteacher figuratively draped around her shoulders.

Charles wondered if Meenie could withstand Miss Poole's inquisition, but he decided he was too tired, too sore, and too pressed for time to wait for the outcome of that power struggle. Besides, it would probably end in a draw, and Miss Poole would be after him again. "I was hit with a cinch," he said, hoping to head off any more questions.

Miss Poole was not easy to head off. "If I'm not mistaken, Sheriff, a cinch is a strap for holding a saddle in place. I don't understand how a strap could inflict such an injury."

Meenie aimed for the spitoon beside Miss Poole's desk and Charles saw the old lady flinch. In the nine months she'd worked as dispatcher, she'd never known Meenie to miss, but Charles guessed she had enough working knowledge of the law of averages not to want to be in range when it happened.

Meenie grinned. "You want me to call old Judge Nourse, Sheriff?"

Charles grabbed the change of subject with all the enthusiasm of a droning man grabbing a life preserver. "Yes, ask him if I could talk to him about seven tonight."

"I certainly hope you shower and change clothes first, Sheriff," Miss Poole said. "And you might come up with a better story to account for that eye. Judge Nourse won't believe that one any more than I do."

"Did someone hit you with the cinch? Is that how it happened, Sheriff?" Slim wasn't about to give up.

Charles had never realized just how tenacious the young man was. "No," he said.

"Then how did it happen?" Slim clenched his fists, his hero worship showing in his eyes. "If someone did it on purpose, Sheriff, you just tell me and I'll take care of it. I'm younger than you, and I'm pretty good in a fight."

"That's enough!" Charles roared. "I was taking a saddle off a horse, slipped and fell, and the cinch ring hit me in the eye."

"You needn't be so defensive, Sheriff. These freak accidents happen," Miss Poole said. "I'm sure everyone will understand."

Charles doubted that since the accident was the logical result of trying to carry a heavy saddle over his shoulder. He'd seen movie actors casually toss saddles over their shoulders, carrying them only by the saddle horn. He concluded those saddles had to be made of lightweight plastic. His own saddle had gone over his shoulder all the way to the ground, taking him with it. He might have been able to preserve his dignity, if the damn metal end of the cinch hadn't flipped up and hit him in the eye as he'd heaved the saddle up and over his shoulder. Thankfully, J.T., his manager, and Rodriquez had elected to stay at the branding pens and thus hadn't witnessed his fall. But Johnny Brentwood had, and Charles had no doubt he would tell his father with all the necessary embellishments. He wished Willie Russell had never found the crucifix, and thus never been murdered, or if both things had to happen, why did they have to happen on the Branding Iron Ranch?

Charles clutched the manila folder a little tighter and squinted at the door in search of a doorbell. Either there wasn't one, or his vision was so impaired, he couldn't see it.

It was amazing how little one could see out of one eye, if one was used to two. Giving up, he opened the screen and knocked on the door.

Stepping back, he waited, gingerly stroking the blisters on the palms of his right hand with his thumb. Somewhere on his body there must be a square inch or two that didn't hurt, but he hadn't discovered it yet. When the door opened a few inches, and a watery gray eye peered through, Charles quickly reached for his hat. "Miss Nourse," he began, and found his words completely drowned out by a high-pitched squeal.

"Dad! There's a man out there!"

A voice that managed to be both raspy and rumbling at the same time reverberated through the partially open door. "Does he have a red nose and a black eye?"

The gray eye reappeared, ran quickly up and down Charles, and vanished again. "Yes! And he's big!"

"Well, let him in, you silly girl. I'm expecting him."

"But, Daddy," the disembodied voice squealed.

Charles heard the raspy voice interspersed by several loud thuds. "Damnation, girl! I said, let him in. It's the sheriff."

The door closed, and Charles heard the rattle of a chain. He arranged his face in what he hoped was a pleasant expression. Whomever the gray eye belonged to was obviously easily frightened, and his appearance certainly wasn't going to win any beauty contests in the next several days.

Reflecting later, Charles was proud of his self-control in holding his painfully sunburned face in a smile for never had he seen a woman who looked more like a mouse than Judge Nourse's daughter. Possessed of a sharp nose, sharp chin, gray-brown hair frizzed around her face, a plump body, and long, skinny feet shod in fuzzy pink house shoes, she only needed a tail and whiskers to twitch to look at home peering out of a hole in the baseboard.

"Don't stand there staring, young man. Come in and let

me get a good look at you.'' The rumbling voice sounded
testy. ''Girl, go bring that coffee into my office. And mind
you bring a bottle of whiskey with it.''

The mouse squealed in disapproval. ''But, Dad, the doctor
said—''

A polished oak cane hit the floor with a resounding thud.
''I've outlived doctors smarter than this new whippersnap-
per. Now you get me my whiskey.'' Two enormous, knobby
hands folded themselves over the cane and two piercing blue
eyes examined Charles. ''Think you know how to carry a
saddle now, young man?'' Judge Nourse asked, and a chuckle
came rumbling its way up a cavernous chest.

Charles felt his hot, red skin become even brighter.
''Meenie has a big mouth,'' he muttered as he followed the
judge into a small office.

The judge settled himself in a large leather chair in front
of the largest rolltop desk Charles had ever seen. He waved
his cane at another chair. ''Sit down, son.''

Helplessly, Charles looked around. Shelves choked with
books covered all four walls, books lay piled on end tables,
in precariously balanced stacks on the floor, and almost completely covered the couch and remaining chair. Finally, he
cleared off the chair and sat down, and examined the judge
in turn.

Large-framed would be an inadequate description for the
extraordinarily tall, broad-shouldered old man. His shirt and
jeans hung loosely, as if age had stripped him of extraneous
flesh, leaving only ropy muscles over his skeleton. His hair
was iron-gray, as was the handlebar mustache that completely covered his upper lip. Blue eyes undimmed by age
were deep-set under bristly eyebrows. Charles could understand Meenie's telling this man about the black eye. Charles
doubted even Miss Poole could face down the judge.

The old man reached in a humidor and pulled out a black,
foul-looking cigar. ''Well, son, what do you think?''

Charles blinked. "About what, sir?"

"About me," answered the old man, clearing a space on the top of the desk for the tray his mousey daughter brought in.

"Well, sir, I really don't have an opinion," Charles began.

"Nonsense," the Judge said briskly, then glared at his daughter. "Set that damn tray down before you drop it, then go to bed. I'll let the sheriff out and lock up." Impatiently he watched his daughter skitter out of the room. He chuckled as he filled a cup with one part coffee to ten parts whiskey and handed it to Charles. "Drink up, son, and tell me why you've come to see an old reprobate like me."

Charles took a cautious sip from his cup. He felt his tenseness dissolve along with the linings of his throat and stomach as the whiskey seared its way through his system. Carefully he sat his cup on top of a stack of books next to his chair. A little of the judge's whiskey went a long way. "Willie Russell was murdered today out at Red Barn Cave."

"I know," interrupted the judge, who chuckled at Charles's expression. "Sooner or later, I find out everything that happens in Crawford County. I don't get out much anymore. They took away my driver's licence—said I was too old to be driving a car, but I still have a telephone, and I know a few people. And Willie was a friend of mine," he added somberly. "But what does Willie's murder have to do with me? I'm not a suspect, am I? There's lots of people I wouldn't mind killing, but Willie wasn't one of them."

Charles smiled, then winced. His face was just too sore for any expression. "No, Judge, you're not a suspect; although, at this point, if you'd care to confess, I'd be glad to arrest you."

"The case's a tough nut to crack, is it?"

Charles looked at his blistered hands. "The evidence seems to point to someone, but I don't think he did it. Not that I don't think he might kill, but not for *this*." And he

opened the manila folder and handled the sketch of the crucifix to the judge.

The old man sat motionless, then carefully placed his cigar
in an already overflowing ashtray. "The Santiago Crucifix,"
he said softly. He looked up at Charles, his face suddenly
old. "I never thought I'd live to see it." The judge smoothed
the creases where the paper had been folded. "I probably
know more about the Santiago Crucifix than anyone living.
I even wrote to the church in Spain where the crucifix came
from to get a description of it. But Willie never saw that
letter, and I never told him about it."

He pointed to the sketch. "See the sign above Christ's
head? It's inlaid with tiny rubies and diamonds. And here is
a heart-shaped ruby representing Christ's heart. And the
whole cross is outlined in rubies and emeralds and diamonds. Willie actually saw the crucifix to be able to paint it
so perfectly."

Charles looked at the sketch. "And it's the motive for
murder, just as it was a hundred years ago."

The judge looked at him curiously. "What makes you say
that, Sheriff?"

Charles handed the other sketches to the judge. "Willie
tells the story very clearly in his sketches: the family with
the woman staring at the door, the priest and the husband
holding the cross, and this one of the faceless horsemen outside the hut. The men came to take the cross and murdered
the family in the process. But apparently they never found
it."

The judge sighed. "That's the story everyone knows. It's
the one Willie was familiar with. But like your evidence,
Sheriff, what looks to be true and what is true can be two
different things."

The old man arranged the sketches in a line across the
surface of his desk, heedlessly sweeping books onto the floor
to make room. "Listen carefully, son, because you're about

to hear of Juan Santiago and the crucifix of gold, and it's the first time the true story's been told in over seventy years.''

Pointing at the sketch of a large, one-story structure constructed around a central plaza or square, Judge Nourse began his story, his voice raspy, but hypnotic, drawing Charles backward in time to a little-known period of Panhandle history. ''This is a view of a plaza, or little square on the Canadian River owned by a Mexican sheepherder named Juan Santiago. After the army chased the last of the Comanches onto the reservations in Oklahoma, and the white hunters had pretty well wiped out the buffalo, tales filtered into New Mexico about the rich grazing to be found in the Panhandle. Now some of the Mexican sheepherders saw an opportunity to increase their wealth by grazing their herds on the free grassland and moved into Texas. They built their homes of sandstone and adobe mortar, or sometimes just adobe brick, around an open area. The cowboys called them plazas. Then more cattlemen came. For a while, cowman and sheepman lived side by side. But then more cowmen moved and bought or leased the grasslands. They bought the plazas and the sheepherders grazed their herds across the Panhandle and back into New Mexico where there was still free range, and that was the last of sheep in the Panhandle. By 1884, the Panhandle was cow country.''

''The ranchers used the plaza for line shacks for a while, until the rains and snows melted the adobe. Can't find much trace of them any more, just a mound of thin sandstone, and that just if you know where to look. The whole history of the sheepherders in the Panhandle might've just melted away like the adobe if it hadn't been for Diego Casados and Juan Santiago's daughter, Dolores.''

''Just a minute,'' Charles said. ''What about the crucifix?''

''I'm getting to that,'' the Judge said testily. ''Now, you just quit interrupting.''

The old man waited until Charles sank back in his chair, then continued. "Diego Casados was a half-breed, the result of a Mexican Comanchero getting too friendly with a Comanche woman. Nowadays some would say Diego was a victim of his upbringing, but that ain't true. Some people are born mean, and Diego was one. His dad's family tried to civilize him, after the Comanches got a belly full of him, but they'd done better tying him up and throwing him in the river. Still they tried. You have to give them that."

"The Casados family were good people, so when Diego got caught with a few cows he couldn't account for, the cowboys dragged him through a few yucca plants, back to the plaza, and his uncle paid for the cattle. They should've hung him, but his uncle said he'd see that Diego stayed out of trouble. 'Course Diego didn't stay out of trouble. A couple of the cowboys got shot from ambush, and everybody knew it was Diego behind the gun, but nobody could prove it. Señor Casados didn't care if it could be proved or not. He knew Diego. The upshot of the thing was, he threw Diego out of the family plaza. Diego didn't kill his uncle, which was probably the only decent thing he ever did."

The judge paused to puff at his cigar, then continued. "Diego moved over to the Hogtown section of old Tascosa and took up gambling for a living. It was the closest thing to honest work he ever did because I heard tell he didn't cheat. He didn't need to—he was a born gambler, a smooth-talking bastard, Sheriff, and handsome if you didn't get a close look at his eyes. Had eyes just like a rattlesnake, cold and dead. Looking into them was like looking into hell."

"A little while after that Juan Santiago's daughter Dolores gave birth to her first child, and old Juan threw a big party to celebrate being a grandfather for the first time, invited every Mexican family, and half the cowboys in the Panhandle. Including Diego Casados. The Mexican community was only about three hundred in 1880, and real close-knit, so

Juan knew Diego was a mean'un, but maybe he didn't realize he was inviting the fox into the henhouse. Or maybe Juan was feeling generous. At any rate, Diego Casados met Dolores. Now Dolores was the most beautiful girl in the Panhandle according to the men who saw her, and Diego fell for her. But Dolores was a respectable married woman with a father, a husband, and a brother to protect her from the likes of Diego.''

"None of that bothered Diego. He wanted Dolores, and he set out to get her. He used his gambling money to lease a bunch of land, hired the worse young toughs in Tascosa as cowboys, and acquired a good-sized herd of cattle, probably by rustling them from his neighbors.''

The judge refilled his cup with whiskey, added a trace of coffee for color, and sipped the mixture with appreciation. "Next thing anybody knew, Diego, all prosperous looking and smooth talking, called on Juan Santiago. Now a charitable man might say that Diego's asking permission to court Dolores less than a week after her young husband fell in an arroyo and broke his neck was a sign of bad manners, not culpability. Juan Santiago was a charitable man, but he wasn't a fool. Maybe Juan didn't suspect Diego of killing his son-in-law, but he distrusted coincidence and was a proud Spaniard to boot and wasn't about to welcome a half-Comanche and a thief into his family. I don't know exactly what was said between the two men, Diego never talked about it, and Juan didn't live long enough to, but Diego left the plaza so mad he was fit to be tied.''

"Soon after that meeting, Juan Santiago started finding his sheep with their throats cut. Then one of his sheepherders was found in an arroyo with *his* neck broken. The next week, another sheepherder had a so-called accident. Santiago's men started moving out of his plaza and heading back to New Mexico. Within a month, only three families besides Santiago's still lived at the plaza.''

"By this time Santiago was dead certain that Diego had killed Dolores's husband and would kill anyone who stood between him and the woman he wanted. He sold his plaza to a neighboring rancher and made plans to go back to New Mexico. Diego heard about the sale and turned up at Santiago's, told him he would never leave Texas with Dolores. But Juan figured he was smarter than Diego, and he planned to sneak away that night with Dolores and her baby. His son and the other members of the plaza were to follow in a week to throw Diego off the track."

The judge scowled, and Charles felt a sense of foreboding. "It might have worked, too," he continued, "if a Franciscan priest bearing a three-foot-tall, solid-gold crucifix hadn't stopped that night at the plaza to visit the Santiago family. He was on his way from Spain to the church in Santa Fe by way of Mexico City, and no one really knows why he was in the Texas Panhandle—it ain't exactly the direct route from Mexico City to Santa Fe. So Santiago and Dolores didn't leave as they had planned, and by midnight it was too late. Diego Casados was outside the plaza demanding that Dolores be given to him. Juan's answer was a bullet. Too damn bad Juan wasn't a better shot 'cause he just got Diego in the shoulder."

The judge peered at Charles from underneath his shady brows. "I suppose you know, Sheriff, that if you just step on a rattler's tail, he's gonna be meaner than ever. Same thing with Diego. He just went crazy with blood lust. Him and his men filled the plaza with lead, but it's pretty hard to shoot through a sandstone wall."

"Nobody knows what went on inside the plaza, but Willie Russell may have the story right." The judge pointed to a sketch of the interior of the plaza. "You see the priest holding the crucifix up and praying? Now I don't know if that's what happened, but I figure it's likely. The look of terror on the faces is probably right, too. See Dolores staring at the door like she knew the devil himself was about to bust in?''

The judge pointed to another sketch. ''What went on outside is pretty much how Willie told it in his pictures. Diego's men crouching behind the wagons, and here's Diego, the one with the bloody rag tied around his shoulder.''

''Just imagine, Sheriff, what it was like: gunfire, the smoke from the black-powder bullets they used in those days being whipped around by the wind, the curses from Diego and his men, and maybe Dolores's baby crying from all the noise, and through it all, the moon shining down like it was any other summer night. The Santiagos must have thought they were caught in hell. And it turns out they were. Diego had his men set fire to the plaza, all except Santiago's house, and shot each member of the other three families as they ran out of their houses. Men, women, and children, all dying, and Diego didn't give a damn.''

''Then we come to this picture of Diego throwing a burning branch through the window of the Santigo home. Now that's wrong. Diego stayed back and had a young kid do it. Diego didn't figure on getting shot again. When he saw the flames flickering through the window, he drew a bead on the door. It burst open and Santiago came running out followed by his son and the priest, all screaming at Diego to put out the fire. Diego laughed and shot them all.

''The fire was raging by this time—those houses had cottonwood logs as ceilings—and Diego screamed at Dolores to come out. When she didn't, he rushed in to get her. You got to give him credit for that. He did run into a burning house to save the woman he loved. Of course, if he'd really loved her, he'd have left her and her family alone, but Diego didn't think that way. When he came back out, his hair was on fire and so were his clothes. One of his men slapped a blanket on him and put out the fire, but you could hear him screaming. He was burned bad, and maybe his pain accounted for what he did next, but I don't think so.''

The judge scratched his head and poured another cup of whiskey laced with coffee. ''No, Sheriff, pain didn't account for it at all. Diego was mad, and a man like that generally hurts someone just to work out his temper. He went over the priest who had fainted from his wound and brought him around, mostly by slapping him, and he asked where Dolores was. The priest was dying, and everybody realized it but Diego. There ain't no sense in torturing a dying man, but Diego was so blood-crazed by that time, he was insane. He kept asking where Dolores was over and over again until even the hard cases who worked for him were sickened.''

The judge pulled the last two sketches closer. ''Now this picture with Diego leaning over the priest and the plaza burning like all the fires of hell is just like it was. And the smoke was so bad a man could hardly breath, but Diego wouldn't leave, just kept at the priest. Finally the poor man mumbled something about Delores being with the golden crucifix. That perked everyone's ears up. Diego's men didn't care about Dolores, but they cared like hell about gold. They went at the priest with a will until they knew all about that crucifix except where it was.

To give the devil his due, Diego was still more interested in Dolores than in the crucifix, probably the only time in his life he ever cared about anything except money. He screamed at the priest to tell him where Dolores was. The priest smiled—shot to hell and beaten up—and he still smiled. He looked up at Diego and he said, and this is a direct quote, Sheriff; he said, ''She and her baby are safe, and beyond your reach.''

''He refused to say anything else, and Diego just went crazy. He raised his gun to shoot the priest but never lived long enough to pull the trigger; one of his own men, the young kid who set fire to the Santiago house, shot Diego

Casados. Everybody has his limits and the kid couldn't stomach killing a priest. He kept his gun trained on the rest of the gang and backed away to his horse. He kept his wits about him enough to untie the other horses and chase them off, then he rode hell-bent out of there. Just in time, too. The shooting and the fire had brought the neighboring rancher and some of his hands to investigate.''

"They rounded up Diego's men and tried to save the priest, but he was too far gone. He told the rancher to send word to Santa Fe that the crucifix was safe. He tried to say more but died before he could. The rancher got the story of the crucifix out of Diego's men, and for a while everybody in the Panhandle was looking for it. And the story was that Diego found out about the crucifix and killed everybody in the plaza for it, but that wasn't true. The crucifix wasn't the motive at all.''

CHAPTER

8

JUDGE NOURSE SHUFFLED THE SKETCHES TOGETHER in a pile, then spread them out again. "Willie was quite a painter, wasn't he, Sheriff? I see he used the Brentwoods as models for the Santiagos, but I don't know this man," he said, pointing to the priest.

"That's Rodriquez, J.T.'s foreman," Charles replied, a shudder running through him. Angie's face on the figure of Dolores made the judge's story all the more horrifying. The thought of Angie's being threatened by an animal like Diego Casados made him sick.

The judge frowned. "I don't know him. How long has he worked for J.T.?"

Charles shook his head. "I don't know. I haven't really questioned the Brentwoods yet."

Judge Nourse peered at the sketches again, then shook his head in puzzlement. "Diego has no face in several of these, just that bloody bandage to indicate which one he is."

Charles got up to lean over the judge's shoulder. "I'd noticed that, but I thought he hadn't finished those particular sketches yet. See, in this one of Diego and the priest, Willie painted a face."

The judge rummaged in the drawer of his desk and brought out a magnifying glass. "I have a spot of trouble seeing up close." He examined each sketch in turn, scrutinizing the figure of Diego and the priest in each one.

Finally, he handed Charles the magnifying glass. "You look and tell me what you see. Your eyes are better than mine." He grinned. "At least one eye is."

Charles smiled sourly at the old man. He didn't want to admit it, but he wasn't seeing very well. By the time he'd gotten back to his office where he could study the sketches, one eye was swollen shut, and the other smarting in sympathy. Consequently he hadn't really looked at the pictures closely, but he still didn't see any reason for the judge's preoccupation with who Willie had used as a model. Taking the magnifying glass, he studied the sketches. "Diego has Rodriquez's face in this sketch and the priest has light hair and is a bigger man."

The judge exhaled sharply. "At least we're seeing the same thing. And who is the priest now?"

Charles examined the face again, his disbelief growing. "Kurt Reynolds!"

"I thought so. The question is why did Willie change his models?"

Charles gathered up the sketches and tucked them back in the manila folder. Even thinking of Kurt Reynolds in any role other than Diego gave him indigestion. "It doesn't matter one way or the other whose faces Willie Russell used, Judge."

The judge smoothed his mustache. "Willie generally had a reason for what he did, and his pictures tell you more of a story than just what you see."

"He was just experimenting, Judge, trying out different scenarios. I'm doing the same thing. I came to find out about the crucifix because I was hoping the past held some clue. Shows you how desperate I am. But I didn't discover a thing except another mystery. What happened to Dolores, Judge, and if she hid the crucifix, why didn't she ever tell anyone where?"

"I don't know. Dolores and her baby and the crucifix disappeared. Presumably, she got out of the plaza while her father and brother held off Diego because there wasn't a trace of her when the rancher and his cowboys searched the next day. I think she hid the cross in the darkness and made her way to one of the other plazas where she was hidden until she could be sent back to New Mexico.''

''Why should she hide? Diego was dead. She was safe.''

''Was she safe, Sheriff? Every hard case in the Panhandle would've been after her to tell them where the crucifix was, and we had some real desperadoes around Old Mobeetie and Tascosa in those days who would've shot her for the price of a drink. What do you think they'd have done to her for the golden crucifix?''

''So you don't know what happened to her?''

''No, I don't. I just hope she found some peace back in New Mexico and lived out her life without any more hell from men like Diego.''

Charles looked at the judge curiously. ''Why are you so sure your story is the right one? It's certainly more logical to believe the crucifix was the motive.''

''Logic doesn't mean a hill of beans when you're talking about people, Sheriff. Looking at people is like looking in a mirror: the image is perfect, but it's the opposite of what's real.''

However much Charles might agree with the judge's philosophy, it didn't answer his question. ''How do *you* know what the true story was?''

Nourse closed his eyes for a moment, then looked at Charles. ''The young boy who shot Diego told me. He left the Panhandle that night and went back to St. Louis. He was what I guess you'd call a runaway nowadays. He was sick a long time after he got home—never told his parents where he'd been or what happened to him, and I think they were afraid to ask. He grew up, married, was a model citizen, but he never forgot that night. In 1890, he came back to the

Panhandle, bought some farm land, and raised his family. The sheepherders were all gone by then, the plazas dissolving into the earth from where they came, and the golden crucifix already just a legend.''

The judge stopped and drew a deep breath. ''It was my father who set fire to the Santiago home and shot Diego Casados.''

Stunned, Charles groped for words. ''I see,'' was all he managed to say.

''I don't think you do, son,'' the judge said, his raspy voice sounding hoarse after his long story. ''My daddy died with that story on his conscience, and I've lived with it for seventy-five years, ever since I was a young kid, and I never knew the end. Now there's a chance I might. I want to know where that cross is, Sheriff.''

Charles eased onto his chair. He contemplated putting his feet on his desk but decided against it. That position wasn't the best one to assume when questioning a suspect. Besides, he was so stiff and sore, he doubted he could lift his feet that high. Turning his head slowly at the sound of the opening door, he slid forward and pushed himself to his feet. He stifled a groan as his palms stung. He had blisters on top of blisters from hanging on to the saddle horn and the reins yesterday.

''Good God, Sheriff! What in the hell happened to your eye?'' J.T. Brentwood sounded curious but not sympathetic. In fact, Charles sensed that J.T. was sorry whatever happened hadn't been terminal.

''Just one of those things, J.T. I was in the wrong place at the wrong time.'' Johnny had evidently not told his father what happened, and Charles wondered why. It certainly wasn't because he was high on Johnny's list of good old boys.

''Well, your blue suit clashes with all that dark purple.

Face's all sunburned, too, Sheriff. Next time wear a hat."
J.T. believed in rubbing it in.

"Sit down, J.T." Charles said, nodding at Meenie to take
notes and hoping his deputy's spelling had improved over-
night. Egyptian hieroglyphs were easier to decipher. "Did
Willie Russell have any enemies among the other cowboys?"

"I told you yesterday no one had any reason to kill Willie
Russell," Brentwood said, leaning back in the wooden armchair. "Everybody liked him, and it's a waste of my time to
come up here today and repeat myself. I tell you, Sheriff, it
was some tramp that killed him. We get some every now and
then. They walk up the river. They could've gotten as far as
the cave."

Charles leaned back in his chair and looked at J.T. The
rancher was doing everything possible to keep suspicion from
the Branding Iron Ranch and its people. "Why would a
stranger, a tramp, or whoever, kill Willie? Nothing was stolen. Even his food was still there."

J.T. shifted uncomfortably. "Nobody on the Branding Iron
Ranch had any reason for killing Willie. Nobody at all."

Charles reached in his desk and pulled out the manila
folder. He opened it and slid one of the sketches across the
desk.

"God Almighty! It's the Santiago Crucifix!" Brentwood's
ruddy skin suddenly drained of color, leaving him looking
sallow and old.

"You do know what it is?"

The rancher stared at the sketch for a long moment before
looking up. "Yes. My grandfather told me about it. He called
it the Bloody Cross."

"Why?"

"Do you know the story of Santiago and the crucifix?"
asked J.T.

"Yes. Judge Nourse filled me in."

"The judge was always curious about it. I remember when

I was a youngster my grandfather let Judge Nourse search on our land.''

"Why was he searching on your land?"

"Because the Santiago plaza was on our land. Old Juan Santiago sold it to my grandfather."

Charles jerked upright, not even feeling his sore muscles object to the sudden movement. "Your grandfather was the rancher who caught the murderers that night?"

Brentwood frowned at Charles's reaction. "Yes, and he always said that cross was stained with blood, and if it ever turned up again, there would be murder done for it."

"Your grandfather was right," Charles said grimly. "Now that we both know Willie was not murdered because someone was angry at him, who on the Branding Iron Ranch would kill for gain?"

A faint sheen of sweat made Brentwood's skin appear shiny. "No one."

"You mean you pay so generously none of your men have any financial difficulties, or do you mean they're all so upstanding and moral, no one would murder for a fortune?"

Brentwood pulled a handkerchief out of his pocket and folding it carefully in a square, wiped his forehead. "I don't have anything else to say."

"You're willing to let a murderer capable of bludgeoning a man to death go free because you won't admit one of your men might be capable of doing it?"

Brentwood folded his handkerchief and tucked it back in his pocket. He got to his feet, looking curiously shrunken as if some life force had been drained from him. "I'm leaving. If you want me to stay, you'll have to arrest me."

Charles stood, knowing his height and features were intimidating and taking advantage of it. "Not today, J.T., but refusing to talk won't make me go away. This is murder, and I'm not through with you. Sooner or later you will tell me everything about everyone on the Branding Iron."

Dismissing J.T. with a wave of his hand, he turned to Meenie. "Get Kurt Reynolds in here."

Reynolds's first words as he entered the office set the tone for the interview. "Have an accident, Sheriff?"

"Yes!" Charles snapped. "Sit down."

After seating himself in the wooden armchair, Reynolds pulled a small notebook out of his pocket. "Sheriff, I tried to find out where everyone was yesterday, but I don't think it'll help you much." He handed over the notebook.

Charles opened it and ran his eyes rapidly down the pages. "I appreciate the information," he said. And he did. He just didn't appreciate the man himself. "Is this everyone who works for the Branding Iron?"

"Yes, and I want you to know how difficult it was to track everyone down by this morning."

Charles didn't give a damn. "None of these statements are corroborated. And I don't find a statement from you either. Why not?"

Reynolds leaned forward, his familiar easy smile on his face. Charles hated that smile. "I forgot about myself, Sheriff. I didn't kill Willie, so I didn't worry about my own alibi. I was in the computer room printing out some information J.T. needed. I'm sure Angie and J.T. could vouch for me. They were both in the house."

Charles held himself as still as possible. The idea of questioning Angie about anything brought the same burning ache in his stomach that murder caused. Unfortunately, she was the only one whose word he'd trust.

Abruptly Charles reached for the manila folder. He slipped the sketch out and handed it to Reynolds. "Do you recognize this?"

Reynolds stared at the sketch, not offering to take it. "It's a crucifix, obviously," he said, his voice bland.

"You've never heard of the Santiago Crucifix?"

Reynolds leaned back in his chair and crossed one leg over

the other. "I've heard of it, but I always thought it was just a story. Did Willie find it?"

Ignoring the manager's question, Charles asked one of his own. "Who on the ranch needs money?"

Reynolds's face immediately stiffened, his lids veiling the expression in his eyes. "I don't know."

Charles wanted to pound his desk in frustration. "You and J.T. are protecting someone. Who is it?"

Reynolds got to his feet with the same lithe grace with which he did everything. "J.T. Brentwood would never protect one of his men if he were guilty of murder. I've told you all I know, and we do have some damage from the tornado to repair." He lifted his hand to Charles, cast an amused look at Meenie, and disappeared through the door.

Charles let him go. There wasn't any information he could pull out of Reynolds anyway, and he hadn't enough evidence to arrest him. "Meenie, bring Rodriquez in here."

Rodriquez preceded Meenie into the office, and Charles straightened. The foreman was a puzzle, an enigma. He suddenly thought of Rodriquez serving as the model for two different men in Willie's sketches and realized the cowboy artist has been as unsure if Rodriquez was devil or angel as Charles himself. "Sit down, Mr. Rodriquez. I have a few questions to ask you."

Rodriquez sat down on the chair, and for one mild, imaginative moment Charles could see him seating himself on a throne with the same arrogant nonchalance. "Sheriff?" he asked, one arched brow lifting slightly. Again Charles caught the lack of any musical lift to his enunciation.

"How long have you been J.T.'s foreman?"

"About six weeks."

"How long did you work for the Branding Iron before being made foreman?"

Rodriquez placed his Stetson on the corner of Charles's

desk, his movements deliberate. "I never worked for the Branding Iron before being foreman."

Charles heard a stifled sound from Meenie and glanced around. His deputy was shaking his head. "Meenie, do you have a question?"

The deputy shifted his tobacco and aimed at the spittoon sitting at the corner of the sheriff's desk. Charles hoped the janitor hadn't moved it even a quarter of an inch because Meenie was aiming on instinct while his eyes were focused on Rodriquez. "How come old man Brentwood made you foreman then? These ranchers 'round here don't bring in outsiders. They give the job to their top hand."

Rodriquez nodded his head. "You'll have to ask Mr. Brentwood about that. I merely answered an ad in one of the ranching magazines, met Brentwood, and was hired."

Charles interrupted. "Where are you from?"

Rodriquez named a county to the south of Crawford County, and Charles was even more intrigued. Cowboys with Mexican sir names weren't nearly as common in the Panhandle as they were in South Texas; in fact they were almost unheard of. "How well did you know Willie Russell and the other cowboys?"

"You learn a man fast cowboying, Sheriff. It doesn't take long to learn who can't be depended on, who won't do that extra little thing that needs done. Russell was a good man to ride the river with, as were most of the other men."

"You said 'most of the other men.' Who wasn't a good man?"

Rodriquez hesitated a moment, the first time Charles had seen him surprised. "You have a quick mind, Sheriff. But there is always someone you don't like. It doesn't mean he's guilty of murder."

"What about Johnny Brentwood?" Charles asked quickly.

"He's a good cowboy," Rodriquez shot back.

"And Kurt Reynolds?"

"Reynolds and I share responsibility for the operation of the Branding Iron. It's natural there would be some friction between us."

"What exactly does a foreman do? How do you share responsibility with the manager?" Charles asked. It really didn't have anything to do with the murder, but he was curious.

"I assign the individual duties to the cowboys, such as who fixes the fence on the south section by the creek, and who does the tally on the herd every morning. The manager may say to bring the herd to the branding pen on Thursday, but I'm the man who picks the cowboys who round them up, and checks on the job. Presumably, Mr. Brentwood gives the original orders."

"Where does Johnny fit into all this?" Charles asked.

Rodriquez blinked, but not before Charles caught a flash of raw emotion. "He doesn't."

"Johnny doesn't help his dad run the ranch?"

The foreman's lips thinned. "You need to ask the Brentwoods if you want to know anything about who can give orders on the ranch."

Charles laced his fingers together and rested his elbows on his desk. It was obvious Rodriquez wasn't going to say anything more about Johnny and his father, and he didn't think this was a man who would talk even if a rubber hose were used on him. Time to question him about his own actions. "Where were you during the tornado?"

Rodriquez smiled, a gracious winner on the subject of the Brentwoods, but accepting that the challenge of another round with Charles might well bring about his own defeat. "When Johnny drove out to tell us to let the cattle out of the branding pens, I followed the herd into the breaks. The gullies, washes, canyons, arroyos, whatever you want to call them, that branch off from the Canadian River," he explained patiently.

"Were you in the canyon or break, where Red Barn Cave is?"

"I was, but at the other end. I wasn't busy killing Willie Russell."

"Did anyone see you?" Charles asked.

Rodriquez thought for a moment. "I saw Skinny Jordan heading back up the break toward the branding pens right after the tornado, but I don't think he saw me. And I saw Johnny taking Willie's body back to headquarters, but he was so blind with shock I don't think he even knew where he was."

"You say Johnny with Willie's body, and you just calmly rode up to the branding pens. Then you acted as if you knew nothing about the murder. Why in hell didn't you go help the kid?"

"He's not a kid, and he didn't need my help."

"Good God!" Charles exclaimed, feeling at a loss. On the one hand the foreman seemed to like Johnny Brentwood, while on the other he'd deliberately not offered the boy help.

Rodriquez's eyes narrowed. "It's time for the boy to walk like a man."

"Is that some Spanish proverb?"

Rodriquez shrugged. "I wouldn't know, Sheriff. My Spanish is rusty."

"Then maybe you can answer this question, Rodriquez. Why didn't you mention your seeing Johnny to Reynolds when he was collecting information from the cowboys?"

"I wasn't aware that Kurt Reynolds was your deputy."

"He's not, damn it," Charles said furiously.

"Then I don't see a problem. You asked me where I was and who I saw. I told you. My not telling Reynolds has no significance."

Charles shivered. Of all the people involved in this drama, he could picture Conrad Rodriquez as the most likely to have the capacity to commit murder. He had the necessary coldness. The next question was motive.

Charles opened his folder and passed Rodriquez the sketch of the crucifix. "Have you ever seen this before?"

The reaction was almost imperceptible. Charles was never able to pinpoint any physical sign, no sudden paling, no involuntary tightening of facial muscles, no dawning recognition. But the foreman seemed to still, as if every physical process had halted for a split second. "It's the Santiago Crucifix, isn't it, Sheriff?"

"How do you know about the crucifix, Rodriquez?" Charles asked quickly.

Rodriquez seemed amused, but Charles noticed the humor didn't extend to his eyes. "Sheriff, not all the sheepherders went back to New Mexico. Some sold their plazas and stayed on in Texas."

CHAPTER

9

"DAMN IT, MEENIE!" CHARLES EXCLAIMED, SLAPPING his hand on his desk. The next instant he uttered an expletive that brought his deputy out of his chair.

"What's wrong, Sheriff?"

Charles wrapped his handkerchief around his hand. "I broke every blister I had when I hit the damn desk." He glared at Meenie. "I'm a physical wreck, nobody has an alibi, J.T. is worried as hell about something, and now Rodriquez turns out to have had family living in a plaza along the Canadian at the time of the Santiago massacre. Every man and his dog knows the story of that crucifix. I'm expecting to fall over an illegitimate son of Diego Casados at any moment. Everywhere I turn the past is staring me in the face. Everyone talks about that massacre as though it happened yesterday."

Meenie aimed a stream of tobacco juice at the spittoon, shifted his wad, and spoke. "Well, Sheriff, you see it kinda did."

Charles groaned, and ran his fingers through his hair. "Not you, too."

"You got to understand. This was pretty much frontier even fifty years ago. We got people living right here in Carroll that remember goin' to all-night dances at the courthouse in Old Tascosa after the turn of the century. Hell, we got people who remember visitin' with Charlie Goodnight. We even got people whose daddies cowboyed for the XIT Ranch. To a lot of folks around here the past, if it ain't yesterday, it's late last week. Willie knew that, and that's why he used real people's faces in his pictures.''

"He did that in all his paintings?"

Meenie squinted his eyes in concentration. "None that I ever saw. Just if he was paintin' from real life—a real cowboy, or somebody like that."

"Good God! Do you know what that statement implies? You're saying Willie used real victims, and real villains from the present to represent the past."

"I don't know as how I said that. You got a real good head on your shoulders, but you want to watch lettin' your imagination run away with you."

Charles sighed. As usual Meenie was right. He was imagining things. He was letting himself get caught up in a mystery a hundred years old when he had a brand-new one to solve.

"Go get Johnny, and let's listen to his story. I hope he hasn't been drinking Miss Poole's coffee, or he'll be so high on caffeine, he'll float in."

"More 'un likely he'll have a hole in his stomach so big you can stick your fist through it, and be hurtin' so bad, he can't answer questions. Did I tell you I dropped a cup of that stuff in the cell block last week, and it ate a hole in the concrete? Hell, the prisoners wouldn't drink any coffee for a week, and one of them said he was fixin' to sue us for violatin' his civil rights by tryin' to poison him."

"Meenie, just go get Johnny. I promised to take Angie to the cemetery today."

Meenie turned around and stared at him, his usual cynical face shocked. "Hell, Sheriff, if you ain't got your usual bellyache from Miss Poole's coffee, you're sure goin' to have one after watching Mrs. Lassiter cry over L.D.'s grave."

* * *

Charles squinted his one functional eye at Johnny as the young man came in.

"Sit down, Johnny."

Johnny hesitated, biting his lip in indecision. His shoulders slumped, and he sank back onto the chair.

Charles dreaded this questioning more than the others if for no other reason than Johnny hadn't revealed how he received his black eye. Someone had killed Willie, and the physical evidence pointed to Johnny.

"Do you have anything else to tell me about finding the body?"

Johnny shook his head. "No, it happened just like I said yesterday."

"Did you go in the cave at all?"

"No. I saw Willie's body, and when I realized he was dead, I picked him up and carried him down to the horses."

Charles picked up a pencil and toyed with it, reluctant to ask his next question. "Did something scare your horse while he was tied up?"

"No."

"Did you see anyone on your way to the cave, or on the way back to the ranch?"

"Sheriff, I didn't see anyone," he started. "No, that's not right. There was someone near the branding pens, but I didn't know it at the time. It's hard to explain. I can remember seeing someone now, but then I just wasn't thinking about anything but getting back to headquarters."

Charles put his pencil back in his pocket. "Can you think of anyone who had a motive to kill Willie? Had he been unhappy with anyone, or had a fight with someone?"

"Willie never fought with anyone; he was barely fryin' size, and he stayed away from fights."

Charles cocked an eyebrow. "Frying size?"

A small grin appeared on Johnny's face. "He was short.

That's why he didn't fight. He always said that was a good way to get stepped on.''

"So Willie didn't fight, and he wasn't unhappy about anything?''

Johnny rubbed his hands together as if he just remembered they were attached to his body. "Well, not exactly. He had something on his mind, but I'm not sure what. He was going to tell me, but, well, you know what happened.''

Charles opened the folder and pulled out the sketch of the crucifix. "Could it have been about this?'' he asked, as he placed it on top the desk facing Johnny.

"Where did you get this?''

"Do you recognize it?'' Charles asked, hoping he didn't.

"Yes, it's the Santiago Crucifix. Willie told me about it. He also told me to keep quiet. Where did you find it?''

"Willie told you about the crucifix, yet you're telling me he still had something on his mind? He was hiding something worth tens of thousands of dollars, yet that wasn't what was worrying him. Just what do you think was worrying him?'' Charles asked.

"I don't know, Sheriff!'' Johnny cried, raking his fingers restlessly through his hair and staring at the sketch. "Where did you find it?'' he repeated.

"The sketch or the crucifix?'' Charles asked.

"The sketch.''

Charles put the watercolor back in the folder, carefully aligning the edges with the other sketches. "We found it in his saddlebags,'' he finally said.

Johnny sighed. "He put everything there. When I was a kid, he used to let me look through his saddlebags. He always had something in there for me: a picture he'd painted, a rock he'd found. Once it was a rattlesnake skin, and I made a hatband out of it. Angie had a fit. She hates snakes. I used to chase her waving my hat, until Willie caught me and tanned my hide.''

"Johnny, did you murder Willie Russell?" Charles asked softly.

The younger man wiped at his eyes and swallowed. "No, Sheriff."

Meenie slammed his note pad on Charles's desk. "Damn it to hell, Sheriff! Why'd you let him walk out of here? There weren't no footprints around the body 'cept his; he knew about the crucifix, and he's the only one who admits that; he brings the body in 'cause he just happens to find Willie's horse while he's sittin' in a canyon during a tornado, and you just let him go! I think all that sun yesterday baked your brain."

"Where's the motive?" Charles asked calmly.

"Why, that damn crucifix!"

"How much do you think the Brentwoods are worth? Just a conservative guess will do."

Meenie lifted his hat and scratched the bald spot on the back of his head. "I don't know. Maybe two or three million? Old J.T. owns a lot of land, and some of it has got oil and gas on it."

Charles shook his head. "I'd guess ten or twelve million. What I'm saying is that Johnny Brentwood wouldn't murder someone he liked for a golden crucifix. He doesn't need the money."

Meenie eyed Charles. "Are you sure you ain't looking for reasons why he didn't do it, 'cause he's Angie's brother?"

Charles was on his feet and leaning over the desk so quickly he was unaware of his sore muscles. All he felt was a rage that seemed to send the blood pounding to his head. "Don't you ever accuse me of deliberately refusing to see the truth because of my personal feelings. If any other man but you had said that, I would have beaten hell out of him."

Meenie backed off, his Adam's apple bobbing up and down as he swallowed convulsively. "I'm sorry, Sheriff. I ain't accusin' you of doin' anything on purpose, but damn it all, I just don't see who else could'a done it.''

Charles sank back in his chair. He felt sick, and it wasn't because he could taste the coppery acid of his own rage. It was fear that Meenie might be right. He'd twisted justice once before to protect Angie—never mind his claims that it was best for all concerned—he'd done it for Angie. But not this time. Johnny was innocent. Both his logic and his gut told him so.

''I'm sorry, too, Meenie. I understand what you're saying, but Johnny doesn't have a motive.''

Meenie let out a deep breath of his own. ''You know, Sheriff, maybe money ain't the motive. I mean, there might be something we don't know about. There's damn sure something goin' on at the Branding Iron. That setup out there just don't make sense.''

Charles wiped his forehead, his temper under control again. ''What do you mean? What's wrong with the Branding Iron?''

Meenie aimed another brown stream at the spittoon, shifted his tobacco to the other cheek, and slid into a chair. ''In the first place, no ranch has a manager and a foreman if the owner is living right there on the place. You don't need both of them. Plus, J.T.'s got a son that could be the manager or the foreman, but Rodriquez said Johnny don't have nothin' to do with running the ranch. That ain't natural. Something ain't right, and what ain't right's got somethin' to do with Johnny.''

''What else did you notice at the Branding Iron that is different from most ranches?''

''Computers! I read an article about the Branding Iron in one of the ranchin' magazines, and the whole operation is on computer. That ranch don't have no scrub cattle on it, Sheriff; J.T. Brentwood has got prime breedin' stock. He sells a bunch of his stuff to other ranchers. Yet he's runnin' around screaming about the branding like he goin' to make a steer out of every male calf. And the way he was takin' on about that tally book like he didn't have every head of cattle on the place already on his computer.''

Charles leaned his elbows on the desk. "Just what is a tally book, Meenie?"

"It's just a little notebook that you put down the number of cattle in a particular herd every day, or every two days, or whatever. That way you know how many cattle you got on your place. But Brentwood's herd is so valuable, the cowboys run the heifers back to the pens when they're ready to calf. They ain't allowed to just run wild all over the breaks like most cattle. Every calf is counted practically before it's on the ground, so how come he don't have any idea how many calves he's got to brand?" Meenie shook his head. "Something funny is going on out there. You take my word on that."

Charles lifted the telephone receiver. "I don't know about tally books or calves, but you're right about one thing. Something funny is going on, and that's murder. I'm calling the pathologist to get some idea of what the murder weapon might be."

He dialed a number and waited, counting the rings. "Hello, Dr. Akin, this is Sheriff Matthews from Crawford County. Do you have anything on Willie Russell yet?"

Dr. Akin's voice was loud and testy. "Well, he's sure as hell dead. That's about the only thing I'm positive of other than he's a white male with a bad disk in the lumbar region. I can't tell you what killed him, but I did get an interesting reading from a spectroanalysis I did of the wound. There were traces of iron in it, Sheriff. And the weapon was something with a pointy end that broadened into a wider object. And mind you, I wouldn't want to take an oath on that. Why don't you ever send me something simple, like a gunshot wound. Or a knifing. I can do a lot with a knife wound: angle of penetration, width of blade, length of blade. But not Crawford County. Now you find a piece of iron with blood and hair on it, and I can tell you if it's the murder weapon, but I can't tell you what to look for."

"Thanks, Dr. Akin, and if I'm not wrong, you'll have your murder weapon by tomorrow."

Charles hung up and looked at Meenie. "What do you have on a ranch that's made of iron and wouldn't attract undue attention if someone noticed blood and hair on it?"

Meenie slapped his hand on the desk. "A branding iron!"

"Tell the county attorney to draw up a search warrant, and have the district judge sign it. We're about to delay J.T.'s branding, because I'm confiscating every branding iron on the place."

Meenie grinned as he walked to the door. "You sure know how to get on J.T's good side."

"I've had a lot of practice lately," Charles said. "Come get me when you have the search warrant."

Meenie nodded in agreement and left, and Charles continued staring at his closed office door. A branding iron—a commonplace object around a ranch this time of year and something one could carry on horseback. It was also something that could be wiped off and put back with the knowledge that in a few days all the traces of human blood would be burned out of existence. The murderer was a very clever man.

Charles picked up the sketch of the crucifix and opened the folder to replace it. Instead he removed the rest of the sketches and arranged them in story form.

He studied the sketch of the priest and Diego, wondering why Willie had changed his mind. Had Willie not been able to decide which man was evil? Charles covered his swollen eye, which had suddenly begun to throb in unison with his head. He must be losing his perspective to be sitting here assigning some sort of symbolism to Willie's sketches. Willie had just used familiar faces. He wasn't saying that Angie was actually threatened, or her family in danger.

"Sheriff, I got it. You ready to go?" Meenie's voice interrupted Charles's thoughts.

Charles got to his feet, but very slowly, and walked as lightly as possible to the door, picking up his Stetson off the filing cabinet on the way. "We'll take two cars. I still have to take Angie to the cemetery."

Meenie frowned as he passed the dispatcher's desk. "You're walkin' funny. Did you hurt your legs?"

Miss Poole turned her head to watch Charles's slow progress through the squad room. "I don't believe it's his legs that are hurting, Meenie. He's walking very much as my older brother did after being caught poaching watermelon."

"What's watermelon got to do with the way he's walkin'?" Meenie asked.

"The farmer who owned the watermelon also owned a shotgun filled with rock salt. My brother could have been badly injured had he not been leaning over at the time the farmer fired."

"Miss Poole," Charles said through gritted teeth, "Meenie and I will be at the Branding Iron. Call me there if you need something."

Miss Poole made a note in her precise handwriting. "I gather Johnny and his father are not on any better terms than they were when he was a boy."

Charles stopped by her desk. "What do you mean?"

"Mr. Brentwood never seemed to spend enough time with the boy. He was always more worried about his cattle and his oil leases than in either of his children. I've always thought that was why Johnny was always in so much trouble. It was the only time his father noticed him. And Mr. Brentwood always had such high expectations. Johnny must be the best at everything, and nothing would do than he attend the best university. Whatever Johnny wanted to do, his father could think of a hundred reasons why it wasn't the right thing to do. Johnny wanted to go to Texas A & M and major in some agricultural related field. His father made him go to the University of Texas at Austin instead and major in computer science. Of course, Johnny retaliated by flunking out. It's really terrible the things people do to their own children.''

"Did Johnny ever finish his degree?" Charles asked.

"Several years, and a few colleges later," Miss Poole replied. "Basically, he's a good boy, but I've always felt sorry for him. He deserves a chance, but J.T. has never let him prove himself.''

Charles smiled, and patted Miss Poole on the shoulder. "Thank you for the story. Is there anyone in Crawford County you don't know about?''

Miss Poole tucked a nonexistent wisp of hair back into her bun. "Excepting yourself, Sheriff, I doubt it. Will you be near your radio, or should I try to reach you by phone should something come up we can't handle?''

Charles doubted there was anything Miss Poole couldn't handle. "I'll be near my car. I may tear it apart driving on that ranch, but I refuse to ride a horse again.''

Miss Poole looked at his stiff posture. "I definitely advise you to stay away from horses, Sheriff. I don't belive you have any natural talent for riding.''

Charles smiled sourly. "I'll keep your advice in mind," he said as he shuffled halfway toward the stairwell before changing his mind and heading for the elevator.

"That elevator ain't been working real well, Sheriff," Meenie warned.

Charles pushed the button for the first floor, then leaned thankfully against the wall. "My legs aren't working real well either, Meenie. I'm not up to three flights of stairs. I wonder what our chances are of getting a new sheriff's department on the ground floor?''

" 'Bout like a snowball's chances in hell," Meenie said.

"That's what I thought, too," Charles agreed as the door slid open. He found himself looking at the unfinished wall and dirt floor of the courthouse subbasement.

"Damn!" he exclaimed, and hit the first floor button again.

CHAPTER

10

CHARLES KEPT THE ACCELERATOR AT A STEADY FIFTY miles an hour and cursed himself as a fool for driving at all. He hugged the right shoulder of the road because he felt as if he were driving blind. Not exactly blind, maybe, but visually impaired. He vowed to try the raw beefsteak treatment on his swollen eye as Judge Nourse had advised. He always thought that was a waste of a good steak, but he was ready to do anything, including witchcraft, if it would help.

He slowed until he was scarcely moving to make the turn onto the ranch. On top of everything else, his depth perception was impaired. He'd never really appreciated the problems of the blind until now, and he made a resolution to donate next month's salary to the Society for the Prevention of Blindness. One of the few advantages of being independently wealthy was he could afford to be generous whenever he felt like it.

He parked in front of the ranch house, but well back from the fence, since he wasn't altogether sure where the fence was, and climbed laboriously out of the car. He squinted at the house in time to see J.T. Brentwood slam the door on the way out.

"What the hell do you want now, Sheriff?" the rancher demanded.

Charles waited until Meenie parked, and silently joined him, before pulling out the search warrant. "Mr. Brentwood, I have a warrant to search your property for a metal object believed used in the murder of Willie Russell. In other words, J.T., I want to see all your branding irons.''

The rancher's mouth gapped open. "What the hell!''

"The pathologist has reason to believe an iron object pointed at one end, broadening toward the other, was used to kill Willie. If I recall, your brand is a replica of a branding iron, is it not? Your brand comes to a point on one end to represent a handle, and broadens to a large BI on the other end. Is that correct?''

"Well . . . yes,'' Brentwood stammered.

"Where are your branding irons, J.T.?'' Charles asked.

Kurt Reynolds stepped onto the porch, a puzzled frown creasing his bronzed forehead. "What business do you have with our branding irons, Sheriff?''

"The sheriff thinks Willie was killed with a branding iron,'' Brentwood said.

"Branding irons today and fence stretchers tomorrow, Sheriff?'' Reynolds asked. "Surely a murderer would have more sense than to use something that could be traced back to the ranch so easily.''

Charles looked at Reynolds, wondering if he'd ever disliked anyone so much. "I think it was a good choice, and I wouldn't have been able to prove a thing except the tornado interfered.''

"What do you mean?'' Brentwood asked. "What's the tornado got to do with anything?''

"The murderer counted on the branding going off on schedule, and once that iron was heated, the evidence was gone. But your branding pens were destroyed by the tornado, so I'm betting the murder weapon is still around, and still wearing Willie's blood. Now where are your branding irons, J.T.?''

Brentwood's shoulders sagged, and he again appeared shrunken and defeated as he had when he saw the sketch of the crucifix. "They're all at the branding pens. We were all ready to start when the tornado warning was broadcast. I guess everything is still up there." He started toward his pickup. "Just follow me."

Halfway to the pens, Charles wondered if he shouldn't have taken a horse; at least the motion would have been just up and down. And it was he'd been jostled in every conceivable direction. This wasn't a road—it was a cow trail. When Meenie stopped by the partially reconstructed branding pens, Charles congratulated himself on even being able to move.

Gingerly he climbed out of the car and leaned against the door until he felt it would be safe to try walking. Straightening his shoulders, he walked over to J.T. "Where are your branding irons?"

Supported by Reynolds on one side and Johnny on the other, Brentwood seemed to recover his fire. "Rodriquez"— he called over his shoulder to the foreman—"where's the branding gear?"

Grinding out a cigarette under his heel, the foreman motioned toward a pile of equipment, only half of which Charles knew the function of. As he drew closer, he decided he didn't want to inquire too closely into what purpose some of the tools served, although his imagination supplied him with a pretty good idea. He decided he was glad he wasn't a male calf.

Then he sank to the ground, his knees bent, weight resting on the balls of his feet, his eyes focused on the two branding irons. Meenie knelt beside him, already opening the evidence kit and removing the fingerpoint powder.

Charles changed positions to try to block the wind, and Meenie leaned over and began brushing. After a moment, he started cursing. "Damn it all, Sheriff. Can't do nothin' in this wind. Powder's blowin' all to hell."

"Wrap one of those plastic evidence bags around them,

and take them over to the car.'' Charles gestured at one of them. ''I think this is the one we're interested in.''

Meenie squinted at the end of the branding iron. ''Somebody weren't very careful. Sure looks like a few hairs and tissue caught there on the side. And some grass. I guess he tried to clean it off by rubbing it on the ground.''

Brentwood's voice interrupted their conversation. ''You two are jumping the gun again. Just what the hell do you think you're going to find on a branding iron but hair and tissue.''

Meenie tilted his head back. ''You got any cattle with curly gray hair, J.T.?''

Brentwood raised his hat and ran his hands through his own hair. ''No,'' he admitted. ''But you're still going to have to prove that's what killed Willie. And even if you do, so what? Those irons were laying up here in plain sight. Anyone could've picked one up.''

Charles rose to his feet. ''If you're going to tell me some stranger just happened to ride by here, saw the branding irons, just happened to know where Willie was, and just happened to know he had a valuable good crucifix, don't waste your breath. Someone who knew Willie killed him, and it was somebody from his ranch. Now how many knew the branding irons were here?''

Rodriquez answered, his voice quiet and expressionless. ''Everyone, Sheriff.''

''Who was here at the pens just before the tornado?'' Charles asked, determined to cut down his list of suspects.

Again Rodriquez answered. ''I was, and Johnny. Mr. Brentwood had been here but left. Reynolds was here earlier in the day.'' He waved his hand at the group of silent cowboys who were unabashedly eavesdropping. ''All the men here. So you see, Sheriff, anyone of us could be guilty. Anyone, that is, who was willing to risk being out in a tornado.''

Charles involuntarily glanced at Johnny. There were only

two men who by their own admission had taken that risk: Johnny Brentwood and Conrad Rodriquez. His glance moved on to the tall, thin cowboy who had asked him about Willie. Skinny Jordan had also been out during the tornado. Both Johnny and Rodriquez had mentioned seeing him just afterward. And he had been at the branding pens.

"Skinny Jordan," he called, moving toward the man.

The cowboy jerked, his eyes darting around as if looking for an escape. Realizing there was nowhere to go, he swallowed and hooked his thumbs in his belt. "You want to talk to me, Sheriff?"

Charles walked back toward the patrol car, motioning Skinny to follow. "Yes, I do. Let's sit in the car out of the sun."

He opened the passenger door for Skinny, then went around and slid in the driver's seat. Out of the corner of his eye he saw Meenie get in the backseat and take a notebook out of his pocket. "Skinny, what were you doing by the branding pens just after the tornado?"

The cowboy didn't seem to know what to do with his hands. He rubbed them together, then grabbed his belt, and finally polished his palms on his demin-covered thighs. "I just wanted to see if everything was all right; I mean, if any of the cattle had been killed."

"I thought the cattle had been released from the pen and chased away."

Skinny licked his lips. "Well, they had, but some of them might've come back. You never know what cattle will do. They're kinda dumb."

"Did you see anyone?"

The cowboy clenched his hands together and looked at the floorboards. "No. I never saw anybody."

"You didn't see Johnny Brentwood riding by with Willie's body?"

Skinny's eyes darted toward the sheriff, then away. "I never saw nobody, Sheriff. Nobody."

"Did you kill Willie Russell?" Charles asked softly.

Skinny's head swung toward Charles, his eyes wide and shocked. "No!" he cried. "I wouldn't kill anybody, Sheriff, and especially not Willie. He got me this job after the drink got me and I had to quit rodeoing. Told me if he ever caught me drinking on the Branding Iron, he'd beat the hell out of me. He was only half as big as me, but I believed him. He'd come by the house sometimes, give the kids some treats, and ask how I was doin'. He saved me, Sheriff. My wife was about to leave me on account of my drinkin', my kids was scared of me. If it hadn't been for him believin' in me, I'd have cashed in my chips a couple of years ago. I ain't gonna kill somebody that saved my life. I might not be a very good man, but I ain't that low."

"But you know who did kill him, or you suspect somebody, don't you, Skinny?" Charles asked.

The cowboy looked away, clenching and unclenching his fists. He cleared his throat, and spit out the window, remaining still as he looked at the small group of men still around the branding pen. Finally, he turned back to Charles. "I don't know anything, Sheriff. I didn't see nobody."

Charles sighed with frustration. "Skinny, if you know something, it's dangerous not to tell me. As long as the murderer is free, he can kill again."

"I don't know anything, Sheriff," Skinny repeated dully.

"All right, you can go, but take a piece of advice. Don't volunteer to ride herd or whatever by yourself. Stay close to people."

Skinny got out of the car, and stood irresolute, shifting his weight from foot to foot. "Thanks, Sheriff," he said finally, and turning on his heel, walked back to the other cowboys.

"I think I'll arrest him," Charles said thoughtfully.

"What the hell for, Sheriff? 'Cause he won't tell you anything? Most of the men on this place won't tell you anything.'' Meenie leaned out of the car, and spit at a dried cow chip.

"I think I'll lock him up as a material witness. That'll keep him safe until we catch the murderer."

"Just how are we goin' to do that? The only evidence we got points to someone you don't want to arrest, and if it ain't him, it could be anybody standing out there by the branding pen."

Meenie dumped the branding irons on the backseat.

"We'll find the right one the only way we can: character and motive. We just don't know enough about these people yet."

Meenie finished dusting the branding irons. "There ain't nothin' but smudges on these, Sheriff. I keep tellin' you, cowboys wear gloves. Ain't nobody about to leave prints on anything."

"Tie a plastic bag around the business end of the one with the hair and tissue—and send it to Amarillo. The Potter County Sheriff's Department can run a test on it in their lab. Thank God the sheriff over there's willing to help us. If we had to send everything to Austin, we'd be next month getting a report."

"Next year's more like it," Meenie said darkly, as he wrapped the branding iron. "When you goin' to arrest Skinny?"

"Not until after the weekend. I can only hold him seventy-two hours, and I don't know what questions to ask. Do you realize how little we know of these people? We have to investigate the Brentwoods, Reynolds, and our mystery man, Mr. Rodriguez. Otherwise, we might miss asking the one question that would actually make Skinny talk."

"Do you think Rodriquez could've done it?"

Charles took off his Stetson and raked his fingers through his hair, noticing he still had his handkerchief wrapped around one hand. "I don't know if he could be guilty or not. I don't know anything about the man except he seems to like Johnny. I'm going to call the sheriff of his home county and find out everything he knows about Conrad Rodriquez. While I'm doing that, I want you and Raul to question Johnny's friends. I'll handle Kurt Reynolds myself."

"How you gonna do that?" Meenie asked.

"There are two people in Crawford who know which closets hold the skeletons: Judge Nourse—and everyone's favorite sixth-grade teacher."

Meenie grinned. "Miss Poole."

"You're psychic, Meenie," Charles said climbing out of the car. "I'll tell J.T. we're leaving, then you can bounce me back to the ranch house."

"Headquarters or the big house?"

"All right, headquarters. Sometimes I feel like I need a dictionary just to understand the language in the Panhandle."

"Just takes a while for a greenhorn to get broke in good," Meenie said, sliding into the driver's seat.

Charles walked toward Brentwood, thinking that greenhorn was a good description of himself. He knew nothing at all about ranching, and "he couldn't ride nothin' wilder'n a wheelchair" to quote Meenie, and his knowledge of cattle was limited to knowing the difference between a ribeye and a T-bone, and that only after one or the other reached his plate. He suddenly felt his wealthy, urban background had been deprived. He had never known the joys of learning to ride, of living life by the never-ending cycles of nature, of using physical and mental strength to maintain dominance over beasts larger, stronger, and, in the case of the horse he'd ridden, probably smarter.

By all the standards of society, he was one of a privileged class: wealthy, intelligent, well-educated, sophisticated, and physically attractive. Yet, as he felt the heat of the sun filter through his sports coat and shirt and smelled the tang of sagebrush, he wondered if he were lucky at all. He shrugged his shoulders. He was too old to be wishing he could grow up to be a cowboy. He was a Texas county sheriff, and that was nearly as good.

He could tell by J.T.'s glowering expression that he didn't consider county sheriffs worth any more than a sterile bull in a pasture full of cows. "J.T., we'll be back Monday—" Charles started.

"What the hell you going to do with my branding irons in the meantime?" interrupted the rancher.

"I'm sending them to the lab. I'm certain one is the murder weapon."

"And if it is?" Brentwood asked. "What are you going to do then?"

"I'll be back, J.T., and I'll want some answers this time." Charles started toward the car, then turned back. "I'm taking Angie to the cemetery this afternoon," he said, and braced himself for Brentwood's reaction.

J.T.'s mouth opened and shut several times as if he had misplaced his voice. "The hell you say," J.T. said, when he was able to say anything at all. "Well, don't get any big ideas. My daughter's not marrying any one so ignorant, he couldn't drive nails in a snowbank. This time, she's marrying a rancher, or at least someone who knows about ranches, and that sure as hell isn't you. And just remember, her first loyalty's to her family." Then he deliberately turned his back on Charles to watch his cowboys rebuilding the branding pens.

Charles stood grinding his teeth together, then turned and walked back to the car. He had been warned off in clear, not-to-be-misunderstood English. And what made it worse, Kurt Reynolds had overheard the whole conversation and preened himself like a sleek tomcat. He had every reason to: J.T. certainly had him in mind with his comment about Angie marrying someone who knew about ranches. And who was better suited than the man who already managed her ranch?

Charles slid onto the car seat, feeling as if a black cloud had taken up permanent residence right above his head. He was in love with a woman who thought of him only as her dead husband's best friend, the father of that woman despised him, and there was a remote possibility that he would have to arrest her brother for murder. Compared to his love life, Romeo had no problems at all.

"Let's go, Meenie, before J.T. changes his mind and takes after me with a shotgun."

"You must've told him you were taking Mrs. Lassiter to the cemetery," commented the deputy, leaning out the window to spit at a yucca plant.

Charles thought Meenie was the one man in history who could spit out the window of a moving car and never miss his target. The logistics involved boggled the mind. "Looking at it from his point of view, he has a right to be upset. As a suitor, I'm a poor prospect for a rancher's daughter."

"Who's better? That manager of his? J.T. ought to know you can't have but one boss. When Johnny takes over the ranch, he don't need to be havin' his decisions second-guessed by a brother-in-law. And Reynolds don't appear to me to be the kind that'll take orders. You, on the other hand, would keep your nose out of somethin' you don't know anything about. Besides, you have some feelings for Mrs. Lassiter, and I ain't sure about Reynolds. He smiles too easy, and I never did trust a man older than five who didn't consider before he smiled."

"You have a unique way of judging people," Charles said, bracing himself against another jolt.

"I'm older'n you, Sheriff. I've seen people give themselves by the little things they do. Like the man who gives a lot of money to some charity, but don't pay his men a good wage."

"What about J.T.?" Charles asked.

"He always paid decent, Sheriff, but there ain't nothin' that means more to him than this ranch, so he hires the best and pays them. He ain't never begrudged money."

"Meaning he begrudges something else?"

Meenie frowned as he tried to explain. Sometimes the sheriff was damn hard to talk to. "J.T. just sees one thing, and that's the Branding Iron Ranch. Everybody is kinda judged by how they see the ranch. That makes him hard, but it don't make him cruel."

"You mean he considers land more important than people?" Charles asked incredulously.

"No, it ain't exactly that either. You see, Sheriff, a ranch up here, or anywhere else for that matter, ain't just a bunch of dirt and grass and cattle. It's family and responsibility and history and livin' a decent life. Money don't have a lot to do with it. It's workin' to deserve something your grandfather made and passin' it down to your son and knowin' it's permanent. The land don't rust, and it don't get stolen, and it gives you back what you put into it. It lasts, is what I'm tryin' to say." Meenie was silent, a dissatisfied look on his face.

Charles caught sight of the ranch headquarters, the red-roofed building nestled under the spreading cottonwoods, serene and peaceful under the hot sun, and for the first time appreciated J.T. Brentwood's feelings. A man would risk a lot for what the ranch represented. "Would J.T. Brentwood murder anyone who threatened the Branding Iron?" he asked abruptly.

Meenie parked in front of the white board fence and spit out the window as he considered Charles's question. "Yeah, he would," he said reluctantly.

CHAPTER

11

"CHARLES, WHAT HAPPENED TO YOUR EYE?" ANGIE demanded before he even had a chance to knock on the door.

"I had an accident." He slipped inside the open screen door. "Where are the girls?"

"The baby is still napping and Jennifer's in the kitchen trying to pester Consuela into giving her a cookie. What kind of an accident, Charles?"

He crossed the living room with its huge fireplace of native stone and the locked cases of antique firearms. "A freak kind of accident," he said. He passed through the dining room to the kitchen. "Jennifer!" he said, bracing himself as a three-foot-tall replica of Angie launched herself at him.

"Uncle Charles, you didn't see me." A pout rounded a childish lip.

He picked her up and hugged her. If he had to curtail his feeling about Angie, he could compensate by loving the daughter. "I see you now, sweetheart."

A cool, but very sticky hand touched his swollen eye. "Does it hurt?" the little girl asked.

Charles smiled. "You can kiss it and make it well," he suggested.

Jennifer tilted her head and considered. "I'll try," she said, plainly doubting she was capable of such a magic cure.

Charles felt the butterfly touch of the little girl's lips, and felt again the twisting anguish that she wasn't really his. He smiled and carried her over to the cabinet. He surveyed the expanse of cooling cookies and confiscated two. "Have a cookie with me?"

"Charles!" Angie cried. "You'll ruin her supper."

A stout Mexican woman joined us. "She don't eat enough. Now she won't eat nothing."

Charles ignored the two glowering women as he handed the cookie to the little girl and lowered her to the floor. He knelt down. "Jennifer, do you promise to eat your supper tonight?"

The little girl looked down at the floor. "How many bites?" she asked, reluctant to give her word.

"Four bites of everything," Charles said promptly. "Big bites," he added, and held out his hand. "Shall we shake on it?"

Jennifer held out her hand, then stared at the handkerchief wrapped around his palm. "Does it hurt, too?" she asked.

"A little," he admitted.

"You need an ouchee," she said soberly.

He rose and looked at Angie. "An ouchee?" he asked.

"She means a Band-Aid," she answered. "Tell Charles goodbye, Jennifer."

The little girl wrapped her arms around Charles's legs. "No!" she cried.

Charles looked helplessly at Angie. Coldly walking away from Jennifer was something he couldn't bring himself to do. "Help," he mouthed silently.

Angie knelt down and unwrapped the little girl's arms. "Charles will bring Mama home tonight, and maybe he can stay and play with you then."

Jennifer wiped at her eyes and looked up at Charles. "Promise?" she asked.

"I promise," he said softly as he took Angie's arm and escaped from the kitchen.

"Just a minute, Charles," Angie said, leading him to a bathroom. "I want to look at that hand."

"That's not necessary," he protested, but obediently unwrapped his handkerchief.

Angie gasped at the raw blisters. "Charles, they must hurt!" She looked up at him, hazel eyes brimming with tears.

He cupped her chin with his other hand and gently caught a tear with a finger. "Don't cry, Angie, honey"—the endearment slipping out before he knew it—"it's just a blister. You don't want to smear your makeup."

Her smile was tremulous as she washed and disinfected his hand. "Oh, Charles, it's not that—it's how you got them. You rode a horse, and I don' think you really know how to ride. Willie's dead, and you're trying so hard to find out why and how, and Dad's acting so strange about it all. And he threatened you, didn't he?"

Charles felt uncomfortable talking about J.T. "He was just a little upset and said some things he didn't mean, Angie. People react like that sometimes when a friend is murdered."

Angie bandaged his hand with quick efficient movements. She looked up at him with wet eyes, her lashes clustered into little spikes from her tears. "I'm so glad you're not angry at the Brentwoods, Charles. I don't think I could stand that."

Charles hadn't planned his next move. But it seemed so natural to bend his head and kiss her. He'd fantasized about it for so long, it seemed just another dream until his lips actually touched hers. He recognized in some subconscious region of his brain that he was experiencing something few men were privileged to know: he was discovering reality to be more magnificent than fantasy.

Yet as suddenly as he had kissed her, he released her and stepped back. He'd come to take her to visit her husband's grave, and he ended up kissing her in the bathroom like a teenage Lothario at a party. He studied his bandaged hand, unable to meet her eyes. "I guess we'd better go." He cursed the husky tone of his voice.

"I'll meet you at the car. I need to touch up my makeup." Her voice was quiet, and Charles dismissed its breathy quality as shock.

He cleared his throat. "Do you have anything you want me to carry? Flowers or something?"

Angie darted a look at him, a blush tinting her cheeks a hot pink. "L.D. hated flowers, don't you remember? He picked at you for weeks when you sent me roses for my birthday one year." She bit her lip and fell silent as if she knew her dead husband was not a topic for conversation. Her blush deepened, and Charles mentally damned himself.

"Angie, girl, don't be embarrassed. I'm sorry." He turned quickly and walked toward the front door, his goal to reach his patrol car where his hands would be occupied, and he wouldn't compound his error by touching her again.

He eased into the car, turned on the ignition, and flipped the air conditioner on high. Angie had been a widow for almost a year, and L.D. Lassiter was still as much between them as when he was alive. He rested his forehead on the steering wheel and shivered in spite of the heat. Please, God, there had to be a way out of his dilemma.

He lifted his head as Angie opened the car door and slid in with a rustle of silk. "Are you ready?" he asked, proud of how impersonal his voice sounded.

Angie slammed the car door and slid across the seat. Startled, he turned to stare at her. His breath caught at the sight of her bright, determined smile, then left him altogether as she leaned against his shoulder and wiped his mouth with a lace-trimmed handkerchief. "What?" he stuttered.

She waved the handkerchief with its coral smudge. "Lipstick," she said with a tremor in her voice, then scooted back across the seat. She calmly folded the lacy piece of cloth and tucked it in her purse, then faced him, her hazel eyes almost green with what he guiltily recognized as anger. "I don't care if everyone in Carroll and Crawford County knows you kissed me, but since you're obviously embarrassed about the whole thing, I thought I'd remove the evidence."

Charles was too stunned to reply, and Angie continued her tirade.

"Don't look at me like you don't know what I'm talking about. You should have seen your face afterward; you were so stiff and disapproving. I am not ashamed of myself, and I won't let you make me feel guilty because I kissed you back!"

Charles found his voice. "What did you say?"

She glared at him defiantly. "I said I wasn't ashamed of myself."

He slid out from under the steering wheel to grasp her shoulders and turn her toward him. "Not that part, I heard that. What did you say last?"

She tilted her head back to look up at him. "I kissed you back."

He moved his hand up to thread his fingers through her auburn curls, cupping the back of her head comfortably in his hand. "That's the part I was interested in," he whispered, and kissed her, testing reality again, and discovering, if anything, it was better than the first time. He indulged himself leisurely, not wanting the test invalidated because of rushing to a hasty conclusion based on insufficient evidence. There was a lot to be said for the scientific method.

Charles concluded the test, not because he had any desire to do so, nor for lack of cooperation on the part of his subject, but for the simple reason that his kneecap was pressing into the sharp corner of the radio, and the pain had reached an unbearable level. "Angie, honey, my knee's killing me."

She looked dazed for a moment, then shifted away to let him ease back under the steering wheel. She looked at his hand rubbing his mistreated knee, then examined his sunburned face and swollen eye. She grinned, her eyes sparkling with mischief. "If I offered to kiss everything and make it well, we'd be here all day. Charles, you look like you've been in a gang fight. And lost."

He looked at her smiling face and felt a gust of love sweep over him. "Aren't you supposed to be wiping my fevered brow and telling me how brave I was?"

"And aren't you supposed to be saying something like your heart aches for me, instead of complaining about your knee?" Her laughter died as she saw his expression.

He clasped her hand. "It does, you know."

"What?" she asked, although she knew.

"My heart," he replied, stroking her fingers. Suddenly he stopped, his thumb resting on the diamond solitaire of her engagement ring. He slowly shifted it to reveal the smooth white-gold wedding band. However much he might love her, and however much she might return it, there was still a lie between them. He'd concealed her husband's murder, and if faced with the same choices, would make the same decision again. But he could never tell her why.

He released her hand and started the car, made a wide circle, and drove toward the highway. He could feel her waiting for an explanation of his abruptness, and knew he couldn't give her one. He pressed his stomach where the familiar burning had begun again.

"Charles, what's wrong? You've got that stiff look on your face again." Her voice was light, but he could detect the hurt confusion.

"I have to concentrate to see where I'm going," he lied.

"What happened to your eye?" she asked.

"I told you: a freak accident."

"What kind of freak accident?"

Charles wondered if Angie was related to Miss Poole. Neither one of them would leave a subject alone. "It's not worth talking about. It wouldn't happen again in a hundred years." It certainly wouldn't because that was how long it was going to be before he ever rode another horse.

"Charles, are you going to tell me what happened, or do I have to ask Miss Poole?"

He glanced at her. "What makes you think Miss Poole knows?"

Angie grinned. "Because Miss Poole is persistent."

He cocked an eyebrow at the understatement. "And I suppose you're not?"

"What happened to your eye?"

He sighed. Angie and Miss Poole were definitely sisters under the skin. "I was unsaddling that horse and the cinch hit my eye."

"I don't understand. How did the cinch buckle hit you in the eye?"

"I fell," he said. "Can we change the subject? How long will you be staying at the ranch?

"I'm going back to Carroll next week. I can't stand the tension much longer."

"What kind of tension?"

"Dad and Johnny are hardly speaking anymore. Johnny's been gambling, and Dad told me he wouldn't pay his debts again; in fact, he threatened to disinherit him. They had a terrible fight last week, and Johnny came to me to borrow money. He got involved in a poker game in Amarillo and lost badly. He can't tell Dad because he knows Dad meant exactly what he said. The ranch means everything to him. And he's a good rancher—he really is. The men respect him, and he has some good ideas for the future."

Charles felt numb. "Did you loan him the money?"

She didn't answer, and he glanced at her. Angie sat staring through the windshield, twisting her wedding band around and around on her finger. Her eyes were unfocused and shadowed with pain. "Did you loan him the money?" he asked sharply.

She looked down at her rings and shook her head. "I couldn't, Charles. I didn't have the money."

"What do you mean? How much was it?"

"Twenty-five thousand dollars," she answered, then looked at him. "Charles, I went to the bank to cash in a C.D., and I didn't have any. L.D. had cashed them in the day he was killed. And the saving account was gone, except for the insurance money I deposited. I was so numb, and so busy just trying to survive from one day to the next, that I never paid any attention to the bank accounts. I have a small trust fund from my mother's estate, and the house and car are paid for, so I just never needed any money. I mean, all I needed was household money, so I never realized until now that household money is all I have. I couldn't loan Johnny any money, because I don't have it to loan."

Charles turned into the cemetery, his stomach burning with both hatred and fear. He realized suddenly that his ambivalent attitude toward L.D. was ambivalent no longer; he hated him with an intensity he didn't think he was capable of feeling. But overriding his hatred of L.D. was fear. Lack of motive was his strongest reason for not arresting Johnny for murder. Now he had no reason at all except his own reluctance to see Angie's brother as a murderer.

He parked the car in the older part of the cemetery, next to a family lot. All the gravestones were weathered, except one: a large, red granite headstone with a name and date chiseled on it. "Angie, we're here," he said softly. "Do you want me to go with you?"

"Do you want to?"

He shook his head, almost nauseous from the burning pain in his stomach. He couldn't stand by L.D.'s grave with a respectful demeanor when his only inclination was to spit on it. "No. I've already said my goodbyes." And he had. Almost a year ago on a hot, windy August day when L.D.'s plane exploded, and he was left to organize a conspiracy of silence.

He watched Angie's slender figure as she stood alone by the grave and grasped the steering wheel until he felt the raw blisters on his bandaged hand crack and bleed. As he watched her reach out to the headstone, he wanted to scream out at her not to mourn him. The next instant, he jerked upright. Angie hadn't touched the headstone. She had brought the back of her left hand down on the corner of it.

He never remembered opening the door, nor getting out of the car. But he must have; otherwise, he wouldn't be standing next to her, reaching for her hand with its cut and bleeding knuckle.

She turned away from him. "No! Wait!" she cried, and twisted off her wedding band and engagement ring. She dropped them and ground them under her foot into the dirt of L.D.'s grave.

"My God, Angie! What are you doing?" Charles grasped her shoulders.

She looked at him, her eyes full of anguish and betrayal. "Take me away, Charles—out of here, and away from him!"

He put his arm around her to support her. She seemed so pale, he doubted she would be able to walk without falling. He helped her into the car and drove off. He couldn't take her back to the ranch. She was in no condition to face J.T. Instead, he took her to the only place he could think of where he could help her—his office.

He led her through the squad room and into his office. "Miss Poole, bring me the first-aid kit," he said brusquely as he passed the dispatcher's desk.

He closed his office door and picked up Angie. "No one will ever know," he said grimly, and carried her into his bathroom. He didn't know how the sheriff of Crawford County had rated a private bathroom, but he was grateful as never before.

Setting her on her feet, he turned on the water and washed her injured hand. His breath hissed between his teeth. Her ring finger was scraped raw and badly swollen. "Angie, you need an X ray; this finger may be broken."

"It's not broken. I can move it."

"My goodness!" Miss Poole said from behind them. "What happened to your finger?"

"I hit it," Angie said flatly.

"What in the world with?" Miss Poole asked, opening the first-aid kit and placing disinfectant and bandages on the sink.

"I hit it," Angie replied again.

Miss Poole glanced at the younger woman's face, then at Charles. She seemed to read some message on their expressionless faces, because she hesitated, a bottle of antiseptic soap in her hand. She cleared her throat and handed the bottle to Charles. "Wash it thoroughly, Sheriff. An injury like that can become infected very easily. I would also recommend a tetanus shot, Mrs. Lassiter."

Angie bit her lip as Charles began to cleanse her finger. "You may be right, Miss Poole."

"Miss Poole, bring Mrs. Lassiter some coffee, please."

"Of course, Sheriff." The old lady gave each a sharp glance and departed, clearly puzzled, but equally determined not to ask any more questions.

Angie closed her eyes and Charles wanted to cry out when he saw the tiny beads of sweat on her forehead. "Finish, please, Charles. I need to sit down."

He rapidly bandaged the whole hand and, picking her up again, carried her into his office and placed her in his chair. It wasn't the most comfortable in the world, but at least it was upholstered, unlike the wooden armchairs in front of his desk. Sitting on the corner of his desk, he held her uninjured hand, content to let her rest for a moment. He had to know the reason for the scene at the cemetery, but he could wait.

Miss Poole entered, carrying a tray with coffeepot, cups, and cream and sugar. She set it on the desk and poured a cup. "I think you better dispense some of the brandy from that flask you carry around, Sheriff. Occasionally alcohol serves a useful purpose."

Charles added brandy to Angie's coffee. "You realize, Miss Poole, that it's illegal to dispense alcohol on the premises."

Miss Poole sniffed. Miss Poole could convey a wide range of opinions merely by sniffing loudly. "Sometimes it's necessary to overlook minor infractions of the law. Sit up, Mrs. Lassiter, and drink your coffee. Let go of her hand, Sheriff. She can't hold her cup with the other one."

Charles released Angie's hand. He had the feeling Miss Poole would rap his knuckles if he didn't. He looked up at the old lady and smiled. "Thank you, Miss Poole."

She inclined her head, as aware as he that the gratitude was not for the coffee. "If you or Mrs. Lassiter need anything, just tell me." If there was any emphasis on the word *anything*, it was so faint as to be almost nonexistent, but Charles heard it, and knew Miss Poole was offering unlimited, uncritical assistance.

After the dispatcher had carefully closed the door behind her, Charles turned back to Angie and grinned at her horrified expression. "The coffee has character," he remarked blandly.

Angie looked up. "My God, Charles, no wonder you have an ulcer. That coffee could rust stainless steel."

"I don't have an ulcer," he stated emphatically.

She smiled, faint color returning to her cheeks. "Then why do you have a desk full of big white pills?"

"How do you know that?"

"L.D. told me."

Like a strobe light flashing intermittently, a series of images flickered across Charles's mind: L.D. chiding him as a pill pusher, L.D. calling him an antacid freak, L.D. berating him as a fool for taking life so seriously. He passed his hand in front of his eyes as if to wipe away the sudden vision of cynical blue eyes.

He took Angie's injured hand and held it gently in his own. "Why, Angie?" he asked softly. "Why did you do it?"

She sat forward in the chair, her body stiff and awkward looking. "L.D. didn't intend to come back that day, did he, Charles? That's why he took every cent we had except what was in the checking account."

She laughed harshly and without humor. "I guess I should be grateful he left me that. Not knowing about the other, I was at least able to cry at his funeral."

She looked at Charles, her eyes confused. "Why was he leaving me? What was the matter? What had I done?"

He tried to draw a breath. His chest felt tight, as if it were expanding from the pressure he felt. God, what to tell her?

"Angie, you didn't do anything; it was L.D. A lot of men just leave for no apparent reason at all. I get missing persons reports every day, and many times, relatives can't give any reason why a husband, or wife, or child has left."

She considered, then shook her head. "We're talking about L.D. We're talking about a man who never did anything without a reason. You know something, Charles. Otherwise, you wouldn't freeze up every time his name is mentioned. Why won't you tell me?"

He got up and paced the room. He lifted his hand and discovered he was still wearing his Stetson. He took it off and carefully placed it on the filing cabinet, his mind working furiously. He couldn't tell her why L.D. was leaving. She would feel obligated to atone for his sins, and all he'd done would be for nothing. Her life would be destroyed, and her children's lives.

He turned to face her. He would tell her a truth, not the truth she was searching for, but a truth, nonetheless. "Did you ever think I might be ashamed? I committed the old biblical sin of coveting another man's wife. What kind of a man would I be if came to you bearing tales about L.D.? Of course, I freeze up every time his name is mentioned—I fell in love with his wife—but at least I have the decency to feel guilty about it even if I can't help myself.''

She looked at her hand, the bandage startlingly white against her skin. ''I guess I've always known how you felt. I just never consciously admitted it to myself. God, I'm so ashamed.''

''Don't, Angie, honey. You never did anything you need to be ashamed of.''

''Didn't I, Charles? Wouldn't you call being a hypocrite and a fool good enough reasons to be ashamed? I lived with a cold, uncaring stranger for eight years. I told myself I loved him because, well, I was his wife. After he died, I kept telling myself how much I missed him. It wasn't until yesterday that I realized I was deluding myself. I didn't miss L.D. I missed you. You were always there. You came by every morning for coffee, and you ate dinner with us two or three times a week. You talked to me, you teased me, you gave me a sense of being important. You even fixed the damn plumbing! I survived the last four years of my marriage because you filled the empty places, and I was too big a fool to admit it.''

''Angie,'' Charles began.

''No, Charles, please don't interrupt. I have to finish this. L.D. never loved me or the girls. We were a convenience, the little wife and family an ambitious politician needed, and there I was standing by his tombstone still playing my dutiful role. Suddenly I couldn't stand it. I buried my rings because I won't be a hypocrite any longer.''

When he didn't move, she did, walking toward him with hesitant steps. Circling his waist with her arms, she rested her cheek against his shoulder. ''Don't feel guilty, Charles, please. Your caring for me didn't hurt L.D. You were a loyal friend, and I suspect you're still being loyal, still protecting him.''

He put his arms around her then and held her. It wasn't L.D. he was protecting, it was her, and he'd do it the rest of his life. He stroked her back, thinking how delicately made she was, how fragile, and what a damn fool L.D. had been. He tipped her head back. ''Angie, honey—'' he started, when the door burst open.

''Sheriff, someone just shot Skinny Jordan!'' Meenie exclaimed.

CHAPTER

12

J.T.'S FACE WAS GRAY, AND HE LOOKED OLDER THAN
he had earlier in the afternoon. He stared at his daughter with
a curious expression of defeat and pain as Charles helped her
out of the patrol car. "Angie, go in the house. I don't want
you seeing this. There's nothing you can do anyway."

Charles watched her slender figure until she disappeared
into the house, then he turned to J.T. "Where's the body?"

The rancher licked dry lips. "He's up in the pasture, Sheriff. You can follow me in your car."

Charles looked past him at the tableau of cowboys clustered near the corral. Kurt Reynolds stood near the pickup
as if declaring he wasn't a member of the common herd.
Johnny Brentwood and Rodriquez, he noticed, evidently felt
no such social distinction; in fact, Johnny seemed to be
shrinking back into the crowd.

Charles frowned. Johnny looked terrified and desperate,
an expression that triggered a memory. That damn sketch of
Willie's! Santiago's son had just such a looked on his face.
But that boy had been caught in a web of circumstances.
That boy had been totally innocent. No outside force was
threatening Johnny Brentwood, but something was scaring
the hell out of him all the same.

He felt the pain spiraling up from his belly and gritted his
teeth. If only Johnny didn't look so much like Angie, if only
he didn't have a motive, if only he didn't look so damn guilty.

If only—the two most hopeless words in the English language.

Wiping the clammy sweat from his forehead, he cautioned himself not to jump to conclusions. Johnny could very well have an alibi for this murder; if he did, he was innocent of the first one. Whoever shot Skinny Jordan almost certainly killed Willie, and he hoped like hell it wasn't Johnny Brentwood.

He drew a deep breath. Time to stop spectulating and ask questions instead. "Who found the body?"

Kurt Reynolds answered. "No one found it, Sheriff; one of the other cowboys was with him." He pointed to a pale, sweating man.

"Why didn't you tell Meenie there was a witness?" Charles snapped, and walked over to the cowboy without waiting for an answer. "What's your name?"

The young man stared up at him without answering. "This is Bud White, Sheriff." Rodriquez detached himself from the crowd of other cowboys, his face and voice expressionless.

"Bud, come with me in the patrol car. I want to hear what happened."

The cowboy followed him docilely to the waiting car. Charles motioned him into the backseat. Sliding in next to Meenie, he slammed the door. "Follow J.T.," he said tersely.

Through the mesh screen separating the front and backseats, he turned to look at Bud White. The young man—Charles judged he couldn't be much more than twenty-five—sat clasping his hands together, unsuccessfully trying to still their tremor. "Now tell me what happened, Bud."

"You ain't going to believe it," he began earnestly. "Nobody else has."

"Just start at the beginning, and tell me everything that happened," Charles said.

"Well, we were riding back toward the big house when it happened."

"Just a minute. Where was everyone else, and what were you doing riding back to the house before dark?"

Bud looked startled for a moment. "The other cowboys was still building on that damn corral."

"Who was still at the corral?"

Bud looked thoughtful, then named several men, counting each off on his fingers. Charles interrupted again. "Where were the Brentwoods, and Reynolds, and your foreman?"

"I don't know exactly, except I know Johnny went back to the house for some spare brandin' irons I guess you didn't know nothin' about, and Rodriquez went to town for some antibiotics. He was mad as hell about it, too. He and Reynolds got into a real hassle over it till Mr. Brentwood told Rodriquez to go on. And I guess Mr. Brentwood and Reynolds went back to the house. I didn't listen too close. Mr. Brentwood looked like he was ready to fire anyone that crossed him. I don't know how Skinny ever had guts enough to tell him he was goin' into town."

"When did Skinny tell Brentwood that?" Charles asked.

Bud scratched his cheek. "Oh, musta been thirty minutes to an hour after you left. He was working along side me, and he was sweatin' like a pig. He was scared. A man could tell 'cause he stank. A scared sweat smells different than a work sweat. Finally, he threw down his hammer and walked over to Mr. Brentwood. Told him he was goin' to town. Well, Mr. Brentwood cursed and said he couldn't spare him, but Skinny said he was goin' anyway, that he had to. The old man kinda looked at him and got real quiet and still, like a steer when you hit between the eyes with a bois d'arc post. He kinda slumped and told Skinny to go ahead. Then Rodriquez and Reynolds got into it, and Mr. Brentwood roused some, enough to tell them to both shut up."

"Rodriquez heard Skinny say he needed to go to town? I thought Rodriquez was gone?"

"No, he was there. I just got mixed up."

Charles wished that one day he could interview a witness that could put events in sequence. Somewhere there had to be a witness like that. "What about Johnny? Was he still there, too?"

"Sure. Everybody was."

"So Skinny announces he's going to town, and four people suddenly find errands to do?"

"I don't know about that, but they all left. I don't know what the all-fired hurry was for the brandin' irons or the antibiotics. We ain't gonna be able to start before tomorrow anyway."

"So then you and Skinny left?"

"No, we didn't. Rodriquez told Skinny to finish that side of the corral before he left. We worked, oh, maybe another half hour, forty-five minutes, then Skinny just up and quit. He came over to me, and said I had to go back to the ranch with him. I asked what the hell for, and he said you told him not to go anywhere alone. There wasn't any boss there to tell me I couldn't, and I'm was sick of hammerin' nails, so I went."

He stopped and pointed ahead. "There's where it happened, Sheriff. The body's right there by Mr. Brentwood's pickup."

Charles scrambled out as soon as Meenie stopped and ran toward the body. A lone cowboy stood a little way off, his back pointedly turned toward the body. Charles understood why a second later. He heard Meenie's expletive.

"Damn it, Sheriff. That's the biggest hole I ever saw in a man! You could stick your fist through it!"

Charles spit out the bile that suddenly filled his mouth. He'd seen some terrible wounds in Vietnam, but he saw their equal for the second time on the Branding Iron Ranch. "It looks almost as if he'd been hit by a small artillery shell. I haven't seen anything like it before. Get the camera and take some pictures.''

He heard a rattling and a sound like gears being stripped. He wondered if someone should suggest to Mrs. Jenkins that she might consider buying a car with an automatic shift. He met her halfway. Someone had to warn her before she saw the body. ''Mrs. Jenkins, this is worse than the other.''

Viola Jenkins walked past briskly. ''I've seen gunshot wounds before, Sheriff. I thought my husband was going to kill himself until I finally forbade his going hunting anymore. Silly old fool shot himself through both feet and one hand at various times.'' Her voice broke off, and Charles grabbed her arm.

''Good God Almighty,'' she said weakly, grabbing the flask Charles handed to her. She swallowed noisily, considerably lowering the level of liquor.

Handing the flask back to Charles, she pulled out her dainty handkerchief and wiped her mouth. ''I'll call the pathologist, Sheriff.''

''Tell him I want a report tonight, Mrs. Jenkins, and I don't care how late it is,'' Charles said. ''Are you going to be all right? I have some more deputies on their way. Do want one of them to drive you back?''

Mrs. Jenkins straightened her shoulders. ''Sheriff, in case you haven't noticed, I'm not of a delicate disposition, and I haven't fainted in thirty years. Save your sympathy for the County Commission; they're going to faint when they get the Parker brothers' bill for two runs out to the Branding Iron and then to Amarillo. They'll probably be charged for a tune-up, too. That cattle trail I had to drive over to get up here put a new rattle in my old Ford. Just imagine what it'll do to a hearse. And they brought their best one again,'' she added, as the long black vehicle parked smoothly beside the body.

''Thanks again, Mrs. Jenkins,'' Charles said.

"Oh, Lord, call me Viola. Mrs. Jenkins sounds like you're talking to my mother-in-law, the interfering old biddy." She waved her hand and climbed back into her car.

Charles motioned the morticians back. "Are you through with the pictures, Meenie?"

Meenie spat at a prickly pear cactus. (Charles noticed he picked the closest one to the Parker Brothers.) "Yeah, and I went through his pockets, too. Ain't nothin' on him that shouldn't be. A can of chewing tobacco, an extra bandanna, that's all." He jerked his head toward the morticians. "We can let them buzzards have him now, I guess."

Charles nodded at the Parker brothers and watched as they removed the body. He noticed even they looked a little pale. It was nice to know they were human. And they weren't the only ones. Johnny was leaning against the pickup, his face ashen.

"Meenie, get Bud out of the car. We need to know where that shot came from. I don't see enough cover for a jackrabbit to hide behind, much less a man with a gun."

Bud walked up, shaking his head. "I know what you're gonna ask. You want to know where the shot came from— and you ain't gonna believe me when I tell you."

Charles was getting tired of hearing the same thing. "Just show me," he snapped.

Bud pointed back toward the headquarters. "Over there. I know, 'cause I saw the smoke."

"Over where, damn it? There's not a tree, or a rock, or even a prickly pear in that direction."

"The shot came from the top of that mesa," the cowboy said, pointing toward a small, flat-topped hill with steep sides.

"It couldn't," Meenie stated emphatically. "That mesa's a good half mile away."

"I tell you the shot came from that mesa. I saw the smoke."

"What are you talking about?" Charles asked. "What smoke? Even if there was smoke from a rifle, you couldn't see it from this distance."

"I did, Sheriff. I ain't lyin'. It wasn't much, but the wind's kinda quiet today, and the smoke just went straight up."

"Well, son, you was seein' things," Meenie said flatly. "That shot came from a lot closer than that mesa. It had to, or Skinny wouldn't have such a hole in him. Ain't no gun I know anything about that'll shoot that far and have enough poop left to make a hole that big."

"All right, just leave it, Meenie. When the pathologist calls, we'll know what kind of a gun was used, then we can decide how far away the murderer was. In the meantime, have the other deputies escort everyone back to the ranch and hold their hands for a while."

Meenie jerked his arm at three deputies who had just arrived. "Take them back to the house, and don't let them blow their noses unless they ask you first."

An excited Slim straightened up as if he were on military parade. "Yes, sir. All right, everybody back to the ranch."

"Oh, God," Charles said.

"Are you prayin', or just cussin'?" Meenie asked.

"Both," Charles said. "Why didn't Miss Poole send Raul out here?"

"Did you want to leave Slim in charge back in town?" Meenie asked dryly.

"Oh, God," Charles said again. Slim in charge of the sheriff's department was too awful to contemplate.

"Now what are we goin' be doing while Slim plays sheriff?"

"We're going to search the top of that mesa."

"Hell, Sheriff, you don't believe that story, do you?"

Charles climbed back in the patrol car. "Do you have any better suggestions as to where to look?"

Meenie shrugged his shoulders. "It's a good day to climb

a mesa. Probably only about ninety-five degrees out there. At least you got your hat on today. Any more sunburn on that nose of yours and you'll have a blister on the end of it.''

''Leave my nose out of this. Just drive.''

Meenie drove to the base of the mesa, muttering under his breath. ''All right, here we are. Now what?''

Charles got out of the car. The walls of the hill were not as rough as they looked. A man could very easily get to the top, and quickly, too. The mesa was not more than thirty feet high. ''We climb,'' he said, and started up.

Very quickly he discovered that he still hurt like hell. His back and legs protested every move he made. Dust gritted between his teeth and eased under the bandage on his hand to create a stinging that made him wish he'd never heard of the Panhandle of Texas, much less pointed his car in that direction when he impulsively left Dallas.

By the time he reached the top, he realized the mesa was higher and larger than he thought. In Bud's words, he was sweating like a pig. He stood up, locking his knees so his shaky legs wouldn't collapse. ''If the shot really came from here, the murderer had to be on this side, and fairly close to the edge.''

''Well, we've got a view of the whole mesa, and I don't see anything,'' Meenie said.

''We'll start from here. I'll take the edge and five feet in from it. You take the next five feet. We'll repeat until we cover the mesa.''

''All right,'' the deputy grumbled, ''but I tell you, there ain't nothing here.''

Five minutes later Charles agreed with him. There wasn't a gun, but he did find a very faint area where the grasses bore the imprint of a body. ''Here it is, Meenie,'' he called.

The deputy came over, his short, bowed legs moving faster than Charles had ever seen them. ''Where's the gun?''

Charles traced in the air above the faint outline. ''He was

lying here, and if he crawled backward, he could simply climb down the back of the mesa and be gone.''

"The mesa slopes down to a creek that runs right behind the ranch, Sheriff. I went over to the other side and looked. The way the house is facin', a man could come up on the back of the house and sneak in the back door. That part of the house's been added on and there ain't nothin' back there but an office and another room and one great big old bedroom on the second floor. But that don't help us none. I still say there ain't no way a fellow can hit a man from this distance even with a scope, 'cause the damn bullet's gonna slow down to next to nothing, and be way off target before it gets there.''

Charles pointed to two sticks, tied together in the middle with a rawhide band into the general shape of a capital X, and stuck in the ground. "Did you ever see anything like that?" he asked Meenie.

His deputy lifted his hat and scratched his bald spot. "I ain't never seen anything like it, but a fool could tell that must be what he rested his gun on. He must have gotten up in a hurry and forgot it. That is, provided you believe this whole thing.''

"What's your explanation, Meenie?" Charles asked quietly. "I'm willing to listen to any ideas at all, because a jury will never believe a man was killed from a half mile away.''

Meenie turned his head and spit in disgust. "Hell, Sheriff, I ain't got no explanations. I just sure as hell don't.''

Charles sat on the passenger side clutching the sticks. "Damn it, Meenie, I should've arrested him this afternoon. At least he'd be alive now. Instead, all I did was paint a bull's-eye on him and dare someone to kill him.''

"What do you reckon he saw?"

"If I were guessing, I'd say he saw someone put a branding iron back. But why wouldn't he tell me this afternoon?"

Meenie rolled down the window, shifted his tobacco, and spit. "If somebody bashed a friend of yours over the head with a branding iron, would you be in an all-fired hurry to talk about it? Drinkers ain't usually real brave, and Skinny was a drinker. It'a been his word against somebody else's, and even a reformed drunk ain't a very dependable witness. Maybe he didn't want to take a chance of endin' up with a branding iron buried in his skull if nobody believed his story."

Charles rubbed his forehead where a dull throbbing was beginning. "No, I suppose not, but I still should have arrested him. It's just one more part of this investigation I've screwed up royally. I should've searched for the crucifix. I certainly had enough cause to believe it was still on the ranch."

"Where was you plannin' to look?" Meenie asked dryly. "In every draw and prairie dog hole? You could lose a tank on this ranch and never find it. No tellin' where that crucifix is now."

Charles shook his head, thinking of Willie's sketch, of the beauty of the cross, not to mention its obvious value. "That cross may be hidden, but no one threw it away. It's a legend and seemed to hold almost a mystical fascination for everyone. I'm beginning to be superstitious about it myself. I keep trying to draw parallels between what happened to the Santiagos and what's happening on the Branding Iron, and that's ridiculous. The crucifix wasn't even the motive for the massacre at the plaza."

Meenie nodded. "I reckon there ain't no reason to doubt what Judge Nourse told you, but it sure don't help us none."

He shifted his tobacco and glanced at Charles. "What do you suppose happened to Dolores Santiago, Sheriff?"

"I don't know, Meenie. I wish I did." He didn't mention why he wished he knew—because he couldn't explain to his practical, unimaginative deputy that whenever he thought of Dolores Santiago, he saw her with Angie's face.

Meenie parked the car in front of the house. "Looks like a damn meeting of the Sheriff's Association of Texas. I didn't know we had so many patrol cars in Crawford County."

"I think Miss Poole was exceeding her authority again," Charles said dryly. "I don't recall telling her to borrow men from the Carroll Police Department."

"You want to send them back?"

Charles climbed out of the car and started toward the house. "No, we're going to need all the help we can get. We're not leaving this ranch until every person on it makes a statement. And if the damn horses could talk, I'd take statements from them, too."

CHAPTER

13

CHARLES BRACED HIS ELBOWS ON J.T. BRENT-wood's desk and dug his fingers through his hair. He rotated his neck, trying to loosen the stiff muscles, and glanced toward an adjoining room that held another desk. The focal point of that room was a computer with a printer and various other pieces of modern technology Charles didn't recognize. Briefly he regretted that Raul had been left in town; Raul was computer crazy. He read catalogues from each of the major companies and carefully compared each computer. Not that he owned one. The chances of Raul ever being able to afford a computer on a deputy's salary were slim to none.

Charles, upon hearing Meenie expectorate, shuddered. "I hope you don't miss that spittoon. If your spitballs land on the carpet, J.T. will turn in a bill to the County Commission, and they'll take it out of your hide."

The deputy looked wounded. "I wouldn't do that to Mrs. Lassiter."

"Let's go over what we have so far," Charles said, ignoring Meenie's comment about Angie. Angie was a subject he was blocking out of his mind.

"All the cowboys said just about the same thing Bud did. J.T. was spittin' nails at everybody until Skinny told him he was goin' to town. Then he quieted down until Rodriquez and Reynolds got into it. Nobody seemed to know why

Skinny was so dead set on goin', but they all agreed he was nervous as a calf about to be branded.''

"Did anybody else say Rodriquez was the one who told Skinny to finish what he was working on before he left?''

"Yeah, a couple did. Most of them weren't close enough to hear.''

"What about the times involved? Did you get verification of the times?''

Meenie shrugged his shoulders. "You know how it is, Sheriff. Nobody was lookin' at their watches, but they figured Skinny didn't stay quite an hour after the Brentwoods, Reynolds, and Rodriquez left.''

Charles sighed and leaned back in J.T.'s comfortable chair. "It seems to check out. The ones I interviewed told me the same thing. So we have Skinny telling J.T. he's goin' to town in the hearing of everyone at the branding pens. A few minutes later four people leave, the same four people who went to Red Barn Cave with us. Two of those people admit to being out during the tornado, and one of those people has a motive.''

"Who's got the motive?''

Charles closed his eyes momentarily. "Johnny does,'' he admitted. "Angie told me he'd been gambling and J.T. threatened to disinherit him. Johnny asked Angie for a loan.''

Meenie finally broke the silence. "Well, did she give it to him?''

Charles looked at Meenie. "She doesn't have the money. She went to the bank and found out L.D. had cleaned them out.''

Meenie's face twisted with sympathy. "Is that why she was a mite upset today?''

"She thinks he was deserting her.''

"That's better than her knowin' why he was really leavin','' Meenie said. "Besides, she needed to know he wasn't no saint. Now she can get on with her own life, hitch up with a good man.'' His expression clearly said who he thought the good man ought to be.

Charles looked at the bandage on his hand, now dirty from the climb up the mesa, and remembered the softness of Angie's touch then and later. It was illogical to keep hoping nothing would change between them. He was the sheriff and his most likely murder suspect was her brother.

He looked up again and knew his face must be revealing something from the expression on Meenie's face. ''I don't need any sympathy,'' he snapped. ''Go get Bud White.''

Meenie pushed himself off the couch. ''Hell, I wouldn't waste my time feelin' sorry for you. You're doin' a good enough job yourself.'' He stormed out, closing the door with exaggerated care.

Charles leaned back in his chair and clutched the arms. Damn Meenie for his forthrightness. And damn him for being right. He sat staring at the door until it opened abruptly and Bud White came in. The cowboy stood uncomfortably, holding on to his Stetson as if it were a lifeline.

Charles motioned to a chair in front of the desk. ''Sit down, Bud.'' He waited until Meenie came back and took out his pad. ''I want you to tell me everything that happened today, so Mr. Higgins can take notes. We'll type your statement, and you can read and sign it. It's just something a witness has to do, rather like branding cattle. We have to have a record others can read.''

''Sure, I understand, Sheriff,'' Bud said earnestly, and launched into his story.

Charles listened carefully, but Bud's story was the same. As he told of hearing the shot and seeing Skinny fall, Charles stopped him. ''How loud was the shot?''

Bud wrinkled his forehead in thought. ''A sharp crack, like a limb breaking,'' he finally said. ''But like a long way off. You know, Sheriff, I would've thought it woulda been louder than that. I mean, to kill Skinny from that far away, a man would think the noise'd pop your ears. And it sure knocked Skinny off his horse.''

"What did you do then?" Charles asked.

"I was off my horse, and tryin' to crawl in a prairie dog hole. I looked over to where the shot came from, and that's when I saw that smoke on top the mesa. If the wind had been blowing like it usually does, I wouldn't have seen it. But I saw it all right, and that shot came from the mesa.''

"Did you see anybody on the mesa?" Charles asked, leaning forward in his chair.

"Not then. I was too busy tryin' to make myself small.''

"You mean you did see someone and you just now thought to mention it?"

"Well, I just thought I did, oh, about five minutes later. The shot had spooked the horses, and they was headin' for the corral, and I was right after them. Damn horses. You think you got 'em trained and then the first little thing, they run off.''

"Who did you see?" Charles asked, fighting the urge to reach across the desk and shake the cowboy.

Bud looked surprised at the question. "Hell, Sheriff, I don't know who it was. I couldn't tell from that distance. But he was driving a pickup. I saw the dust from the wheels. Whoever it was got in a pickup and drove back toward the big house.''

"How the hell do you know that?"

Bud looked wounded. "Ain't no place else that road goes but to the big house. He couldn't take off across the pasture toward the highway; there's a big draw just this side. Ain't nobody gonna drive across it.''

Charles sighed. "Okay, Bud. We'll call when we want you to sign your statement. Ask J.T. to come in, will you?"

Bud grinned and got up. "Sure thing, Sheriff," he said. He tilted his head to one side and looked at Charles. "You know you ought to try a raw beefsteak on that eye.''

"Thanks, Bud. I'll remember that. Now tell J.T. I want to see him."

Charles waited until the door was closed before speaking to Meenie. "So somebody grabbed the gun and came back to the house. I think it's safe to assume he came from the house in the first place."

"And we got four people at the house," Meenie said. "J.T., Reynolds, Rodriquez, and Johnny."

"Rodriquez was in town picking up antibiotics. Remember?"

"There's somethin' funny about Rodriquez, Sheriff. He don't act like no ranch foreman I ever saw. And he sure does act independent for a man that ain't been working for an outfit any longer than he has."

"I know it, Meenie. I'm not dismissing Rodriquez as a suspect." He called a brusque "Come in" as a faint knock sounded on the door. A second later he flung himself out of his chair and around the desk.

Grabbing a heavy tray, he kicked the door shut, and glared. "What the hell are you doing carrying anything with that hand, Angie? You let Consuelo do it, or one of my deputies."

Meenie grunted, but for the first time Charles wasn't able to define his deputy's noises. He glanced over Angie's shoulder and thought he saw the hint of a smile on Meenie's face. If so, it was the second time he'd smiled in as many days. It was a record of sorts.

"You can set the tray down, Charles," Angie reminded him gently.

He obeyed and circled around the desk to sit down. He cleared his throat. "Thank you for the coffee, Angie. Now if you'll excuse us, Meenie and I have several witnesses to interview."

"I know," she said, following him around the desk and

proceeding to fill a plate with a variety of sandwiches. "But I told everyone to stay out until you'd eaten."

Charles heard another snort from Meenie's corner of the room. "Angie, I don't have time to eat. I have two dead men—"

"Who won't be resurrected simply because you refuse to take five minutes to eat." She handed him the plate with a suddenly shaking hand. "Please, Charles, let me do this for you," she whispered. "You've done so much for me."

He stared at the plate in front of him. Gratitude! She wanted to do something for him in exchange for his help. He didn't want *gratitude*, damn it. He looked up at her. "It isn't necessary to feed me," he said stiffly.

She thrust a cup of coffee at him. "Just eat your sandwich," she snapped, and ran to the door.

She opened it, then whirled around. "Sometimes I don't understand you at all, Sheriff Matthews!" Charles was left staring, a half-eaten sandwich in one hand, a cup of coffee in the other.

Meenie filled his plate. "Sure were polite, weren't you? You coulda at least said thank you."

Charles swallowed a bite of roast beef sandwich. "I didn't mean to hurt her. I just don't want—"

"You know, for a college man, you sure as hell don't know how to tell people what you *do* want."

Charles shoved his plate away, the roast beef suddenly tasting like cardboard. "Shut up, Meenie!" he snapped.

"Yes, sir. Don't want to rattle your cage none. I ain't in the mood to get my head chewed off like you done to Mrs. Lassiter."

Charles threw his napkin on the desk and stomped to the door to throw it open. "J.T., I'm ready for you."

The rancher seemed shrunken, as if he'd lost inches and pounds. His lips looked pinched, and he moved stiffly. He sank into a chair. "All right, Sheriff, I'm ready to give my statement or whatever the hell you call it."

"Statement is the proper word, J.T. Now tell me about this afternoon."

"Hell, Sheriff, there's nothing to tell. Somebody shot Skinny Jordan."

Charles slammed his fist on the desk. "Damn it! I know that! What I don't know is what you were doing just before he was shot. What I don't know is what you were doing while he was being shot. In other words, what's your alibi, J.T.?"

The ranger wiped a handkerchief over his face and stuffed it back in his pocket. "I was at the corral, Sheriff. And I admit I was mad as hell. I was yelling at everybody. But damn it! It's bad enough that Willie was killed, and then to find out my own branding iron was used. It's like someone spit on me and everything I stood for. Then Skinny came up and told me he was going to town, that he needed to see you. It was too much all of a sudden. Now one cowboy was going to tell off on another. I tried to make myself believe he hadn't seen anything, and told him I couldn't spare him. He said he was going anyway, and that's when I knew he was scared."

"Why then?" Charles asked.

"Skinny Jordan couldn't have found another job cowboying, Sheriff. He was a drinker, and I was the only one who would take a chance on him. If he was scared enough to threaten to quit, then he knew something. I told him to go ahead, but Rodriquez jumped in and told him to finish what he was doing first. At that point I just didn't care; I was sick about the whole thing."

"What did you do then?" Charles asked.

"I got in the truck and came back to the ranch."

"What about the argument between Rodriquez and your ranch manager?"

"Well, Kurt was trying to get everything lined out so we can start branding tomorrow. He told Johnny to get the spare irons, and he told Rodriquez to run into town after more antibiotics. You have to give these calves a shot just to be on the safe side. Don't want to lose any from an infection they might pick up during the branding. Rodriquez said he'd send someone, and Kurt flew off the handle at that. He and Rodriquez don't see eye to eye sometimes anyway, but I couldn't let the men see Reynolds's authority challenged, so I backed him up.''

''Who is Rodriquez and why did you hire him, J.T.? I understand if you have a manager, you don't need a foreman, and vice versa.''

''Rodriquez serves a function,'' Brentwood said.

''Who is he? He told me he answered your ad in a ranching magazine. I'd like to see that letter.''

''I'm not showing you my private papers, Sheriff. You just take my word for it. Rodriquez is a good man.''

''You're hiding something, J.T., like you hid the fact you had spare branding irons, and I want to know what it is. I damn well intend to know everything about every man on this ranch, including what kind of underwear they prefer. Now what do you know about Rodriquez?''

''I know he didn't murder anybody.''

''Then who did, J.T.? Who hated enough, or was desperate enough, to smash Willie's skull with a branding iron and blow away a big part of Skinny's chest? Was it you, J.T.? Where were you when Skinny was shot?''

J.T. closed his eyes. ''I was asleep. I didn't hear a thing until Kurt woke me up after Bud White came screaming back to the house.''

Charles rose and leaned over the desk. ''You're telling me you didn't hear the shot? You're saying you slept through a gunshot Bud White heard a half mile away? You expect me to believe that?''

''I don't give a damn whether you believe me or not, Sheriff. You can arrest me and I still wouldn't change my story.''

Charles sat down. "I'm not going to arrest you for murder because I don't think you have a motive, but I won't hesitate to arrest you for obstructing justice if I find out you know something that would solve these killings and aren't telling me. Now let's back up a little. Where were Johnny and Reynolds?"

"Johnny went to the shed to get the branding irons, and Kurt came in here to run off the tally of calves to be branded. Since we can't find Willie's tally book, the only record we have is on the computer."

"If you have a computer record, why are you so worried about the tally book?" Charles asked curiously.

J.T.'s face was stiff and expressionless. "It's always a good idea to have a check on a machine."

Charles nodded, his curiosity satisfied. "So you were in your room asleep, Johnny was in the shed, and Kurt was working on the computer. Who else was in the house?"

"Consuelo," J.T. said, "but you surely can't suspect her?"

"No, but I'm a lot like you with your tally book, J.T. I like to have a second opinion on testimony." The ringing of the telephone interrupted him.

He waved at the phone. "It's your house, J.T. Answer it."

Brentwood leaned over and picked up the phone, and Charles noticed his forehead looked clammy with sweat. Something was bothering J.T., and he'd give a year's salary to know what.

Brentwood handed the phone to Charles. "You should have answered it in the first place, Sheriff."

"Go to bed, J.T," Charles said, taking the phone. "You look like you need the rest."

"Do you really think I could sleep, Sheriff?" Brentwood wearily left the room.

"This is Sheriff Matthews," Charles said, half his attention still on J.T.'s testimony.

"Dr. Akin here," the pathologist said brusquely.

"What kind of a gun was it?"

"Don't push me, damn it," Dr. Akin snapped. "I have a question for you first. How far away was the victim when he was shot. And don't tell me you don't know. I'm not in the mood."

Charles drew a deep breath. "About a half mile."

Akin's reaction was immediate. "Damn it to hell, Sheriff!" Charles heard the pathologist take a deep breath of his own. "I'll call you back," he said, and hung up.

Charles looked at the receiver, then at Meenie. "That was Dr. Akin, and I don't think he believed me."

Meenie aimed another stream of tobacco juice at the spitoon. "No reason why he should. I don't much believe it myself."

Charles didn't like to believe it either, but unfortunately there didn't seem to be a choice. "Go get Consuelo, and let's hear what she has to say."

He tapped his fingers on the desk while he waited for Meenie to bring in Consuelo. It wasn't going to be an easy interview. He was the law, the policía, the Anglo authority, and thus to be feared, particularly since he suspected that Consuelo, like half the Mexican-Americans in Crawford County, had never bothered to get a visa.

He got up and seated Consuelo in a chair. She was a good woman, and he wanted her to feel comfortable. "Now, Consuelo, I don't want you to be nervous, or afraid of me."

"I am not afraid. Why should I be afraid of someone who steals cookies to give to a little girl. And Miss Angie talk about you. All the time she talk about you. The sheriff is a good man, she say. You going to marry her, Sheriff? She need a husband bad. She need you."

Charles felt his mouth fall open. "I don't know. That's up to Angie."

Consuelo nodded emphatically. "She marry you. Now I

go back to kitchen. Lots of coffee and sandwichs to make. You don't worry about Miss Angie.''

"Wait, Consuelo. I have some questions. And not about Angie," he added quickly when he saw her grin. "You know Skinny Jordan was shot this afternoon."

She nodded. "Bad, very bad thing to do. He have a wife and three babies."

Charles decided that everything boiled down to family with Consuelo. "I need to know who was in the house this afternoon and where they were."

Consuelo thought a moment. "Mr. Brentwood, he lying down in his room. And Mr. Reynolds, he in that room going click, click on the machine. And Johnny, he come to house for a drink. Say he going to work on branding irons in shed. I tell him too hot to work like that, but he don't listen. He is a crazy boy, that one, all the time crazy. He drive crazy, too—drive the pickup right up to the back door. Pickups belong out front on dirt, not at the back door."

Charles straightened, a premonition sending a wave of pain through his belly. "When was this, Consuelo?"

"This afternoon. I was in big bedroom at the back, rocking Miss Angie's little baby. I hear big crack, like thunder, and think it will rain. Not much rain this year, Sheriff. Mr. Brentwood, he worried about the grass."

Charles gripped the edge of the desk, trying to calm himself. "It has been a dry spring," he agreed. "Now when did Johnny drive up to the back door?"

"Little while after the crack, Sheriff," Consuelo said.

CHAPTER
14

"YOU WANT ME TO GET JOHNNY?" MEENIE ASKED, after Consuelo had left, smiling and happy at having helped Miss Angie's man.

Charles paced the office, running his fingers through his hair. "Damn it, Meenie. I don't think he did it!"

"Just who the hell do you think did it?" the deputy demanded. "You got Johnny's footprints at the cave; you got Johnny at the house at the right time; you got Johnny drivin' up to the back door like a crazy man a few minutes after Consuelo hears the shot. What else do you want? His fingerprints on the gun?"

Charles whirled around. "Yes, damn it! Maybe I do. He had a motive, and he had the opportunity, but he just doesn't have the character to murder someone for a few thousand dollars."

"It wouldn't be a few thousand dollars. If old J.T. was gonna cut him out of his will, it was a few million dollars. Now just who else's got a motive like that?"

"I don't know, but there's a lot I don't know. Who is Rodriquez? And what about Reynolds? And what happened to the crucifix? Hell, we don't even know what kind of a gun was used to kill Skinny, and even if we did, we don't know if Johnny is even a good shot."

"He is," Meenie said. "That antique gun collection out in the living room is his. And all those damn trophies out there have his name on them. I looked while you were talkin' on the phone this afternoon."

"I'm not arresting him yet, Meenie. Not without a gun or that crucifix. We can't go to the district attorney with what we have. He'd throw us out of his office. There's just too much reasonable doubt."

"Well, who do you think did it, Sheriff?" Meenie repeated. "Diego Casados's ghost?"

Charles saw again the sketch of Diego Casados with Rodriquez's face. Murderer or priest? Why couldn't Willie make up his mind whether Rodriquez was the priest or Diego? And why did he use a face in only one sketch of Diego? Why not all of them? He rubbed his forehead. The dull ache had progressed to a sharp pain that made him grit his teeth. He wished he could stop thinking about those sketches. Willie's vision of the past had nothing to do with the present.

"I don't know who did it, Meenie," he admitted, "but I'm not ready to settle for Johnny. Get Reynolds in here—I need somebody to yell at."

Charles quickly lifted his head when Reynolds came in. Fighting the enervating exhaustion that made him feel rumpled and unwashed, he straightened, looking at the ranch manager with a jaundiced eye. The man even looked as if he'd just stepped out of a shower.

"Sit down, Reynolds," he said abruptly.

Reynolds sat down heavily and rested his head against the back of the chair. "God, this feels good. It's been a hell of a past two days, Sheriff, and I'm tired. In fact, I'm too damn tired to try to intimidate you."

"You don't intimidate me," Charles said.

Reynolds grinned, his elusive dimples appearing in his cheeks. "I've noticed, Sheriff. It's one of the things that almost makes me like you."

Charles cocked an eyebrow. "Almost?"

Reynold's blue eyes locked with Charles's brown ones. "I don't think we can ever be friends, Sheriff, not when we both want the same thing."

Charles didn't have to ask for an explanation. He knew what they both wanted. But he didn't intend to discuss Angie. "I want to know about this afternoon, Reynolds, and we'll start with your argument with Rodriquez. Why did you send him to town? Why not one of the cowboys?"

"I sent the man we could best do without."

"You could better do without your foreman, than a cowboy?"

Reynolds's mouth parted in a disarming grin. "I'll admit to being obstinate. I don't like the man, so when he suggested I send someone else, I was determined he go and be damned. The cowboys could build six corrals without any help. And Rodriquez, he's just a figurehead. I don't know why J.T. ever hired him. He never takes orders, and half the time he isn't where he's supposed to be. The first two weeks he was here, he spent exploring the ranch, but did he fix a fence he found down, or chase a stray in? Hell, no, he sent some cowboy to do it. I even caught him messing around the computer. But when he broke the cowboys up into shifts and assigned some to ride herd at night, I'd had enough. He and I had it out."

"Who won?"

Reynolds's face tightened. "He did, but I cut him back to two men a night. We just don't have enough cowboys to split them up like that, and we don't need to. If you ever find Rodriquez murdered, you won't have to look far to find the guilty party."

"I'll keep that in mind," Charles said dryly. "Why did you come back to the house."

"J.T. was ready to come back, and I needed to run a list of cattle to be branded."

"Where was Johnny?"

"He came back with us and went to the shed."

"And you and J.T., what did you do?"

"I went to the computer room, and J.T. went to his room."

"What did you do when you heard the shot?" Charles asked.

"I didn't really hear it."

"What do you mean you didn't hear it? Consuelo heard it."

I was in the computer room with the printer going. All I heard was a crack and I didn't hear that very clearly. In fact, I took a shower when I finished the printout, and I had just stepped out when Bud came pounding on the door. That's when I found out what I'd heard was a shot."

"Where was Johnny?" Charles asked.

Reynolds' steady gaze wavered, and he glanced down at his hands. Johnny was here."

"Where is here? In this office? In the kitchen? Where?"

"He was at the back door."

"Tell me something, Reynolds," Charles said. "Why are you the manager of the ranch? Why not Johnny? Why are you the one operating the computer? Johnny has a computer science degree?"

"I don't believe those questions have anything to do with murder, Sheriff," Reynolds said cooly. "The personal lives of the Brentwoods are none of your business."

"Everything is my business, Reynolds. Now I want to know why Johnny Brentwood isn't trusted by his father."

"What makes you think he isn't?"

"If he were, you'd be the figurehead, Reynolds. You'd be an employee again, instead of giving orders like a surrogate son," Charles said, taunting the manager, hoping to see his composure crack.

Reynolds jerked upright, his lips thinning until Charles was reminded of an animal at bay. "Johnny Brentwood would gamble this ranch away in a year, and J.T. knows it! I've lived on this ranch since I was sixteen years old. J.T. took me in after my father died. He educated me, taught me everything about ranching. I've given twenty years of my life to the Branding Iron Ranch, and I'll be damned if Johnny Brentwood will destroy it. And J.T. won't let him do it either.''

"So you'll marry the crown princess and inherit the throne,'' Charles stated.

"Something like that, Sheriff,'' Reynolds said, a glint of sympathy in his eyes.

Charles felt a gust of rage. "Be damned if you will,'' he said softly.

Reynolds rose to his feet and walked to the door. "Be damned if I won't,'' he said equally softly. He closed the door behind him.

Charles slammed his fist on the desk. "That damn bastard!''

"You sure can't say he's hidin' his intentions,'' Meenie said. " 'Course, neither one of you roosters is asking what the hen thinks.''

"What is that comment supposed to mean?''

"Mrs. Lassiter ain't no prize at the fair. She's got some say about who she marries. The way you treated her tonight, she oughta kick you right where you live.''

"My love life is none of your business,'' Charles snapped as he rose from his chair.

Meenie snorted. "You ain't gonna have one the way you're goin', snapping her head off when she brought you coffee and sandwiches just to be nice.''

Charles whirled around. "Don't you think I want to be nice back? Don't you think I want to promise her everything will be all right? But if I do, how will she feel if I arrest her brother?''

"I don't know,'' Meenie answered dryly. "Why don't you ask her?''

Charles paced the room again. "I don't have to—I already know. She's not over feeling betrayed by L.D. I don't want her to feel betrayed by me, too.''

Meenie rubbed his chin thoughtfully. "If she can't see the difference between L.D. doing murder and you doing your duty, she ain't as smart as I think she is."

"She still doesn't know L.D. was a murderer."

"And you still ain't gonna tell her, are you?"

Charles sat down behind the desk. "Let's change the subject, Meenie. Go get Johnny, and let's hear what he has to say."

When Johnny came in, Charles studied him. There were subtle differences between Angie and her brother, made more apparent by Johnny's haggard face. His jaw was more square, his eyes more deeply set, but he had an air of hopelessness that caused an ache in Charles's chest.

He looked more closely at Johnny and detected a hurt in his eyes that Angie's had never had. The nearest Charles could come to describing it was that Johnny looked like an abused child ready to strike back. "Johnny, where were you this afternoon during the murder?"

"I was in the shed trying to fix up the old branding irons. One of them had a bent shaft, and I was trying to straighten the damn thing."

"Were you in the shed the whole time?"

Johnny rubbed his hand across his eyes. "Yeah, I was—no, wait a minute. I came into the house to get a drink of water. Consuelo landed on me with both feet when she found out what I was doing. She said it was too hot, I should wait until it was cooler. As if I could. Dad would have had my hide. He wanted those damn branding irons back at the corral, and I'd rather work in the heat than listen to him. Of course, it doesn't really matter, I suppose; he'll find something wrong. Or if he doesn't, Reynolds will point out something to him. Sometimes, Sheriff, I'd just like to chuck it all and leave. But if I do that, what'll happen to Angie?" He stopped, as though waiting for Charles to answer his question.

"Why should anything happen to Angie?"

Johnny pounded his fist on the arm of his chair. "Damn it, Sheriff, Angie can't run this ranch by herself. She'd have to either marry or hire somebody she could trust. This place is huge, and it takes every bit of energy a man has to keep it going. Angie's no cowgirl. She's helped work cattle before, but only because she's had to when we were shorthanded. If she had to give everything she had to this ranch, she'd end up old and bitter. You have to love ranching if you want to be a rancher. You've got to fight the weather and worry about the cattle market and whether some idiot of a politician is going to call for a freeze on prices just when you think you might be able to pay off your loan at the bank. You've got to be a jackleg vet and a business man and sometimes a fireman if some damn fool throws a cigarette out of his car window and sets your best pasture on fire. What I'm saying, Sheriff, is that Angie doesn't want to be a rancher, and I don't want her to have to try."

Johnny leaned forward and clasped his hands loosely between his knees. "I'll stay here because I love all those things and I love the Branding Iron; I'll stay in spite of my father and Reynolds."

"Then why do you gamble, Johnny? Why are you risking losing the ranch?"

Johnny's face paled. "How do you know about that?"

"I know your father threatened to disinherit you, and he can do it. Texas law allows a parent to disinherit his children. Is that why you killed Willie? Did you need the money the sale of the crucifix would bring to pay off your debts?"

"Damn it! I didn't kill Willie! I was going to get the money from . . . from someone."

"Where?" Charles asked. "Angie couldn't loan you any. Where were you going to get twenty-five thousand dollars?"

"Angie told you, didn't she? Damn L.D. anyway for leaving her broke. But I'll get the money somewhere. I'll sell something.''

''A gold crucifix?'' Charles asked.

''No! I told you I didn't kill Willie. I don't know where that damn crucifix is, and I wish to hell Willie had never found it.''

''But he did find it, Johnny, and you're the only one who knew he'd found it. You're the only one whose footprints were found at Red Barn Cave. You're the only one who's admitted being there.''

''Well, I'm not the only one who could've killed Skinny. Everybody at the corral saw you talking to him, and everybody heard him ask to go into town.''

''But only four of you besides Skinny and Bud left that corral, and so far you haven't offered any alibi as to where you were when the shot was fired.''

Johnny licked at his lips as if discovering suddenly they were dry. ''I—I was in the pickup when I heard the shot. I was on my way back to the corral. I'm not a dumb kid, Sheriff. I knew you suspected me of killing Willie. I heard that shot, and I panicked. All I could think of was that I was out there by myself with no one to vouch for me, and I headed back to the ranch. I drove up to the back and got out and just shook.''

''You stood by the back door and shook until Bud came running toward the house? Why didn't you go inside? Why didn't you find Consuelo? And why did it take so long for you to get back to the house? It was several minutes before you drove up, long enough for you to grab the gun and climb back down the mesa. What's your explanation for the time span, Johnny?''

Johnny braced his elbows on his knees and rested his face in his hands. ''I don't have an explanation,'' he admitted, his voice muffled. He looked up at Charles, his face pale and stiff. ''I didn't shoot Skinny. You've got to believe me.''

''Where's the gun, Johnny?'' Charles asked.

Johnny shook his head. "I didn't shoot Skinny," he repeated. "I don't know what's happening, I don't know why everything looks so bad for me. But I didn't kill anybody, and I'm not going to jail for something I didn't do." He looked at Charles, his face desperate. "I won't go to jail, Sheriff."

"Then why don't you tell me the truth, Johnny. You're hiding something. Either you shot Skinny or you know something about it. That mesa is only a half mile from the house. It wouldn't take you several minutes to get back here after you heard the shot. What were you doing in those several minutes?"

"I didn't shoot Skinny," Johnny doggedly repeated.

Charles slammed his fist on the desk. "Damn it, Johnny, you're backing me into a corner. If you don't tell me something, I may have no choice but to arrest you. Trust me to help you."

Bitter lines etched themselves around the younger man's mouth. "I don't trust anybody, Sheriff."

Charles closed his one unswollen eye. "Meenie, take Johnny out and tell Slim to watch him. And bring Rodriquez with you when you come back."

Meenie took Johnny's arm. "Let's go."

Jerking his arm free, Johnny rose and walked to the door, his back straight and proud. "I'm not a criminal, Sheriff. I can go back in the living room without being held on to." He stalked from the room, leaving Charles with a bitter taste in his mouth.

Charles let himself slump in defeat and reached for the phone. Dialing a number, he traced circles on the top of the desk with his finger until he heard Raul's lilting voice on the other end of the line.

"Raul, this is the sheriff. Get the county attorney out of bed and have him draw up a search warrant for that damn crucifix."

"He's not going to be very happy, Sheriff, and neither is

the judge when I have to wake him up to sign it. It's two o'clock in the morning.''

''I don't care who's unhappy, just do it, and bring it out here as fast as you can,'' Charles snapped, and hung up the phone.

Forcing himself to sit up straight, he arranged his features in the familiar harsh lines, as Meenie escorted Rodriquez into the room. And escorted was the right word, Charles decided. A lord of the realm didn't possess the self-confidence or aura of majesty that the foreman of the Branding Iron Ranch did.

''Where are the antibiotics?'' Charles asked.

Something flickered in the brilliant blue eyes and a faint smile of amusement parted the foreman's lips. ''Very good, Sheriff,'' he said softly.

''You can skip the compliments, Rodriquez.''

Rodriquez inclined his head. ''Very well, Sheriff. I don't have them because I didn't go pick them up, a fact I'll willing admit since you can check it easily. I drove to town, made a few phone calls, and came back. Skinny would still be alive if he'd followed orders. As it was, I didn't make it back in time.''

''Are you telling me you knew he was in danger?''

''I'm not a stupid man, Sheriff. I knew when you were talking to him that he was an important witness. He was at the corral just after the tornado, and he was scared of something.''

''Was it you, Rodriquez? Did you kill Willie Russell for a golden crucifix? You said you saw Skinny Jordan at the corral. Did he see you? Did he see you put a branding iron back with the branding equipment? Is that why you killed him?''

Charles had seen glaciers warmer than Rodriquez's eyes. ''I didn't kill him, Sheriff. And I didn't kill Skinny either. I got back to the ranch just as Bud White got to the house.''

''Driving a pickup?'' Charles asked.

"I certainly didn't walk to town," Rodriquez replied.

"Did you bypass the house and go on to the mesa, Rodriquez? Did you shoot Skinny Jordan, drive across the pasture back to the ranch road so you could innocently appear just as Bud arrived to announce the murder?"

"Very clever reasoning, Sheriff. Unfortunately, you can't prove it, any more than you can prove Johnny's pickup was the one Bud saw."

Charles clenched his jaw until he could feel a muscle jerk. There was a surplus of arrogant bastards in this case, and the one sitting so nonchalantly in front of him was worse than Reynolds. "How did you know that, Rodriquez?"

"I'm good at asking questions, too, Sheriff," he replied.

"Just who the hell are you, Rodriquez?"

"At present, I'm the foreman of the Branding Iron Ranch."

Charles rose and braced his hands on the top of the desk. "According to Reynolds, that might be a very temporary job."

"Reynolds is a very ambitious man," Rodriquez said obliquely. "And very dangerous to anyone who got in his way. He wants the Branding Iron, Sheriff, any way he can get it."

"And what do you want, Rodriquez?" Charles asked softly, thinking that if anyone were dangerous, it was this cool stranger.

"Justice," the foreman replied, his face totally implacable.

"So do I, Rodriquez. And *I'm* very dangerous, too."

The foreman unfolded himself from the chair and walked to the door. "I've known that from the beginning, Sheriff." He closed the door quietly behind him.

CHAPTER

15

"HE'S RIGHT, MEENIE. I CAN'T PROVE A THING against Johnny. Not in Skinny's murder. And if I arrest him for Willie's murder, any decent defense attorney can get the whole thing thrown out. We've got to find the crucifix—and the gun." Charles grimaced. "That is, if we knew what kind of a gun we were looking for. And if we found it, we'd still have to prove Johnny was the one who fired it."

"I don't hardly see how anybody else coulda killed Willie. Rodriquez's a strange bird, but he don't have a motive. Reynolds wants this ranch so bad he can taste it, but killin' Willie ain't gonna help him none. Now if Johnny'd been found with his head bashed in, I'd look real hard at Reynolds, but that ain't the case."

When the phone rang, Charles automatically reached for it, motioning Meenie to silence. "Hello, this is Sheriff Matthews."

"Sheriff." Dr. Akin's voice sounded tired. "You can't even send me a simple shooting, can you? Hell, no, you have to fancy it up. Crawford County's getting a reputation. Did you know that? Every time I go to a convention, the rest of the pathologists in the country want to know how the latest victim from Crawford County was killed. Don't bother to send me a knifing—the murder weapon would probably turn out to be an Egyptian embalming knife, or some such thing.

Do you know what my telephone bill is going to run this month?''

"Dr. Akin, I don't give a damn what your telephone bill is. That doesn't have anything to do with my case. Now what kind of gun am I looking for?''

"My telephone bill has everything to do with you, Sheriff, because I've been phoning every damn pathologist in this country and Canada trying to find someone who's seen something like this. I finally called a friend of mine in Virginia. He's a Civil War buff—spends his time reading journals and diaries of army doctors on both sides of the fence. I described the wound, the bullet, the distance you claim the gun was fired from, and listened to a lecture on Civil War wounds. He referred me to somebody right there in Crawford County who's an expert in antique guns. You know, I've seen people who thought they were Napoleon, or Caesar, or even God, but this is the first time I've run in to anybody who thought he was Billy Dixon.''

"Wait a minute," Charles said. "Who is Billy Dixon?''

"*Was*, Sheriff. The man's been dead for years and years. I'm surprised you haven't heard of him. He had a little ranch down there on the Canadian River. He's real famous around the Panhandle.''

"He may be, but I don't know anything about him, and I don't see what he's got do with the murder.''

"Billy Dixon shot an Indian off his horse at the Battle of Adobe Walls in 1874 from a distance of fifteen hundred eighty-three yards. He said afterward it was plain damn luck, but what I'm saying is that a half mile is not unreasonable under the circumstances.''

"What circumstances? What are you talking about?'' snapped Charles.

"What I'm saying, Sheriff, is that—barring some military weapon I don't know anything about—no modern gun has that accuracy at that range. We got a lot of guns floating around that might get a bullet that far, but sure as hell not with that kind of accuracy, and it sure wouldn't make that big a hole.''

''Dr. Akin,'' Charles said with all the patience he could muster, ''what kind of gun am I looking for?''

''Same kind Billy Dixon used: a Sharps buffalo gun, probably a .44-90, rather than a .50 caliber, according to Judge Nourse. You'll have to talk to him. Seems there's some dispute about exactly which Sharps Dixon used, but there's no dispute at all about that being one damn big, damn heavy bullet that hit the victim. You look for an octagonal-barreled, single-action, side-hammer rifle that's been fired recently—and you got your murder weapon.''

''You're willing to testify under oath that it was a buffalo gun?'' Charles asked.

''I am not,'' Dr. Akin said testily. ''I'm willing to testify to the extent of the injury, the size of the entrance wound, the weight of the bullet, and its probable caliber. The local ballistics expert will back me up. Judge Nourse is your expert on the type of gun that fired said bullet, and I don't think any defense attorney is going to be able to shake him. He's evidently an expert on buffalo guns in general, and the Sharps in particular. You've got what you need to find the gun, Sheriff, so I'm going to bed. I'll need a lot of sleep to be ready for the next little mystery from Crawford County. God knows, it sure won't be something simple. Oh, by the way, the Potter County crime lab called me about your branding iron, so I took a look at it. I'm about ninety-five percent sure it's your murder weapon for the first victim. It matches the wound—tissue and blood are the same. You know, Sheriff, you people are caught in the nineteenth century. Buffalo guns and branding irons are not your commonplace twentieth-century weapons.''

''I'm aware of that, and you don't know the half of it,'' Charles said, thinking of the sketches of another nineteenth-century object involved in the murders. "Sometimes I don't know which century I should be investigating myself."

"Always thought you'd look good in a flock coat with a pair of revolvers strapped on your hip, Sheriff. Well, good-night, and stay out of range of that buffalo gun."

Charles heard the click as Akin hung up. Bemused, he dialed a number. Unconsciously he sighed with relief as Raul answered instead of his night dispatcher. "Raul, get a warrant for a Sharps buffalo gun." He heard a gasp from Meenie.

"Did you say buffalo gun, Sheriff?" Raul asked, the lilt in his voice more pronounced.

"That's what I said, and hurry it up. I want to get this over with."

"Okay, I'll be out as soon as I can. Oh, yes, Judge Nourse called. He said he needed to see you tomorrow."

Charles glanced at his watch. "It's already tomorrow, Raul. It's nearly three o'clock. I'll see him as soon as I get back to town, whenever that may be."

He hung up and looked at Meenie. "You heard?" he asked.

The deputy nodded. "A Sharps. I'll be damned. Shoulda known it wasn't no modern gun when I saw the size of the wound, then heard Bud say it was fired from the top of the mesa. But I was still thinkin' of some rifle like the .30-06, but even a .45-70 Winchester ain't goin' carry that distance. An old Sharps buffalo gun was made to stop something a whole lot bigger than a man, and stop it in its tracks. Skinny Jordan probably didn't even have time to know he was hit."

Charles thought of the wound. He certainly hoped Skinny died instantly; no one deserved to have to live even a few seconds with half their chest cavity blown to shreds. "Could you fire a gun like that, Meenie?"

"I guess I could. Mind you, I wouldn't want to. I've seen them big Sharps, and it ain't like firing a .22. I ain't a bad shot, but I don't know if I could hit anything from that distance. Take a steady hand, a good marksman, and I don't think I'm that good.''

"But Johnny is?''

"Yeah,'' Meenie said, "Johnny is.''

Charles was never able to think of that stretch of time between Meenie's comment and Raul's arrival with the search warrants without shuddering. They had each sat without speaking, the silence broken only the low hum of conversation from the next room, and that hardly filtered through the solid oak door.

He never asked Meenie what his thoughts were during that period, but he could sense his deputy's unspoken sympathy, and he'd gotten up to pace the room.

He'd lost count of the number of times he crisscrossed the room, carefully avoiding furniture, feeling dizzy and sick from lack of sleep, his swollen eye throbbing, when a soft knock preceded Raul's entrance.

"You took long enough!'' Charles snapped, holding his hand out impatiently for the warrants.

A flush tinted Raul's olive skin, and Charles drew a deep breath to apologize when Meenie interrupted. "You got to watch out, Raul. The Sheriff's lookin' to chew someone to-night.''

Charles turned on his heel and started for the door, jerking it open with a viciousness his deputies had never encountered, and Charles himself had seldom felt. "We'll search the house while the others check the barn and outbuildings.''

He walked into the huge living room, overflowing with cowboys and deputies, each group silent as they watched the other. J.T. and Reynolds sat on the couch while Rodriquez stood alone, resting an arm on the mantelpiece. Charles quickly surveyed the room, unconsciously tensing when he saw Angie sitting quietly in a chair. Their eyes met, and he looked away. Better not to smile, better to let her think this afternoon with all its touching and soft words was a mistake.

Resolutely he turned around, his eyes finding Johnny. The young man stood leaning against the wall, thumbs hooked in his belt. He looked older, his jaw clenched in determination as he looked back at the sheriff. "I haven't gone anywhere," he said.

Charles nodded and walked over to J.T. "Mr. Brentwood, I have a warrant to search the premises for the Santiago crucifix and a Sharps buffalo gun."

J.T. lifted a trembling hand for the warrants, his face sunken with fatigue and something else Charles couldn't quite define. He licked his lips. "We got a lot of Sharps around here. My, my"—he stopped then went on—"Johnny's a collector."

"I doubt this one will be nice and clean, J.T. I don't think the murderer would've had time to clean it after shooting Skinny Jordan."

Charles turned to face the room and rapidly gave orders, sending most of his deputies outside to start searching the grounds. He grabbed Slim as the young man started for the door, an eager expression on his face. "Slim," he said in an undertone. "Stay close to Johnny."

Slim looked disappointed for a moment, seeing his chance for glory disappearing, then his jaw dropped in ludicrous surprise. "You mean he's the murderer?" he said out of the side of his mouth. Charles was reminded of a bad gangster movie with James Cagney or Edward G. Robinson.

"Just stay with him and keep your mouth shut."

Slim threw back his shoulders, and Charles thought for a moment he intended to salute. "Yes, sir!" he said.

Charles wearily closed one eye, then opened to look steadily at his youngest deputy. "This isn't the army, son."

Slim blinked, and Charles waved his hand aimlessly in the air. "Never mind me, Slim. Just go on."

Charles hoped Slim was capable of watching Johnny. God knew he wasn't trustworthy in a search. He'd either forget about fingerprints and pick something up or overlook it in the first place. Jerking his head at Raul and Meenie, he said tersely, "This room first. It has more guns in it than a National Guard Armory."

Raul followed the two men to the gun case that covered one complete wall. "Sheriff," he said quietly, "what does a Sharps buffalo gun look like?"

Charles rocked back and forth on his heels, his mind a blank. "I don't know, except it has an octagonal barrel, a side hammer, and is .44 caliber. Meenie, would you recognize one?"

Meenie lifted his hat and scratched his head. "I could probably tell you which gun is a Sharps without looking at the manufacturer's mark. I don't know as how I could tell which caliber I was looking at. I just ain't no expert at antique guns." He cocked his head at Charles. "Don't suppose the Brentwoods would help, do you?"

Charles snorted. "I wouldn't in their place. I'd sit back and watch a city boy of a sheriff make a fool out of himself." He started as Angie slipped by him, a key ring in her hand.

"The cases are locked," she said expressionlessly. "I don't trust the girls not to play cowboys and Indians." Swiftly she unlocked the cases, then stepped away, her head tilting back slightly as she looked at Charles. "I know you're not being very considerate of the rest of us, but please don't wake the girls when you search their room."

He wondered if the pain he felt was reflected on his face. He lifted his hand to touch her face, then stopped, letting it drop uselessly to his side. "I'll call you when we're ready for their rooms," he said, then clasped her arm as she turned away.

"Angie, I wouldn't frighten the girls. Think whatever you want about me, but don't think that."

She stood, her back to him, her head turned to glance down at the dirty bandage wrapped around his hand. He held his breath waiting for her answer when another's sharp voice snapped out a command.

"Let go of her, Sheriff," Reynolds said, standing by the couch, his blue eyes looking dangerous. "You can manhandle the rest of us, but I won't let you bully her."

Charles tightened his grip on Angie's arm in an automatic possessive reflex and stepped closer until his chest touched her rigid back. For a split second, he thought he felt her relax against him, before she stiffened. "Shut up, Reynolds. I'm not bullying Angie, and she knows it."

Angie jerked away from him and whirled around. "Aren't you, Charles. There are all kinds of definitions for *bully*." She turned toward Reynolds, her eyes snapping green sparks. "And when I want your help, I'll ask for it." She slammed the kitchen door behind her as she left the room.

Charles cleared his throat, glad again he had his sunburn to hide behind; otherwise, he would be as red as Kurt Reynolds. "Meenie, Raul, take that end of the gun case and we'll meet in the middle."

The hum of voices gradually resumed, but it was subdued. Charles supposed some men would enjoy the feeling of power that came as a result of making an entire room of people uncomfortable and on edge, but he didn't. This was the hardest part of his job, the knowledge he represented authority and could make even the most innocent person feel guilty. He wanted to turn around and scream at the men that he was just ordinary, but he knew he wasn't. He was the sheriff, an armed man with the authority to kill if necessary in the line of duty. He wondered what they would think, these cowboys and their bosses, if they knew he hated violent death so much he seldom carried a gun.

He smiled with ironic amusement at himself. A Panhandle sheriff, a supposedly tough, hard individual in a section of the country where everybody owned a gun, and sometimes several, and he was unarmed most of the time. Systematically his examined the guns, recognizing very few of them. There was a Colt .45, probably one of the first made, and an U.S. Army issue Springfield. There were even several muzzle-loading guns and several pistols he was sure dated back to the eighteenth century, if not before. There were two octagonal barrel rifles, but each turned out to be a Remington.

"Ain't no Sharps .44's, Sheriff," Meenie said. "Not in this case. There are a couple of Sharps, but they got round barrels."

"Okay," Charles said heavily, "let's check upstairs in the bedrooms. If it isn't in this case where the murderer could hope it would be camouflaged, then he must have hidden it."

Charles led the way up the stairs. "We'll take the first door and search each room." A few seconds later, he wished he were searching alone. The room at the top of the stairs was Angie's. As he opened drawers, he felt like a peeping Tom. He'd always managed to control his carnal fantasies about Angie, but after kissing her, he knew that kind of control was a thing of the past. And it certainly didn't help any to be pawing through her nightgowns and imagining how she'd look in them. He corrected himself. How she'd look in them wasn't what was bothering him; it was how she'd look out of them.

Noticing Meenie and Raul standing by the door, their eyes carefully averted, he slammed a drawer shut and looked at them. "Well, what the hell are you waiting for? An engraved invitation?"

Meenie pushed his hat to the back of his head. "We figured if anybody was gonna look at Mrs. Lassiter's underwear, it'd better be you."

Charles finished the search in tight-lipped silence. It was all right for his deputies to be sensitive to his feelings, but they ought to be quiet about it. He finished the last drawer, checked the closet, and opened the bathroom door. He leaned against the door, as the faint scent of Angie's perfume seemed to reach out and touch him. He quickly searched, feeling again as if he were violating her. By the time he pushed past Meenie and Raul and gained the hall he was sweating.

He wiped his forehead on his coat sleeve, and opened the next door—J.T.'s room. Framed photographs of Johnny and Angie hung on every wall. "Okay, you can help me now," he said to Meenie and Raul.

They made short work of J.T.'s room and systematically made their way down the hall to the next room. "Judgin' from the gun cases, this must be Johnny's," Meenie said sourly. "And you don't have to unlock them 'cause I can tell you right now there ain't a Sharps in there."

But Charles wasn't listening. Instead he was staring at a veritable gallery of paintings, Willie's paintings. The room seemed to pulsate with the dead man's personality. Headquarters, branding, cowboys, windmills, decaying buildings—all the subjects of Western art were represented. He eyes passed over a painting of Red Barn Cave, then returned to it.

"Sheriff, here's another one," Raul said, pulling a sketch from a drawer.

Charles grabbed it and frowned. "Why did he change his mind?" Charles asked absently.

Meenie peered over his shoulder. "It's another picture of the inside of the Santiago house, but that's Reynolds!"

Charles shook his head. "No, it's the priest. Willie painted Reynolds as the priest, then he changed his mind and used Rodriquez. Why?"

Raul took the sketch. "You could look at it from the other point of view, Sheriff. This might be a later sketch that Johnny found. He doesn't like Reynolds and might not want him representing a priest. You remember, one of the other sketches has Reynolds as the priest."

Charles folded the sketch and tucked it in his pocket. "I don't know what Johnny thinks, and I'm tired of the past always jumping up in my face. Finish this room. I'll do the one next to it."

Opening the door into the ranch manager's room, he stopped. The walls were covered by photographs of the ranch. Charles recognized the branding pens, the headquarters, the pasture. There was even a picture of Red Barn Cave. Damn! That place was haunting him almost as much as the sketches. But not anywhere, in drawers, on the dresser, or on the walls, was there a picture of a human being. It was a neat room, almost antiseptic, with no personal letters of any kind. He felt a faint sympathy for Reynolds, because it was the room of a lonely man who for one reason or another had cut himself off from human affection. Instead, the Branding Iron Ranch had become a shrine to him, and he didn't even own it. Johnny Brentwood did, or would. Johnny Brentwood and Angie.

Shivering, Charles pulled open a desk drawer. Any man who loved something as much as Reynolds loved the Branding Iron wouldn't have any passion left for a woman. Rummaging through the drawer, he found Reynolds's army discharge papers, idly noting the man had achieved the rank of captain. Slamming the drawer shut, his mouth twisted with self-loathing. He wasn't going to find a buffalo gun in a drawer; he merely had a unhealthy curiosity about his rival.

Rising to his feet, he left the room, closing the door on its sterile atmosphere. He stopped in front of the last door and knew he wouldn't go in. It was the girls' room, and he wouldn't risk wakening them. If they found nothing downstairs, and in the outbuildings, then he would wait until morning to search this room. It wasn't much, but it was as far as he could stretch his duty. He motioned Meenie and Raul to follow him, then he went back downstairs.

* * *

"Where do you want to look next?" Meenie asked.

Charles opened a door just off the kitchen. "Nowhere," he said. "I've just found it."

He stepped inside what was obviously a workroom. Tools of various kinds were neatly hung from hooks on a pegboard wall over a workbench. Cabinets lined the other three walls. But what was important about the room was the gun lying on the workbench: a side-hammer, octagonal barreled rifle. Next to it a box had been overturned, spilling out lethal shells considerably over two inches in length. Charles leaned over and sniffed the barrel. "It's been fired recently."

"I'll get the evidence kit," Meenie said, and disappeared through the door.

Charles jerked open the cabinets, carelessly pulling out whatever filled them. Raul silently joined him, searched more neatly and with less desperation. "Why didn't he clean it, Sheriff?" he asked finally.

Charles started pulling books off a shelf in one cabinet. "No time, Raul. He barely had time to get back to the ranch. He was hoping the pathologist wouldn't able to identify the gun, or maybe he thought he could sneak back here and clean it. But he's never been alone. I've made sure of that. My God," he finished on a tortured note.

Raul turned toward him, his question dying on his lips as he saw what Charles had uncovered. "*Madre de Dios*, is that it, Sheriff?"

Charles sank down to sit on the floor, his expression full of loathing. "Behold the Santiago Crucifix—the Bloody Cross, as Brentwood's grandfather called it—the motive for a murder, the reason Johnny Brentwood buried a branding iron in the skull of one of the few men who believed in him. Damn it to hell, Raul. I wish the cursed thing had never been found."

Meenie came back carrying the evidence kit. His mouth

gaped open as he saw the crucifix. "God Almighty, that's the biggest thing I ever saw."

"Three feet of pure gold," Charles answered. He waved his hand toward the workbench. "Dust the gun for prints and tell me he wore gloves."

Meenie uncapped the fingerprint powder and carefully covered the rifle with tiny, delicate strokes of the brush. He blew gently, then stood back. "He didn't wear no gloves, Sheriff. There's prints, and good ones. See this here thumb print? It's got a thin line through the center, a scar. Makes it easy to remember who it belongs to."

"And who is that?" Charles asked.

"Johnny Brentwood," Meenie answered, as he carefully lifted the prints. "Want me to get that cross, too?"

Charles closed his eyes. It was done. Johnny was guilty beyond any jury's doubt. He felt Meenie kneeling and heard the soft swish of the brush as he applied the fingerprint powder. His stomach was burning like fire.

"Nothing on the cross, Sheriff, or at least no prints I recognize, and believe me, I memorized the prints of our four friends out there. So I'd bet the prints on there belong to Willie Russell, but we'll have to wait until we get the autopsy report back to make sure."

Charles opened his eyes and climbed to his feet. "Bring the gun, the bullets, and the cross, and let's get this over with."

He slammed out of the workroom, through the house, and into the living room. All conversation died as he appeared, his face looking like carved granite. Johnny and Slim stood by the front door. Johnny's face was a mask of hopelessness.

"Johnny Brentwood," Charles intoned, "I arrest you for the murders of Willie Russell and Skinny Jordan."

CHAPTER

16

CHARLES HEARD AN INCOHERENT CRY AND JERKED his head toward the sound. Angie stood pressed against the wall, her eyes full of the betrayal Charles knew she would feel. He froze for a moment, but that was long enough.

"I'm not going to jail," Johnny screamed, and he landed a blow on Slim's jaw. The young deputy's body had scarcely slid to the floor before Johnny was out the front door.

Meenie dropped the buffalo gun and, pulling his revolver, rushed after him. Charles grabbed his arm, whirling him around. "We're not going to shoot him!"

Shoving past his deputy, Charles raced through the door, vaulted off the porch, bellowing at his men whose shadowy figures were emerging from outbuildings. "Stop Brentwood, but no guns, damn it!"

He halted, his glance darting about the yard and corral. The moon was almost full and sent a gentle wash of light on the stucco house. It also created dark shadows where a man could hide until he could slip away into the vastness of the ranch. And once away, Johnny could hide almost indefinitely among the thousands of acres with its breaks and caves. He could not be allowed to leave the headquarters area.

Charles spoke without turning his head, his one unswollen eye still focused on the shadows. "Meenie, Raul, park the cars and turn on the headlights until we have a solid circle of light around the headquarters area. I don't want a jackrabbit to slip through.''

He watched as the headlights of one patrol car after another joined in a circle of light, himself standing alone in its dark center. But he wasn't really alone; he could sense it. Johnny was with him. He could sense the younger man's fear, almost smell its acrid odor. For a moment he had feeling of déjà vu. He was back in Vietnam on patrol, straining for the first sound of the enemy, knowing they were out there in the dark, waiting.

Johnny couldn't escape. And if he tried, then what? Trust the deputies to catch a running figure on his own home territory where he was familiar with every inch of ground? Charles felt the sweat break out on his forehead. He couldn't do that; he had to stop Johnny, and that meant shooting. And shooting in the dark was risky. A single tremor, a single gun sight just slightly off, and Johnny would be dead. He had to persuade him to surrender.

Charles smiled bitterly. How can you persuade a man to give himself up when he's charged with murder? Threaten him with resisting arrest? What would that matter to a man looking at life imprisonment or lethal injection? Tell him you love his sister and don't want to shoot her only brother? That would be expecting saintly behavior, and Johnny wasn't a saint. Realistically, it was also stupid behavior, and Johnny wasn't stupid either.

He turned until he was facing the barn, its huge bulk casting the deepest shadows. ''Johnny,'' he called, his voice seeming to echo off the distant mesas. ''Give yourself up. You can't escape, and I have to take you in. You say you're innocent, that things aren't really as they appear to be. I don't know that, because I can't see through your eyes. You have to tell me. Trust me, Johnny. It's the only chance you've got.''

The silence lay thick and heavy, broken only by the night

sounds of the cicadas. Charles slumped until his silhouette no longer stood straight against the bright circle of light. He bent his head and covered his eyes, knowing he now had no choice. He raised his head to give his deputies the order to shoot if necessary, then hesitated. He couldn't take the chance. His men were good shots, most of them, but none were real marksmen.

"Meenie, where are you?" he called quietly.

A figure detached itself from the circle and silently walked toward him. "What do you need, Sheriff?"

Charles held out his hand. "Lend me your gun."

Meenie hesitated a moment. "If it's gotta be done, let me do it."

Charles snapped his fingers impatiently. "I'm the sheriff, Meenie. It's my responsibility. If I hadn't been so stubborn, if I'd arrested him after Willie's murder, I wouldn't be faced with this choice now. Besides, I'm the best shot in the department. He's got the best chance of living if I'm the only one shooting."

"Ain't nobody gonna kill him on purpose, Sheriff," protested Meenie.

"I know that, but he'd be just as dead if it were accidental."

Handing over his gun, Meenie spit in disgust. "You ought to wear your own. You're gonna need it sometime when I ain't around."

Charles clasped his deputy's shoulder. "You're always around, Meenie. Now go back to the circle. You may be able to tackle him and nobody will have to do any shooting."

Meenie shuffled away. "That ain't likely."

Charles knelt on the ground, his bandaged hand wrapped firmly around the revolver's grip, and he pulled the hammer back. The click seemed like a gunshot in the still air. He drew a sharp breath; it was done, the gun was now a lethal weapon. He pressed his empty hand against his stomach to ease the burning, then stilled, holding his breath. Shifting his position slightly, he raised the revolver. There had been a whisper of sound, a creaking like . . . like—

"Watch it men!" Charles screamed. "He's in the barn, and he's got a horse!"

The horse burst out, the figure on his back bent over until he provided no profile at all, just an indistinct bump. Swinging to the right, the horse and rider slipped between two patrol cars. For a moment they were silhouetted in the headlights and Charles sighted his gun, his finger automatically tightening on the trigger. With a curse he jerked his arm up, firing into the air. Angie's scream echoed with the shot as each seemed to reverberate through the night.

There was a scuffling as the deputies nearest to Johnny ran toward him. The mounted rider disappeared into the shadows along the creek bed, and sound of hoofbeats died away.

Charles did not move as the disgruntled deputies gradually came back. He didn't know how many saw him deliberately miss the shot, and he didn't care. He would not kill Johnny. Duty or no, that was too much to ask of a man. He would not be judge and jury again.

"Sheriff," Meenie said. "What do you want to do now?"

He turned abruptly toward the house. "Let's revive Slim, pick up the evidence, and I'll make a few calls, get some deputies from Potter County. We'll have to wait for light. We couldn't find the Crawford County courthouse in the dark, much less Johnny."

Charles stepped up on the porch. "We're starting the search in the morning, J.T. In the meantime, I don't have to remind you to stay in the house. Don't try to help Johnny."

"You'll never find him, Sheriff. He knows this ranch better than anybody. He can stay hidden forever."

Charles opened the door and paused. "He's unarmed, with no food, J.T. We'll get him. He's only made it worse for himself."

"He has a gun, Sheriff, a rifle," Reynolds said. "That was his horse he took, and he always carries a rifle in his scabbard."

Charles grasped the door frame, a shuddering wave of nausea leaving behind a sour taste. "Then he'll have to be considered armed and dangerous," he said.

He felt Angie's gasp like a stabbing pain and entered the house to escape. He couldn't look at her, couldn't give her false hope. He wanted to strike out at someone to relieve his frustration, and a low moan came from a most deserving target. Slim was sitting upright, leaning against the wall, resting his head in his hands.

Charles stalked over to him. "Get up, and get back to town. I want you back here in the morning to tell me why you let yourself be knocked cold by someone you were supposed to be watching."

Slim scrambled to his feet, a purple bruise already discernible on his jaw. He opened his mouth but quickly closed it again when he saw the sheriff's face. He retrieved his hat and scurried out the door as if he were afraid Charles would change his mind and chew him out in front of everybody.

Picking up the buffalo gun, Charles motioned to Meenie to get the crucifix. He straightened and swayed, fatigue and his aching muscles combining to make him dizzy. "Let's go in the office. Raul, will you see if you can get some coffee."

Reynolds grabbed Charles's shoulder and swung him around. "You're standing on Brentwood land after trying to kill Johnny and you calmly expect us to provide you with coffee? You're a real bastard, Sheriff. You'll get nothing here."

Charles knocked Reynolds's hand away, and grabbed a fistful of the ranch manager's shirt. "Don't ever touch me again, Reynolds, or I'll beat the living hell out of you."

He shoved the man away, sending him stumbling backward until he came up against the wall. "Meenie, tell the men to grab a cup of coffee, then sack out in their patrol cars. We'll start the search at dawn.'' He turned and walked into the office, closing the door behind him.

He sank onto the chair and rested his head in his hands. His head ached abominably, and his one eye felt as gritty and swollen as the other. He would live through this, but he wondered if he wanted to. But he'd done his duty. God, yes, he'd done his duty.

And it had cost him the only woman he'd ever loved.

He shook his head. It was done, and he didn't have the time to be wallowing in self-pity. No one ever guaranteed that making the right choice would result in a happy ending. No one ever said life was fair.

He pulled the phone closer and began his calls, his voice decisive as he made his plans and gathered his forces. He was conscious of Raul's entrance with fresh coffee, and he smiled a quick thank you as the deputy poured a cup. He took a sip before dialing a last number. There was no good reason for making the call, not now, not with Johnny guilty as hell, but damn it, he wanted to know.

The voice that answered was definitely sleepy sounding, definitely grumpy, and somewhat less than happy about being awakened at four A.M.

''Sheriff Winfield, this is Sheriff Matthews of Crawford County—''

''Damn it to hell, Sheriff, I hope this isn't a social call because I'm not feeling very sociable at this time of night. God Almighty, do you know what time it is?''

''I'm sorry about the time, but I need to know about one of your former residents, and I need to know now.''

''Sheriff Matthews, we haven't got any criminals down here to export to Crawford County. You people have the corner on strange murders. All we have are a few Saturday night knifings and a few kids tryin' to hold up convenience stores. Unless one of our former citizens was the victim. Did somebody from this county get himself murdered?''

Charles drew a deep breath. First Dr. Akin, and now Sheriff Winfield—he was growing tired of all the lame quips about Crawford County. "No, he's not a victim, and, although I have heard one witness express a desire to make his stay on earth a short one, he's not likely to be a victim. I can almost sympathize with that feeling. There have been times lately I would like to strangle Rodriquez myself.''

"Rodriquez? Conrad Rodriquez?''

"Yes, do you know him?''

Winfield's chuckle was loud. "Do I know him? Why, Sheriff, his family's been around here for a hundred years or more. I watched that boy grow up. So Rodriquez is in Crawford County. You've got real problems up there, don't you? Well, you couldn't ask for a better man. He smart, and one of the best damn shots around. You give him my regards. Tell him this old jailhouse just isn't the same without him.''

"Sheriff Winfield, just who and what is Conrad Rodriquez?''

"Well, Sheriff, I guess you better ask him. He wears a lot of hats.''

"I'm asking you as a professional courtesy.'' Charles wished he could reach through the telephone wires and throttle the man on the other end.

"Sheriff, I'm not going to tell you. I don't know what's going on up there, but I do know Conrad Rodriquez, and I'm not about to stick my nose in his business. You just ask him, and if he thinks you need to know, he'll tell you.''

"Damn it, Winfield!'' Charles shouted.

"Go cuss Rodriquez, Sheriff. I get cussed enough by my commissioners' court. I don't need it from a fellow officer. Do you know what they're trying to do to my department?''

"No, I don't know,'' Charles declared, secretly hoping Winfield's commissioners were planning to remove the man from office. "I'm sorry I woke you up, Sheriff. If I'd known how helpful you were going to be, I'd have saved the taxpayers a long-distance phone call. Goodbye."

Charles hung up and glared at Meenie, who had come in and was stretched out on the couch with his hat over his face. "Wake up, damn it. I need to talk to someone."

Glancing around the room, he frowned. "Where the hell is Raul?"

"Right here, Sheriff," said the lilting voice. "I was just looking at the computer."

"Unless it can tell me who Rodriquez is and where Johnny is hiding out, I'm not interested in the computer," Charles snapped.

"I take it Sheriff Winfield wouldn't tell you any information about Rodriquez. Not surprisin'. He's a close-mouthed old codger."

"This case has moved so quickly, I haven't had time to even find out about the people involved. Do you realize Willie was killed only day before yesterday?"

"Yeah, I know. But you already got the murderer. What you worryin' about everybody else for?" Meenie asked, pulling a small can of chewing tobacco out of his pocket.

"Because Johnny Brentwood could very well be killed during this search. He's got a gun, and the first time he uses it, I'll be forced to declare it open season. But before I do that, before I send men out with orders to shoot a man, I want to be damn sure I have all the answers. Right now I feel as if I'm looking at one of Willie's sketches; half the faces are missing in this case."

"You're worryin' too much about those pictures, Sheriff. This case ain't got nothin' to do with what happened a hundred years ago."

Charles got up, his restlessness forcing him to pace up and down the office. "I know it, Meenie. But damn it, those sketches are just one more puzzle, one more incomplete answer.''

"You don't want it to be Johnny, do you, Sheriff?" Raul asked softly.

Charles stopped abruptly and turned to face his deputy. "No, I don't," he admitted. "Can you blame me for that?"

Raul slowly shook his head, his eyes sympathetic. "It would be hard for Mrs. Lassiter to forget that you arrested her brother."

"Forget?" Charles ran his fingers through his hair. "I don't expect her to forget. That's asking for the impossible—and I learned a long time ago not to hope for the impossible."

He walked around the desk and sank onto the chair, already sorry he had admitted so much to his deputies. "Raul, get Rodriquez," he ordered.

The deputy brought Rodriquez in, and Charles examined the foreman, turning over in his mind everything he knew about the man. He was curious, a crack shot, smart, a good man to have around if you had trouble, and one who was familiar with the law. All that added up to a very interesting sum—and it didn't equal a foreman.

He leaned forward. He had his question, now to test it. "Sheriff Winfield sends his regards, Rodriquez." He felt a rising sense of elation as he saw the foreman's eyes narrow slightly.

"Just what kind of a lawman are you, Rodriquez, and what are you doing in Crawford County?" he asked. He heard Meenie's muffled exclamation, and smiled.

Rodriquez crossed one leg over the other, and hesitated. "If one of your deputies will get Mr. Brentwood, I'll answer your question." He waited while Charles motioned to Raul, then continued, his voice incisive and commanding.

"I didn't think it wise to confess before now, because quite frankly, I was hoping that Johnny wasn't guilty, and I didn't want to throw suspicion on him. But it appears that hope is futile.''

J.T. Brentwood shuffled into the room, his steps slow and awkward. His hands shook like a palsied old man. He sat down on a chair as if his legs had suddenly given way. ''What do you want, Sheriff?'' he asked, his robust voice as gray as his complexion.

''The sheriff knows who I am, Mr. Brentwood, and I think it's time to tell him why I'm here,'' Rodriquez said gently, a thread of regret running through the texture of his voice.

Brentwood waved his hand vaguely, then pulled a bandanna out of his pocket. 'Go ahead. I can't be shamed any more than I already am. I'm as much responsible for Willie and Skinny being killed as Johnny is. If I hadn't been so damn dead set on handling this myself, he'd never have had a chance to kill anybody. But I'd hoped when we confronted him with proof, he'd admit it like a man. I never thought he'd kill somebody to cover up.'' His voice broke, and he swiped at his eyes with the bandanna.

Charles suddenly wished he had never pushed, never bluffed Rodriquez, because he intuitively knew he was about to hear something that would only sicken him. ''Who are you, Rodriquez?'' he asked again.

Rodriquez sighed, then pulled a wallet out of his back pocket. He extracted a plastic card and passed it to Charles. ''I work for the Texas and Southwest Cattle Raisers Association, Sheriff.''

Charles stared numbly at Rodriquez's identification. ''You're a special Texas Ranger.'' It wasn't a question, but a statement. An investigator for the TSCRA was always a Texas Ranger. Charles was aware of that although he had never had any dealings with that special breed of ranger.

''What are you doing in Crawford County and why didn't you check in with me?'' he asked.

''I'm not required to, Sheriff, and I'm impowered to make

arrests if necessary. Not that Mr. Brentwood wanted an arrest. He only wanted proof.''

"Proof of what, for God's sake?'' Charles demanded.

"Rustling,'' Rodriquez answered simply.

"What?'' Charles shouted. "Do you mean two people were murdered because Johnny stole a few of his own cows?''

"They weren't his cattle, Sheriff. They belonged to his father. And it's not quite so trivial as you think. Mr. Brentwood runs registered cattle. A pair are worth seven to ten thousand dollars each.''

"A pair? A pair of what?''

"A pair means a cow and her calf.''

"Well, how many pair were rustled?''

Rodriquez frowned. "We're not sure. We think ten pair valued at approximately one hundred thousand dollars.''

"You're not sure? Why not? Don't you know how many head of cattle you had to start with?''

"I know,'' Brentwood interrupted in a hoarse voice. "But Rodriquez here wanted to be sure. He wanted to double-check. I should have confronted Johnny at the first; but no, I had to tangle Willie up in my personal affairs.''

Charles held up his hand. "Wait a minute! Start at the beginning. How did you know Johnny was rustling?''

Brentwood nodded toward the other room. "The computer. We have all the records on the computer. All the animals on this ranch have a number tattooed in their ear, and those numbers are in the computer. We can check each animal against the number listed on the computer for a complete tally. But Johnny was erasing some of the numbers. I don't how long he was doing it, but he didn't count on Reynolds's memory. Kurt remembered some of the numbers, those that were a little different. He always was making a joke about cow number so and so. He entered some calves on the computer, and he ran a printout on the cattle. We'd had some power problems, and he was afraid some of the memory had been erased. That's when he noticed some of the numbers were missing. We had a printout from the month before, and I checked it against the new one. There were ten pair missing."

Brentwood cleared his throat, then continued, his voice lower and husky with tears. "I knew Johnny had been gambling again and I'd threatened to throw him out if he came to me for money again. So he didn't. He stole cattle from me instead. He was a computer expert; in fact, he set our program up. He knew exactly how to alter it."

"Where does Rodriquez come in, and Willie? If you knew Johnny was guilty, why didn't you confront him?" Charles asked.

Brentwood looked at Charles. "How would you like to accuse your own son of stealing, Sheriff? I couldn't. I called in Rodriquez instead. I was hoping he would prove Johnny didn't do it."

Charles nodded. "I can understand that. But where does Willie come in to this thing, and why did Johnny kill him? If he was rustling cattle to pay his gambling debts, why did he kill Willie for the crucifix?"

"He didn't murder Willie for the crucifix," Rodriquez said. "The crucifix had nothing to do with it. He murdered Willie for the tally book."

CHAPTER
17

CHARLES WIPED HIS HANDS ACROSS HIS MOUTH, once again feeling out of his depth. Tattoo marks, tally books, computer inventories—the terminology was being thrown at him faster than he could assimilate it. "I'm sorry, but I don't understand why anyone would kill for a tally book."

Rodriquez uncrossed his legs and leaned forward in his chair. "The tally book would tell us just exactly how many cattle and which ones were actually on the ranch. I'm rather old-fashioned, Sheriff. I wanted an actual head count. Computers can only tell you what you program them to tell you; they're only as good as the operator. I had to make sure someone didn't slip up and inadvertantly erase those numbers. I had to make sure the cattle were actually gone. That was Willie's job. He had been checking the tattoo marks on each head, then attaching a tag to those animals. He finished the day he was murdered."

"But couldn't you just have done a tally when you branded? Just checked each calf as you branded it?" Charles asked. "I don't understand why Willie had to check each one?"

J.T. answered him, his voice sounding stronger, as if he'd confessed his shame and had nothing left to hide. "That wouldn't work, Sheriff. Some of those pairs had been branded at the fall roundup in December. They weren't even being rounded up."

"Then all that talk about needing the tally book for the branding wasn't true?"

"No, that was just to keep anyone from getting suspicious."

Charles felt the anger rising slowly like liquid lava until it heated his whole body. "You don't mean anyone, J.T. You mean me. You knew if I'd known about the rustling, I'd have arrested Johnny then. Damn you, Brentwood! You deliberately held back evidence. You're as responsible for Skinny Jordan's death as Johnny is. You knew when I didn't find the tally book that Johnny was guilty of murder, and you didn't tell me."

He switched to Rodriquez, disgust turning his voice into a cutting rapier. "And you, you as a lawman, didn't tell me what you suspected. As far as I'm concerned you're an accomplice to murder, and I intend to make sure the Texas Rangers jerk your badge."

Rodriquez rose, his blue eyes reminding Charles of sun glinting of a frozen sea. "If you're going to throw accusations around, you'd better include yourself. You had enough physical evidence to arrest him without my help, Sheriff. Why didn't you?"

Charles sat staring at Rodriquez as his whole case seemed to turn upside down.

He was as guilty as Rodriquez and J.T. He'd ignored physical evidence because he didn't want to arrest Johnny. He'd walked around feeling so superior because he believed Johnny's character wouldn't permit him to commit murder. He'd let feelings overrule his objectivity. "I didn't arrest him because I didn't think he could commit murder," he confessed.

"I didn't either, Sheriff," Rodriquez said. "In fact, I didn't believe he was really guilty until just a few minutes ago."

"When we found the gun and the crucifix?" Charles asked.

"No. When you didn't find the tally book," Rodriquez said.

Charles rubbed his temples with a circular motion, hoping it might help his headache. With each passing minute Rodriquez's statements increased his confusion, and thus his headache. "Would you care to explain?" He was too tired to care if he seemed dense.

"The gun and crucifix could have been planted for you to find, but the tally book would be the mortal blow. The tally book, along with the computer printouts, would brand Johnny as a cheap cattle rustler. This is ranching country, Sheriff. A jury of his peers would crucify him. He stole that tally book and destroyed it. The crucifix would be harder to get rid of. And, of course, he didn't have time to dispose of the gun."

"But why take the crucifix at all?" Charles asked.

"To draw suspicion away from himself. If you thought the crucifix was the motive, you wouldn't look as hard at Johnny, and he knew that. It confused me, too. After all, we had no way of knowing whether or not Willie had the tally book with him. He might have left it at his house."

"He didn't," J.T. said flatly.

"How do you know that?" Rodriquez asked sharply.

"Because I told him to give it to me before he left. Reynolds told me he came by the house, but I was gone, and he refused to leave it. Kurt gave me the devil about that tally book, said I didn't trust him."

"You mean Reynolds didn't know about Willie doing a tally?" Charles asked.

"No one did," Rodriquez answered.

"Then how did Johnny know about it?" Charles asked.

"Johnny overheard the argument between Kurt and Willie," J.T. said.

Charles felt nauseous. He wanted all the gray areas cleared up, and he got his wish. Everything was black and white. Johnny Brentwood was a murderer, and he, Rodriquez, and

J.T. were accomplices as surely as if they had all known in advance what was going to happen. They'd never be brought to trial for it, but each would have to live with the knowledge that while they couldn't have saved Willie, they could've prevented Skinny's murder.

He looked at the other two men and saw the same awareness of guilt. But he was most to blame. He'd let his feelings for Angie cloud his judgment, and it had cost a man his life.

He squared his shoulders, accepting his burden of guilt. He had to accept it. He couldn't live with himself otherwise. Unlike Johnny, he was a man, and never had he regretted it more.

Finally he broke the silence. "J.T., I'm sorry . . ." He hesitated, realizing he didn't know what to say.

"That's all, J.T. Why don't you go to bed? There's nothing you can do here."

The rancher smiled bitterly, resembling Angie for the first time in his vulnerability. "Someone had to keep the death watch, Sheriff, because you're going to kill him, aren't you?"

"No! I'm not going to kill him!"

J.T. wearily pushed himself out of his chair. "He won't surrender. I know my son well enough to guarantee that. You won't have a choice." He looked at Charles's tortured face. "I'm sorry, Sheriff. You'll lose more than I, won't you? I'll still have a daughter, but you won't have anybody."

Charles knew he was speaking of Angie. "I can't change anything, J.T., not and keep my self-respect."

The older man opened the door, then turned, his face filled with regret and resignation, and strangely enough, admiration. "You're a strong man, Sheriff, and it's a little late to tell you this, but you would've been welcomed here. I thought heroes died out with Charlie Goodnight, but I guess they just wear a coat and tie now, and don't know how to ride a horse worth a damn."

The door closed behind J.T. Charles sat dumbfounded. "I'll be damned," he said.

Rodriquez stirred restlessly. "I'll go with you tomorrow, Sheriff, with your permission."

Charles switched his gaze to the ranger. "If you do, you're under my orders."

Rodriquez nodded his head. "Agreed."

Charles drew a breath, expelling it nosily. "My first order shows you what a lousy hero I am. I'm not quite up to informing J.T. that I'm commandeering his horses to hunt down his own son, but that's exactly what I'll be doing. The sheriff's department doesn't own any horses and we can hardly chase Johnny on foot, so I'm stuck without a choice again. Have them saddled and ready at first light. I just hope my deputies can ride better than I."

Rodriquez shrugged his shoulders and rose. "You haven't had many choices in this case, have you, Sheriff?"

Charles felt his face stiffen with bitterness. "It's probably just as well. I made the wrong decision when I did have a choice."

He nodded his head in abrupt dismissal of the ranger and reached for his coffee. He took a sip and grimaced. He had yet to finish a cup of coffee before it got cold since this case had begun. He put the cup down and rose to stretch his sore, cramped muscles. He heard the raised voices in the other room and presumed Rodriquez had informed J.T. about the horses. He certainly didn't blame the rancher for being upset. He would have been himself.

He jerked when a deafening thud caused the door to shake, but before he had a chance to react, it opened to reveal a tall, white-haired old man. "Judge Nourse?" he asked.

"I'm sure as hell not Santa Claus," the old man said. Charles had a chance to glimpse the twitching nose of the judge's daughter before the door slammed with a resounding crash.

''Whoever said daughters were a comfort in one's declining years was a damn liar,'' the judge said, taking the chair in front of the desk, and resting his cane across his lap. ''Of course, if anybody's declining, it's her. She spent too many years declining offers from good men, and look at her now. Let that be a lesson to you, Sheriff. If a woman plays to hard to get, just skip over her and get to something better. Half the time she'd ain't worth the effort.''

He looked around, politely acknowledging Meenie and Raul, then fixed Charles with a hard stare. ''Where the hell is the liquor, Sheriff? You can't expect a man to talk without a little shot to get him started.''

He turned toward Meenie with the air of a patriarch ordering a poor shepherd to turn in the best of his flock for sacrifice. ''Meenie, go find out where J.T. hides his liquor, and bring me a bottle, some hot coffee, and a clean cup.'' Charles wished he knew how the judge could make his deputy move so fast without a single argument.

''Judge Nourse, what are you doing out here? Do you know what time it is?'' Charles asked.

''Certainly I know what time it is, and don't sound so much like my daughter. I had to threaten to drive myself before I could get her out of the house. I don't know why everybody thinks that just because I'm old I should be tucked into bed with a cup of Ovaltine at eight o'clock. I'll rest when I'm dead. Now, tell me what's happened. I couldn't get much out of your deputy. Excitable kind of boy, that Slim, but he'll be all right when he grows up a little.''

''You talked to Slim?'' Charles asked, thinking that the judge was being a little generous to call Slim excitable; incompetent was more like it.

''Yes, I caught him and Miss Poole at your house. I'd been to the sheriff's department, but that woman you've got as night dispatcher couldn't find what's in her bloomers with both hands. So I went to your house to find Miss Poole's supervising a little breaking and entering. Seems she's sending out some suitable riding clothes with Slim. Anyway, that young man told me Johnny Brentwood killed two men and escaped. Is that right?''

"Yes," Charles admitted.

"You're claiming a boy I've known since he was in short pants killed two men? I want to hear your evidence." The judge turned as Meenie came back in the room with a tray of whiskey and cups.

"Reynolds gave me some lip about the whiskey," Meenie said, "and your daughter said something about your doctor."

The judge looked sour. "Reynolds and my doctor have a lot in common: neither one of them thinks anybody else has any rights." He poured a generous cup of whiskey, topped it with a drop of coffee, and took a sip. "All right, Sheriff, I'm ready."

"Johnny had opportunity and motive for both murders," Charles said bluntly. "By his own admission he was out during the tornado; his footprints were the only ones found at Red Barn Cave except Willie's; the gun that killed Skinny is his; and he's an expert marksman."

"So is Reynolds. And guns have been stolen before."

"Johnny's fingerprints were on it, and we found the crucifix hidden in his workshop."

The judge's bushy white eyebrows drew together in a frown. "Fingerprints are a little hard to argue away. But I don't like to think Johnny killed a man for a piece of gold."

"He didn't," Charles said. "He killed Willie for a tally book."

Drawing a deep breath, he plunged into the story of Johnny's gambling, J.T.'s threats to disinherit him, his growing desperation for money, and finally, the rustling. "The crucifix was just a coincidence in the case, just as it was a hundred years ago. And just as in the case of J.T.'s grandfather, I let myself believe it was the motive. That's why I didn't arrest Johnny after the first murder. I thought he had no reason to steal the cross. I've never heard him described as greedy, and I thought he was wealthy enough to buy six crucifixes. When I discovered he was a gambler, I still believed the crucifix was the motive. That crucifix has been the biggest red herring in this case. But I still should have arrested Johnny after Willie's murder; all the physical evidence pointed to him.''

"Damn shame you aren't perfect, Sheriff. Then you could be like that computer you keep talking about. You could just spit out the facts and never worry about what's underneath. Let me tell you something I've learned about facts over the last ninety years.'' The judge settled back comfortably in his chair, and deep-set eyes focused on Charles. "Facts are just like a mirror, Sheriff. They tell you what's there, but sometimes you're seeing them backward. You got to interpret what you see. You have to turn the facts around and look at them from a different angle.

"Now the evidence said Johnny was guilty, but your imagination, intuitive reasoning, logic, or whatever you want to call it, said there was more to it than what the facts said. Well, you were right; there was more to the story. Don't go wearing a hair shirt like some addlepated martyr. You made a mistake. For once the facts were exactly what they looked like. But there was no way to know that at the time. And I can tell by the way you're looking at me that you aren't taking to heart a single thing I'm telling you.''

"My mistake killed a man, Judge. I don't find that easy to live with.''

"The minute you find that easy to live with, Sheriff, is the day you'd better go into another line of work. Last thing this county needs is a man without a conscience, particularly if that man's wearing a badge.''

Charles slammed his fist down on the desk. The dull thud fell into the heavy silence, stiffening the postures of Raul and

Meenie. The judge's only reaction was a narrowing of his eyes. "Damn it! I was just so sure Johnny didn't have the character to commit murder."

"Goes to show we can't always tell how somebody's going to react. Now show me the Sharps, and I'll get on with what I came out to tell you."

Meenie retrieved the gun from the corner where it had been propped. "Here you are, Judge; one Sharps .44–90." He handed it to the old man.

Judge Nourse laid the long-barreled gun across his knees, brushing his cane to the floor as if it were a pesky mosquito. He ran his long, gnarled fingers up and down the gun, carefully checking the grip, and the length of barrel. Finally he lifted it, resting it carefully on the edge of the desk, and sinking to his knees with the agility of a much younger man, sighted the gun.

Grabbing the edge of the desk with one hand, he pulled himself up and sat back on the chair, once again letting the gun rest on his lap. "I don't know if this is exactly like the gun Billy Dixon used at the Battle of Adobe Walls. Probably not. According to a manual on antique American firearms, there were only eighty-five of this particular gun manufactured. Besides, this gun doesn't appear in the Sharps catalogue until 1875, a year after the battle. Dixon says—or rather, writers say that Dixon said, which is a horse of a different color—that he had a Big Fifty."

The judge laid the gun on the desk. "But what Dixon used is beside the point, except to prove to the jury that a Sharps of this caliber can kill with accuracy from a hell of a longer distance than seven-hundred-fifty yards. But what we have here, Sheriff, is a .44–90 side-hammer Sharps with a thirty-four inch octagon barrel, firing a .44 caliber cartridge, using ninety to one-hundred or more grains of black powder, and with five-hundred-fifty grains of lead."

He pointed to the sight. "You have a rear sight of the peep

type having a Vernier scale with graduation up to thirteen hundred yards. The front sight is a globe and split bar that is used for gauging the wind. The buffalo lived on the Great Plains, and there's a lot of wind. The buffalo hunter had to have a way of gauging the wind, so he could compensate for the wind drift of the bullet. He also had to rest it on something; the damn thing is heavy, at least twelve pounds. You can't just hold it up like an ordinary gun. Even a strong man is going start to shake a little.''

"We found two sticks tied together with rawhide in the shape of an X on top of the mesa.''

"That would be what the murderer used, then. The buffalo hunters used the same thing. Sometimes they used hardwood or iron strips bolted together that would fold up when they weren't being used. And something else, Sheriff. That gun uses black powder, and black powder makes smoke.''

"Bud Crawford said he saw smoke from half a mile away. I didn't really believe him though.''

"Believe him!'' the judge said firmly. "I'm a reader of Westerns, and I can always tell when the writer doesn't know what the hell he's talking about. The gunfight, for instance, where the gunfighter gets off two or three shots, and drops not only the man he's facing, but the one behind the watering trough, one sitting on the hotel roof, and some innocent bystander who didn't have the sense to get off the street. I tell you something, Sheriff, after the first shot, you got a black powder cloud in front of your face, and the only one you're really liable to hit is the bystander, and that would probably be an accident. What I'm trying to tell you is that whoever fired that gun would have a residue of powder on him. In some cases, a buffalo hunter after an hour or more of firing would have an eye that looked like yours. All that greasy smoke and powder would turn his face black. 'Course I expect Johnny would've known enough to wipe his face off before he came back to the house.''

"Weren't no powder on him, Judge," Meenie said from the couch.

The judge reached out and touched the old gun. "So my information didn't help him at all."

Charles shook his head. "No, judge, it only made it worse. Johnny's the only one really familiar with antique guns. He would've known to take a support to rest his gun in. He would've known how to use the sights on the gun. And he had a motive, an opportunity, and no alibi."

"And everybody else did?"

"All but Rodriquez, and I don't think our Texas Ranger committed murder."

Leaning on his cane, the old man got to his feet. His shoulders seemed more stooped, as if what he'd heard were weighing him down. "I'm staying until this is over. My father was there when the crucifix disappeared and murder was done. I'll be here at the end of the story. It's only fitting, Sheriff."

The old man opened the door to reveal Slim. "Young man, you've got quite a bruise there. You're going to have to learn to stay out of fights." Chuckling, Judge Nourse disappeared into the living room.

Slim stepped hesitantly into the room, a bundle of neatly folded clothes in his hands. "Uh, Miss Poole thought you might need some more clothes, Sheriff. There's a razor there, too. Miss Poole said there was no excuse for a man not being shaved. Miss Poole said you were to eat something, too. She said your ulcer would feel better."

Charles felt a flash of irritation. He was getting tired of everyone's concern for his ulcer. Damn it, he didn't have an ulcer, just acid indigestion. He took the clothes and noticed his shirt had a dusty footprint on it. "What's this?" he demanded.

Slim turned white, gulped audibly, and looked at the floor.

"I, uh, dropped your shirt, and, uh, stepped on it before I noticed. But I can dust it off, Sheriff?"

Charles clutched his shirt to his breast. "No!" he said sharply. If Slim ever got hold of his shirt again, he might return it minus both sleeves and all the buttons. "Thank you for bringing the clothes, Slim."

The deputy grinned, wiggling all over like a puppy who'd been forgiven for eating his master's newspaper. "That's all right, Sheriff. Miss Poole just thought you ought to have them."

Charles laid his clothes on the desk well out of the youngster's reach. "Slim, What I want to know now is how you managed to let Johnny surprise you completely."

Slim shifted from foot to foot, studying the toes of his boots as if he'd never seen them before. "Well, Sheriff, you know Johnny and I went to school together—and I know him pretty well. He said things looked awful black for him, but that he didn't kill anybody. He asked if I believed him. He was worried I might think he was guilty, and it bothered him a lot. I mean, we was real good friends and all. Hell, I just said no, I didn't think he was guilty, and not to worry. He relaxed a little then, and we was talking about school and what we used to do, and then you came in carrying that cross and gun. I kinda straightened up to see who you was going to arrest. I mean, I never thought it'd be Johnny, and I just wasn't ready. Besides, he always was a better fighter than me."

"You mean, after I told you to keep an eye on Johnny, you just decided he wasn't guilty because he was an old friend of yours? Did you think I didn't have a good reason for suspecting him? When I tell you to watch a man, I don't mean to have a pleasant conversation about old times, I mean for you to remember you're a deputy sheriff, and as such, you don't have any friends when you're on duty. Do you understand me?"

Slim gulped again. "Well, Sheriff, I just figured Johnny

wasn't the kind to kill somebody. That doesn't make sense somehow. But I wouldn't let him go just because he was a friend. I'm a better deputy than that."

Slim's words stung at Charles. They hit too close to home.

"Sheriff, you do believe me, don't you? I didn't let him get away on purpose. You wouldn't do such a thing, and I always try to do just what you do."

Charles covered his eyes with his hand. "Get out of here, Slim, and see if you can't find somebody better to imitate."

Slim moved with alacrity toward the living room, pausing only to look back over his shoulder. "I'm real sorry I let you down, Sheriff, and I'll make up for it. But he just got the drop on me."

"With his fist?" Charles asked.

Slim had the decency to look embarrassed.

CHAPTER

18

"THAT KID'S GOIN' BE MIDDLE-AGED BEFORE HE EVER grows up," Meenie said as he aimed for the spittoon.

Charles got to his feet and picked up his clothes. "Leave him alone, Meenie. He's not guilty of any more ineptitude than the rest of us. This whole investigation could make the textbooks as an example of what not to do." He changed the subject abruptly. "Hold down the fort. I'm going to take a shower and get into Miss Poole's idea of more suitable clothes. With any luck I can brush the dirt off my shirt so I won't look like I lay down in the middle of a busy street and was stepped on."

"You already look like you been stepped on," his deputy said. "That eye's got a yellow-green cast to the purple now. And I think your face is gonna peel from the sunburn. You better put on some suntan lotion today. You don't want to get burned any worse."

Charles decided Meenie's worse fault, other than complaining about everything, was acting like a scrawny mother hen. "I don't need any damn lotion. I'm a Texas sheriff. I can eat nails for breakfast."

Meenie shifted his tobacco. "Not with your ulcer, you cain't."

Charles stomped out of the room. He closed the door behind him, feeling an immense satisfaction at his strength of character. A lesser man would have slammed it. He glanced about at the tableau of figures in the living room: J.T. and Reynolds sitting on the couch, Rodriquez still leaning against the mantle of the fireplace. Nothing seemed to have changed. Judge Nourse sat in the room's only armchair, his folded hands resting on his cane. His daughter, although standing beside him, seemed to be crouching at his feet. Angie sat unobtrusively in the corner, her head resting against the back of the chair, her hands lying limply on its arms. After a moment's hesitation she walked over to Charles.

"Come with me," she said. "I'll show you where you can get cleaned up." She started up the stairs and Charles followed her. She opened the door to Johnny's room. He hesitated before stepping across the threshold. He felt as if he were violating Johnny's privacy.

"Take a shower, Charles," she said, "and I'll be back. I have a few things to say to you."

Charles dropped his clothes in the middle of the bed and faced her. "Whatever you have to say, say it now."

She flinched, hazel eyes darkening with hurt, then drawing strength from some nearly depleted resource, she shook her head. "No," she said, quietly, and walked out, closing the door behind her.

Charles stood gawking at the door. He felt like a rabbit caught out in the open by a coyote. He had no place to run, no defense to mount, and he couldn't really blame Angie for wanting to see him suffer some of the same anxiety she was feeling.

Grabbing a worn pair of Levi's and clean underwear, he stalked into Johnny's bathroom and stripped. Alternating between hot and cold water, he stood under the shower hoping for some miracle of recovery. When he finally turned the water off, it hadn't occurred. He still felt tired, sore, and used up. Resolutely he shaved, nicking his chin. It was damn hard to shave when you only had one eye. His depth perception was off, and he could have sworn his chin was farther away.

Slipping into his clean clothes, he padded into the bedroom. He stopped abruptly. Angie was placing a breakfast tray on a bedside table. "Who's that for?" he asked.

Angie looked at him, then around the room. "Unless someone else is hiding in the bathroom, it must be yours. You can't go without something to eat. Your ulcer will act up."

"I don't have an ulcer," he said automatically, plucking his shirt off the bed. Maybe he would feel less vulnerable with his shirt on. "And you don't have to be kind to me, Angie. I know how you feel, and I understand. Resentment against someone who is threatening your family is a normal reaction."

"Are you psychic, Charles?"

He sat down on the bed, ostensibly to put on his boots. In reality, his legs were shaking. "Of course not."

Angie crossed her arms against her chest in a curiously defensive gesture, then straightened them, balling her hands into fists. "I see. In that case, Sheriff Matthews, just how can you be so damn sure of what I'm feeling?"

Charles stood up, a sock still clutched in his hand. "For God's sake, Angie, it may be a cliché, but blood is thicker than water. Once I realized that Johnny was my most likely suspect, I—I knew you'd take your family's side against mine. Since we are—were—friends, I know you're feeling confused and betrayed, especially after my behavior yesterday. I knew then that all the physical evidence pointed to Johnny. I never should have touched you. In your emotional state, and with the situation with Johnny, my behavior almost amounts to sexual harassment." He waved his hand toward the breakfast tray. "But you don't have to try to placate me with food and kindness. I'll keep my distance and try to be as objective toward you as possible. I'll treat you as I would any other suspect's family member.''

''Are you always so rude to a suspect's family?''

He flushed. ''I'm trying to be as honest with you as possible.''

''I see.'' She raked her teeth over her lower lip and looked up at him. ''About yesterday. Did you mean it when you said you loved me?''

Charles wet his lips. ''Yes.''

She took a step closer, and he braced himself. ''Then you're either a liar or a blind fool.''

Charles felt his mind reel with confusion. ''I don't understand.''

Her lips trembled, and she wiped at her eyes. ''Only a fool would love a woman as shallow and stupid as you seem to think I am. I can almost understand your thinking I see you as a threat to my family. I can even forgive you for believing I might expect you ignore some of the''—her voice broke and she drew a breath—''evidence against Johnny. But for you to believe I'd twist your kissing me into some kind of sick sexual assault is going too far, Charles Matthews.''

She advanced on his step-by-step like some auburn-haired Valkyrie, and Charles retreated. The edge of the bed caught him in the back of the knees, and he lost his balance, landing spread-eagled in the middle of the bed. ''Now, Angie,'' he said weakly.

Angie followed him down, crouching over him with her hands on his shoulders. ''On the other hand,'' she said in a conversational tone. ''If you are a liar, if you don't love me, then it would make your behavior more understandable. No one could blame you for closing out a resentful, self-centered, childish woman who stands around wringing her hands and whining that she's been betrayed.''

''Damn it, Angie!'' he shouted, grabbing her wrists and rolling over with her until she lay on her back, his body pinning hers to the bed. "You're not shallow or stupid or any of those other traits you mentioned. Why are you calling yourself names?"

"I'm not. You are. You're the one who decided I couldn't possibly feel anything but hate and betrayal. You never asked me how I felt. You never gave me a choice. Johnny's still free, at least for a little while. I'm the one you've locked away, Charles."

Suddenly conscious that his body covered hers like a lover, he freed her wrists and rolled over to sit beside her. "What are you trying to say, Angie?"

She slipped her arm around his waist and tugged at him until he slid down beside her. "Don't jump to conclusions, Charles. I don't hate you and I don't resent you. I need you."

He gathered her closer, breathing deeply of the wildflower and sunshine scent that was uniquely hers. "Angie, do you realize what you're saying is impossible, illogical, almost unnatural? I'm the man responsible for hunting your brother down. Then he'll either be executed or spend the rest of his life in prison because of me. I shouldn't be holding you like this because sooner or later you're going to realize what I'm saying is true, and you'll despise me for taking advantage of your being scared and confused."

A split second later his head rocked back as her fist connected with the point of his chin. "Don't patronize me, Charles Matthews, you damnable, stubborn man. And don't ever make my choices for me again. I know what Johnny's done, and I know what you have to do. There's nothing you or I can do to change what's happened, but do we have to let Johnny ruin two more lives? Do you have to punish yourself and me by rejecting what we both feel?"

He cupped her chin with one hand. "What are you telling me?" he roared.

"I love you!" she screamed back.

Charles had been an athlete. He'd been in a war. Both

experiences taught him to react automatically to certain stimuli without thinking. In this situation, however, all he could do was stare at her. His mind had just received the greatest stimuli of all time and his body short-circuited. Until he saw the tears gather in her eyes and overflow to trickle slowly down her cheeks. Then he kissed her with the voraciousness of a starving man.

He rolled over with her and gathered her closer, feeling her fingers dig into the sore muscles of his back. He broke the kiss and stroked the tears from her cheeks. "You're sure?" he questioned hoarsely. "If you have any doubts, tell me now."

Smiling, she shook her head. "No doubts," she whispered.

He smoothed the hair away from her face. "That was your choice, Angie, your only chance to leave. I won't let you get away now. I won't let anyone come between us, not your family, this ranch, public censure, nothing. And I'm not giving you another choice."

"You're a bastard, Sheriff!" Kurt Reynolds stood in the open doorway, his features having that pinched look anger always brings. "Seducing Angie in the middle of Johnny's bed takes a lot of gall. What were you planning? A little tumble before you go out and shoot her brother?"

Charles heard Angie's scream and the satisfying thud of his fist against Reynolds's mouth at the same time. He rubbed his bruised knuckles as he struggled to control the primitive urge to kill the other man. "Get back downstairs, and don't open your filthy mouth again."

Reynolds wiped the blood from his split lip and looked at Angie. "Have you forgotten who this man is? Have you forgotten Johnny?"

Angie stepped next to Charles and placed her hand in his, clutching it tightly. "No, I haven't forgotten."

"He's going to kill your brother, you know."

Charles felt her hand tighten convulsively on his. "He could have done that last night," she said, "and didn't. He won't kill him today either."

Reynolds looked at Charles, a smile on his swollen lips. "What about that, Mr. Sheriff? Can you promise the little lady you won't kill her brother?"

Reynolds's question was like a barb sinking in his flesh. He saw the malicious triumph in the other man's eyes, and he slumped in self-defeat. "Johnny has a gun, Angie. I can't promise I won't have to shoot."

He watched the horror age her face until he could no longer face her and turned back to Reynolds. "You've won," he said. "Now get out of here."

"Sheriff?" Raul appeared in the doorway. "The Potter County sheriff's deputies are here, and Randall County sent over four. It's daylight, or near enough." His black eyes darted from one face to another. "We're ready," he added unnecessarily.

Charles released Angie's hand and buttoned his shirt. Walking to the bathroom, he retrieved his badge and slipped the leather flap into his breast pocket. He threaded a heavy leather belt through his belt loops and buckled it. Miss Poole had thought of everything. Everything, that is, but a way to do his duty without losing Angie. But even Miss Poole couldn't perform miracles.

Padding out of the bathroom, he sat on the bed and silently pulled on his boots. Out of the corner of his good eye, he could see Angie's slender back as she stood by the dresser holding a picture in her hands. He could sense Reynolds's malevolent stare without looking at him. He rose and tucked Meenie's gun in his belt. He hadn't realized he'd never returned it until just now. He cleared his throat. "I'm ready."

Angie turned around, and Raul took Reynolds's arm. "We'll be downstairs."

Reynolds started to jerk free, but whatever he saw in Raul's eyes stopped him. Casting a last sneering glance over his shoulder at Charles, the ranch manager went with Raul, leaving Charles and Angie alone.

Angie looked at the photograph in her hand. "Dad took this when when he gave me my first horse. I didn't know Johnny had it."

She looked up at Charles. "Is there any way out, Charles?"

He lifted his hand, unable to resist touching her one last time. He could feel the silky warmth of her hair on the back of his hand as he laid his palm against her cheek.

Reluctantly he pulled his hand back. "I don't know, Angie. I'll try."

Rising on tiptoes, she pressed her lips against his, then stepped back. "I'd rather not go down, Charles," she said. "I don't want to see you leave."

He walked downstairs and through the living room, noticing out of the corner of his eye that Judge Nourse was missing from his chair. As he walked outside, he felt as if he were caught in a scene from a movie. The sun was a bloodred ball just above the horizon, and a band of over thirty men waited patiently by their horses. But the figure that stood out from the deputies in their various colored uniforms from khaki to navy, was that of an old man, his white hair ruffled by the silent breeze.

"Just where do you think you're going, Judge Nourse?" Charles demanded, grabbing the horse's bridle.

"This is a posse, isn't it, Sheriff?"

"In a manner of speaking, yes, but a posse of duely appointed deputies. Now get off that horse."

Judge Nourse grinned·at Charles. "It just so happens your predecessor appointed me a special deputy for life."

"That's an honorary title," Charles sputtered.

"That may be," the judge agreed, "but I have the papers

at home, and they don't say a thing about my not being able to arrest someone, or otherwise function as a deputy."

"Damn it, Judge!" roared Charles. "I don't have time to argue. Get off that horse."

The judge folded his hands over the saddle horn. "If I'm along, I might be able to persuade Johnny to surrender, and I'm the only one who might be able to do it. Are you willing to throw away your only chance?"

Involuntarily, Charles looked over his shoulder toward the house, focusing on the second-story window. His only chance, the judge said; his only chance to avoid shooting Johnny. He turned back to the old man. "If you can talk him into surrendering, I don't care if you bought your badge at the dime store."

"I figured you'd be sensible, Sheriff," said the judge dryly. He looked at the revolver stuck in Charles's belt. "I don't know about you, but I wouldn't ride a horse with a gun in my belt. The damn thing might go off by accident and leave you with a squeaky voice."

Charles flushed and pulled out Meenie's gun. "It's not mine anyway," he said. He walked over to his deputy. "Here's your gun, Meenie."

Meenie stuck it back in his holster. "What about you? You gonna go out there without a gun? You think good deeds'll stop him from shootin' you?" Meenie spit at a grasshopper in disgust.

Charles gathered his reins, set his foot in the stirrup, and gingerly climbed in the saddle. "If he's smart, he'll just let me ride myself to death," he said. "Have you broken them into teams?" he asked, gesturing toward the deputies.

"Yeah," Meenie said sourly. "I kept a Crawford County man in each group 'cept this one. The judge and me are goin' to ride with you."

"But I need you to lead one of the groups," Charles objected.

''And what if you find him, and he don't listen to the judge? You ain't got no gun, the judge ain't got no gun, but Johnny damn sure does. I'm ridin' with you, and you might as well stop wastin' time arguing with me.''

Meenie was right about one thing: anybody who argued with him wasted his time. Charles lifted his hand above his head for attention. ''Men, the suspect is Johnny Brentwood. We have reason to believe he's armed. He's charged with murder, but I don't want him killed. Shoot his horse if necessary, but I don't want anybody to shoot Johnny. He's only a suspect; he hasn't been convicted yet.''

''What if he tries to kill one of us, Sheriff?'' asked a Potter County deputy.

Charles could hear the creak of an old windmill down by the corral as he struggled for an answer. He couldn't ask men to risk their lives with no defense; that would be another innocent life lost, another death he would be responsible for. ''We don't know how much ammunition he has, so try to pin him down and draw his fire until he runs out. Now let's ride.'' It wasn't an answer the men wanted to hear, but it was the only one he could give.

Charles kicked his horse, noticing for the first time he had the same mare as he'd ridden before. He gripped the saddle horn tightly. Not that it mattered. One horse was pretty much like another; they all seemed bent on shaking him to death.

''Relax, Sheriff,'' said Judge Nourse, sitting easily on his own horse. ''Go with the horse's rymthm. You're so stiff, you're going to break your back the first time you have to kick that mare into a gallop.''

''You ride your way and I'll ride mine,'' Charles said through gritted teeth, as the mare's first steps managed to locate every sore muscle in his body.

''Stubborn, ain't he?'' Meenie asked Judge Nourse.

''Just like a Missouri mule,'' agreed the judge.

"Shut up!" Charles said. "Which section did you reserve for us, Meenie?"

"We're gonna ride along the bluff by the river," replied the deputy. "I figure he's got to have water. Sure didn't take any with him and he can't get the drop on us if we're on higher ground."

Charles nodded his agreement, and he spent the next hour alternating between scanning the riverbanks and trying to guess which of the hundred different gaits his mare was going to try next. The damn animal belonged in a circus. She had a rumba step that beat any professional dancer he'd ever seen.

The sun had turned from a red ball to a brilliant white one, and the dawn's breeze had grown into a wind that blew the hot, dry air into their faces. Charles flexed his hands one at a time; he wasn't letting go of the saddle horn with both for any amount of money. He suspected the mare was just waiting for him to do that. He noticed both his palms were bleeding. He'd forgotten his gloves again.

"The Santiago Plaza, Sheriff, or what's left of it," said Judge Nourse.

Charles peered over the bluff. That stretch of river bank looked just like the rest: salt cedar, sand bars, very little water, and a few isolated cottonwood trees. He blinked and realized he had the use of both eyes. He still felt as if he were looking through a slit, but his abused eye was at least open. "I don't see any buildings," he said, leaning forward.

He felt the shot like a hot lash across his shoulders before he heard it. Or perhaps he heard and felt it at the same time. It didn't really matter which; the question was purely academic. What really mattered was getting off his horse and behind something. He hit the hard prairie on his shoulder, nearly fainting from the waves of pain being generated by his wound, and flattened himself on the ground. Why? Why was he shot? There was no reason for it. Another man would simply take his place, and another after that. The supply was endless.

Meenie's steady curses as he fought his rearing horse and the judge's pulling his horse to the ground and crouching behind it seemed to happen at some great distance away. He ought to grab his horse, he ought to move toward some cover, and he would, just as soon the first shock wore off.

Meenie and Judge Nourse crawled over to him. "How bad you hit?" the deputy demanded, throwing his revolver to the judge, who took a professional stance on his belly, grabbed his horse's reins so it wouldn't bolt, and fired a quick shot toward a small rise a little over a hundred yards away.

"No time to look, Meenie," Charles grunted. "We've got to find cover."

"There's none around here, Sheriff," the judge said. "We'll have to crawl down the bluff. It's not too steep right here. A hundred yards further on, and we'd break our necks trying to get down."

"Just like Dolores's husband," Charles mumbled.

"Damn it, Sheriff, this ain't a hundred years ago, and you ain't Dolores's husband," Meenie snapped, his face stiff with worry.

Charles's mind grappled with the problem. Angie and Dolores, the sketches, and faces, always faces from the present superimposed on the past. The answer was there if he could only stop hurting long enough to think. "Not Dolores," he said finally. "Angie."

"Well, you won't have a chance to be her husband if you don't get down that bluff. Meenie, you help him, and I'll try to force the horses down. They can make it if they slide on their rumps."

"Forget the horses," Charles said, forcing back the ragged blackness of unconsciousness. The answer was there, the solution to the whole puzzling case, hovering on the edges of his mind along with the blackness.

"Can't, Sheriff. We're about five miles from headquarters and you're too damn big to carry," Meenie said. "I'm goin' over first so I can help you. Put your head on your arms and just let yourself slide. Might scratch your belly some, but it'll hurt a lot less than sliding on your back. You're bleedin' pretty bad."

Charles followed orders, biting his lip as pain ripped through him when he lifted his arms to protect his face. He crawled backward, concentrating all his efforts on reversing normal forward motions. He froze suddenly, ignoring Meenie's shouted encouragement to hurry. Backward! Of course, that was the answer. He smiled, welcoming unconsciousness as he slipped over the edge of the bluff.

CHAPTER
19

UNLIKE A NOVEL, HE DIDN'T FLOAT IN AND OUT OF
unconsciousness, but came awake with an oath as the sting
of something wet hit his back. "Damn it to hell!" he shouted
as he tried to crawl away.

Strong hands held him down. "Settle down, Sheriff,"
Judge Nourse said. "Angie's trying to clean you up a little
before the ambulance gets here."

Charles felt crisp sheets beneath his bare chest, and he
twisted his head around to meet Angie's red-rimmed eyes.
"What's wrong, Angie, honey?" he asked foolishly.

She burst into tears and dropped the cloth she was using.
Judge Nourse made a clicking sound of disgust. "What's
wrong, the man asks. We bring him in, unconscious and
bleeding like a stuck pig, dump him on the floor in front of
the woman whose affections he's been trifling with, and he
wants to know why she's crying. Check his head, Meenie.
He must've been shot there, too."

Charles struggled to a sitting position, swaying from dizziness, and pulled Angie into his arms, winching as his torn
muscles started bleeding again. He buried his head between
her breasts. "Not trifling with her affections," he said, his
voice muffled against her chest.

"Damn him!" cried Angie between sobs. "He could've
killed you! And all for a ranch he doesn't deserve."

Charles lifted his head to kiss away her tears. "That's right,

Angie, honey; it was all for the ranch, and I didn't realize it until he shot me. He was very clever, but he didn't realize until this morning that I was a threat.'' He glanced at the sketch of Red Barn Cave and smiled.

"What the hell are you talking about, Sheriff?'' Meenie demanded. "Johnny wasn't one damn bit clever. He left a trail a blind man could follow. And you ain't any more of a threat than anybody else. Less, in fact; you bent over backward to try to keep from killin' him. Worst thing he coulda done was shoot you. Every sheriff in the Panhandle's gonna be after him. He ain't got a prayer of coming out of this alive unless he surrenders, and he's lookin' at the death penalty if he does that.''

Charles looked at Meenie and caught sight of himself in the mirror over the dresser. He smiled at his reflection, feeling good in spite of the waves of pain from his back. There they all were in the mirror: himself holding Angie, Meenie and the judge hovering by the bed, J.T. and Rodriquez by the door, and Consuelo holding a basin of blood-tinted water. But everything was reversed in the mirror, just like everything was reversed in the Branding Iron murders.

He looked toward the door as Raul burst in, his olive complexion faded to gray. "Relax, Raul, it's just a flesh wound.''

Angie pulled herself out of his arms, blew her nose on a dry bandage, and glared at Charles. "Don't you dare make light of this, Charles Timothy Matthews. My brother shot you, and your back looks awful, and you're sitting there grinning and bleeding all over my clean sheets. And furthermore, you don't know if it's just a flesh wound or not; you can't see it.''

Charles grinned wider. "I can move my arms and shoulders. It hurts like hell, but I can do it.'' He lay back down on his belly, his head turned toward Angie. "Stick a Band-Aid on it, honey. I've got a murderer to catch.''

Raul looked at Charles's back and paled even more.

"Sheriff, I don't think they make Band-Aids that big. That bullet plowed a furrow across your back an inch wide."

"So wrap a bandage around it," Charles said casually. "And round up a couple of aspirin for the pain. I'm going to take that bastard in personally, then I'll figure out a way to break his alibi."

"Johnny doesn't have an alibi," J.T. burst out.

Charles cocked an eyebrow at the rancher. "I'm not talking about Johnny. I'm not a threat to Johnny. I don't stand between him and the ranch."

"Then who the hell are you threatenin'?" Meenie demanded.

Charles motioned to the judge. "It's just like the sketches, Judge, but everything is backward, a mirror image."

"Damn it to hell, Sheriff," Meenie said. "You're always carryin' on about them sketches. That was a hundred years ago."

Charles smiled at his deputy, then cursed as Angie applied an antiseptic to his wound. He drew a deep breath and tried to ignore the stinging. "But you see, Meenie, Willie used faces from the present, and the crucifix turned up, and most of the people involved in this little tragedy were descendants of those involved in the Santiago massacre. The present seemed to rest on the bones of the past. All the elements of the past are also present in these murders: rustling, a woman, the crucifix, and two men being murdered because they were a threat."

Charles sat up and lifted his arms as Angie began to wrap a bandage around his chest. "Raul, what is the one room we didn't search last night?"

"The bedroom where the children slept," Raul answered.

"And where else?"

Raul smiled. "The office."

Charles nodded. "Go search it now. See if you can find a tally book. J.T., what does it look like?"

"A small spiral notebook," the rancher answered. "But, Sheriff, it won't be in there. Kurt and I started locking the doors as soon as we suspected Johnny of rustling, and Johnny didn't have a key."

Charles grinned. "So if we find the tally book, it proves Johnny couldn't have hidden it there. Right?"

J.T. nodded. "I suppose so, but that doesn't explain the crucifix and gun. I don't know what you're thinking, Sheriff, but I'd just as soon not know. I've spent all night getting used to the idea my son's a murderer, and I don't think I can take getting my hopes up on the basis of some wild theory of yours."

"Raul, go see if you can prove my wild theory. Meenie, while he's looking, you call the Department of Public Safety and have them send a helicopter out here, one with a loud-speaker. We've got to give Johnny the all clear, and we've got to let the deputies know the quarry has changed."

"Just when are we going to hear this theory of yours, Sheriff?" asked Rodriquez, pushing himself away from the door and striding further into the room.

"Ah, my friend the Texas Ranger. Tell me, at which plaza along the Canadian did your family live?"

Rodriquez cocked an eyebrow at Charles. "Casados had blue eyes."

"You and Casados are related?" Charles asked.

Rodriquez smiled. "Let's say we shared a common ancestor. Most of my family have been in law enforcement since that day. Perhaps in reaction to what he did."

"That's why you knew about the crucifix?" Charles asked.

Rodriquez paced across the room restlessly. "My great-grandfather died wondering about the crucifix. He knew that wasn't the reason for the massacre, but he thought if the family could find the crucifix, it would help to wipe out what Diego had done."

Judge Nourse stirred and walked to face Rodriquez. "My father believed the same thing."

The younger man looked at the Judge, his blue eyes narrowing. "What interest did your father have in the crucifix? He didn't arrive in the Panhandle until years after the massacre."

Judge Nourse leaned heavily on his cane. "That was his second arrival. He was here as a young boy."

"Your father killed Diego?" Rodriquez asked.

"I'll be damned," exclaimed Brentwood. "That's why your dad was always looking for the crucifix."

"And he never found it," the judge said. "He must have searched every square inch of the area between the Santiago Plaza and the next closest plaza. It had to have been somewhere between the two places, unless Dolores took it with her when she escaped back to New Mexico. Where in the devil did Willie find the thing?"

Meenie and Raul came in, Meenie waving a blue spiral notebook in his hand. "Found it, Sheriff, taped to the back of a desk drawer in the computer room."

Charles flipped it open. "Would you recognize the missing numbers, J.T.?"

The rancher sat down beside Charles. "Yes, I think so."

Charles handed him the tally book. "Look it over quickly, J.T., before the murderer shoots someone else and Johnny ends up getting killed as a result."

Charles passed a hand across his forehead while he waited. He was sweating and his skin felt greasy. He knew he had to hold on; he couldn't give in to the oblivion that was threatening him again.

"Sheriff," J.T. said, "the numbers are all here. According to the tally book, no cattle have been rustled at all."

"Then why the hell did Johnny kill Willie?" Meenie demanded. "Did he want the crucifix after all?"

"Meenie, Johnny didn't kill Willie," Charles said. "And

I'm sure the crucifix was as big a surprise to the murderer as it was to us. The motive was the tally book, not because it proved Johnny guilty of rustling, but because it didn't. Then Johnny aided the murderer without being aware of it by bringing in Willie's body and leaving his footprints at Red Barn Cave. Without those footprints, Johnny might never have been suspected. Not that it mattered to the murderer. The only person he wanted to believe Johnny was guilty was J.T. He knew J.T. would never leave the ranch to Johnny if he suspected him of murder.''

Charles took Angie's hand. ''And that brings us to the second element in common with the sketches: a woman. If Johnny doesn't inherit the ranch, then Angie will, and Angie is a widow. Whoever marries Angie gains the ranch. It was really a very simple plan: get rid of Johnny and marry Angie. Then things got a little complicated. J.T. didn't want to believe his son was guilty of rustling, so he called in Rodriquez. Rodriquez didn't trust the computer and wanted an old-fashioned tally, which set up Willie as a murder victim. Then the murderer was seen returning the branding iron to the corral, and Skinny Jordan had to be eliminated. I believe it was at that point that the murderer began deliberately setting up Johnny. He used a gun that belonged to Johnny, that would have Johnny's fingerprints on it, and that supposedly only Johnny would be familiar with, and he hid the crucifix in Johnny's workshop.''

''Events went as he planned. I found the crucifix and gun, tried to arrest Johnny, but the human beings involved didn't react the way he wanted them to, nor as I expected them to.'' He looked at Angie. ''I didn't kill Johnny when I had the chance, and Angie refused to blame me for her brother's situation. Now I was a threat, and I had to be disposed of. When he tried to kill me, I knew Johnny was innocent.''

''Damn it, Sheriff! Who are you talking about?'' Meenie demanded.

Charles looked surprised. "Why, Reynolds, of course."

"Reynolds!" J.T. cried. "But I raised that boy from the time his parents died. I educated him, trained him, gave him everything."

"But you weren't going to give him the Branding Iron Ranch," Charles said. "And he learned this morning that I stood between him and Angie, but if he killed me, there was a chance Angie might turn to him." He looked up at the others. "Do you know what's wrong with my reasoning?" he asked Meenie.

"Yeah, Reynolds has an alibi, two of them, and both iron-clad. Everything you said makes sense, but you can't prove any of it."

Charles pointed to the tally book in J.T.'s hand. "That proves there wasn't any rustling. And Reynolds was the one who claimed there was."

"So how did he kill Willie?" Meenie asked. That ground leadin' up to the cave had a crust on it, and the only prints were Johnny's and Willie's. If anybody else had walked on that ground, even if they brushed away their prints, they woulda broken the crust. How did he climb that bluff without breakin' the crust?"

"He didn't," Charles replied.

"I know that!"

"I'm sorry, Meenie. I'm being deliberately obscure."

"I don't know about that, but you're sure as hell not bein' plain."

"He didn't break the crust because he didn't walk up to the cave, he climbed *down* to the cave. I never thought of that until last night when we searched this room and I saw Willie's sketch of Red Barn Cave. It was dated last week, and the mesquite tree was whole. Now what happened to that tree between this week and last?"

"The tornado," Meenie said.

"Exactly," Charles said. "I may not have grown up in the

Panhandle, but we do have tornadoes in Dallas, and I know what freaky things they can do. It was well within the realm of possibility for the tornado to twist that tree causing it to split—and not touch the dead cottonwood a hundred yards away. And if a tornado passed that close, what would a horse's reaction be?''

"He'd be spooked," Meenie answered, "and tear hell out of the ground just like we found."

"Reynolds tied his horse to the dead cottonwood, then climbed up the canyon wall and walked on top of the bluff to directly above the cave entrance with its very convenient mesquite tree. Willie would've heard something and come to investigate—and Reynolds killed him. Then Reynolds was caught in the cave during the tornado, and that's when he found the crucifix and decided to steal it. We'll never know, but perhaps he was planning to keep it. The sketches we found were folded away in Willie's saddlebag, which Reynolds didn't think to search any more than he thought to bush away his horse's hoofprints around the tree when he brushed away his own. Once he found the sketches, then he had to plant the crucifix on Johnny just as he was planning to do with the tally book as soon as he altered it. But he never had the opportunity because J.T. was always around or he was busy killing Skinny Jordan. Then, of course, I commandeered J.T.'s office, and Reynolds couldn't get to the computer room."

Charles let go of Angie's hands to push himself of the bed. He clutched the bedpost as dizziness made the room swirl. "That tally book was why Willie Russell was so anxious to get to Red Barn Cave that he took off the busiest weekend of the season. It's why he changed models in his sketches, Judge."

"There you go with them damn pictures again," Meenie said.

"Willie Russell thought Kurt Reynolds was a rustler, that he was Diego Casados."

J.T. interrupted, a disbelieving look on his face. "Just a minute, Sheriff. Willie didn't have any idea I was worried about rustling when I told him to make that tally."

"Meenie wondered why you needed a tally when you had your whole herd on computer, J.T. I think Willie wondered the same thing. I don't think he bought your story of checking your computer records. I thinked he knew the sudden night patrols of the ranch boundaries, plus a secret tally, plus your nervousness added up to rustling by someone you trusted, someone close to you. He knew it wasn't Rodriquez because as ranch foreman Rodriquez had to know about the tally, and I doubt he even considered Johnny. That left Kurt Reynolds, the keeper of the computer, the man who wasn't in on the secret of the tally."

The judge tapped his cane on the floor. "That's a real interesting story, Sheriff, and it might even be true, but the sketches sure as hell don't support it. Diego Casados had Rodriquez's face."

"Only in the last sketch, the one of Diego torturing the priest who was Reynolds. In the first sketch, that of the scene inside the Santiago home, Rodriquez was the priest. But that wasn't the only sketch Willie made of that scene. I found another version when I was searching Johnny's room and in that one Reynolds was the priest. You lined up the sketches found in Red Barn Cave in chronological order according to events, Judge, but that evidently wasn't the order in which Willie painted them. We had everything backward. The first sketch was the last one painted, and Willie Russell replaced Reynolds with Rodriquez as the priest."

"Charles!" Angie's voice was hesitant. "You're wrong. I wish you weren't, but you are. I can't let you arrest Reynolds, not even to save Johnny. Reynolds couldn't have killed Willie. He was right downstairs in the computer room."

J.T.'s voice was raspy. "Angie's right, Sheriff. Kurt didn't come out of the computer room until right before you got here. He was doing a printout for me and didn't even stop until after the tornado. I could hear that printer going for an hour or more."

"But that isn't an alibi," Raul said sharply.

"What do you mean?" Charles asked.

"Did you see Reynolds in the computer room, Mr. Brentwood? Were you in there with him?"

"No, of course not, but I didn't need to be. I could hear the printer."

Raul looked at Angie. "Mrs. Lassiter, did you see Reynolds or did you just hear the computer?"

Angie looked back at him, hope bringing a sparkle to her eyes. "I just heard the printer."

Raul spread his hands out in a Latin gesture. "That broke his alibi, Sheriff. With the type of computer Mr. Brentwood has, it isn't necessary to stand and watch it. It will continue to print out documents without stopping as long as you give it the proper commands. I thought it was unusual when you said Reynolds had the computer on during a tornado alert. A loss of power, or a power surge, could wipe out your programming. Most operators turn off their equipment during a storm just to be on the safe side, even if they have safeguards of various kinds. I think the reason Reynolds didn't turn off the equipment was because he wasn't here to switch it off."

"Raul, I think I'll take up a collection so you can buy yourself a computer. I never thought to ask if anyone had seen Reynolds because it was so obvious no one was lying when they said he was in the computer room. It was where they honestly believed him to be. And as for Skinny's murder, Judge Nourse said something that didn't really mean anything at the time, but is damning now that I know how Reynolds set up his alibi."

''I don't remember saying anything that would implicate Reynolds,'' the Judge said.

''You said the murderer should have traces of black powder on him. Reynolds said he was in the shower when Bud White rode in. In fact, Reynolds was the only one of the suspects who had showered and changed clothes. He had good reason: he had to get rid of the black powder.''

''There's only one thing wrong, Sheriff,'' Meenie said. ''You can't prove a damn thing you're sayin'. You got no witnesses, no physical evidence with his prints on it. Even the tally is worthless as a milk bucket under a bull.''

''Would you care to explain that?'' Charles asked, fighting an urge to shake his deputy. Everything was so clear, so logical, and fit Reynolds's character so well. Reynolds had to be guilty; Johnny just wasn't the type to commit murder.

''Sheriff, I ain't meanin' to make you mad, but you been down on Reynolds all along. I'm not saying I like him much, either, but all your talk of sketches, and his wantin' the ranch—all it's gonna do is make that jury think you lost your good sense the same time you got your eye blacked. He could say he found that tally book in Johnny's room and wanted to check it before givin' it to J.T. Hell, he could even claim he was addin' numbers so the tally would come out right and make it out to look like he was trying' to help Johnny—and you'd have to call in a handwriting expert to prove him wrong. Then the defense would do the same and you know what would happen. They'd cancel out each other. If you gave two handwriting experts the stone tablets with the Ten Commandments on them, they'd testify two different people wrote them. And what are you doing to do about Skinny's murder? You got some kind of explanation that'll cover Johnny's backside on that one? What was he doing in those missing minutes after the shot? It sure as hell wouldn't take him any time at all to turn his pickup around and get back to the ranch unless he had to climb down from that mesa.''

Charles rubbed his pounding head while he grappled with Meenie's question. Damn it, he'd forgotten about those missing minutes. There was no explanation unless Johnny had sat frozen in his pickup, too panicked to act—and that didn't fit with how Johnny behaved. "I think you're right, Meenie," he said slowly. "Johnny was on top that mesa, but he wasn't shooting Skinny Jordan. He heard that shot, recognized the sound as coming from a Sharps, and climbed that mesa to find out who was setting him up. A kid who had the courage to bring in Willie Russell's body when, for all he knew, the murderer was still around, isn't the type of person to run away. That's why Reynolds left the gun rest on top the mesa. He saw Johnny get out of the pickup, and he ran."

"Why didn't Johnny tell you, Charles?" Angie asked.

"He didn't trust me, Angie. Nobody did but you. From his point of view it didn't make any sense to admit he'd been on that mesa, not when he knew how close I was to arresting him."

Meenie interrupted. "But you got no proof of that, Sheriff. It just sounds like more moonshine. I know the people around here. They just ain't gonna believe your theory."

"Do you think Johnny shot me?" Charles asked, feeling the unconsciousness beckoning again. He felt tempted to sink back into it and escape Meenie's logic. Because his deputy was right. His beautiful theory was just that—a theory. He had no proof at all, just conjecture.

Meenie hesitated, studying Charles's still swollen eye. He sighed. "I reckon I don't, Sheriff. I reckon a kid that stayed quiet about how you got that black eye ain't the type to shoot you in the back two days later. Mind you, I ain't saying he's innocent. I'm just sayin' I don't think he shot you."

Charles walked over to Meenie and clasped his shoulders. "Meenie, do you ever completely admit you're wrong?"

Meenie screwed up his eyes in thought. "I guess I don't, Sheriff. No percentage in it. Half the time the facts are what you make of them, and there ain't no sense admittin' you're wrong when it just depends on where you're standing when you're lookin' at them.''

''Then you admit I could be right?''

Meenie grinned sheepishly. ''Yeah, you could be right. But you still ain't got no conclusive proof. It's all just guess work, fancy thinkin', and them damn sketches.''

Charles dropped his arms and turned to Angie. ''Where's my shirt?''

''We had to cut you out of it, Charles. It's in two pieces.''

''Find me another one,'' he ordered as he turned to J.T. ''I need a gun, preferably a rifle.''

''What are you going to do, Charles?'' Angie demanded.

''Is anyone going to get me a shirt, or do I have to steal one?'' Charles demanded.

''No!'' Angie said stubbornly. ''Not until you tell me what you're planning.''

Charles smiled coldly. ''I'm going hunting.'' He walked to Johnny's closet and pulled a shirt off a hanger. He pulled it on and struggle with the buttons, cursing his broader shoulders. Giving up, he stuffed the shirt tails in his Levi's, leaving the front unbuttoned. Picking up his hat, he walked to the door. ''Are you loaning me a gun, or do I steal that, too.''

J.T. looked at him with admiration. ''I've got a nice .30-30 that ought to do, Sheriff.''

Angie grabbed his arm. ''You're not going, Charles. You're wounded. And you're still dizzy. How do you plan to ride a horse when you can hardly stand up?''

Charles leaned down and kissed her, then grabbed her around the waist and moved her away from the door. ''I can't ride a horse worth a damn when I'm not dizzy. Maybe I'll do better when I am.''

Angie glared at the other men. ''Somebody stop him.''

Judge Nourse smiled at her. ''Young lady, never try to

stop a man from doing what he has to do. J.T., you got two rifles to loan?''

Rodriquez started toward the door. ''I never get involved in domestic quarrels, Mrs. Lassiter. Sheriff, I'll just ride along if you don't mind. I know the ranch better than you.''

Angie turned to Meenie and Raul, her eyes beseeching. ''Please stop him.''

Meenie shrugged. ''He's bigger than me, and 'bout twice as stubborn when he gets his mind set on something. Might as well try to lasso a twister as to try to stop the sheriff.''

Raul smiled sympathetically. ''He has to go, Mrs. Lassiter. The rest of us can't do it by ourselves.''

Angie stared at him. ''Why not? What can one wounded man accomplish that the rest of you can't. He's not Superman, even if he thinks he is.''

''He said he was going hunting, and he is. Except he's the bait to flush out Reynolds.''

Angie turned white and grabbed his arm. ''What do you mean?''

''He's hoping Reynolds will try again to kill him so we'll have positive proof he's the murderer.''

''But I don't want him risking his life proving Johnny's innocent for me, and that's why he's doing it,'' she cried.

Raul gently loosened her clutching fingers. ''That's where you're wrong. He's not doing it for you. He's doing it for himself.''

CHAPTER

20

CHARLES GRASPED THE SADDLE HORN AND TOOK A deep breath. His back burned and throbbed with every move of his arms and shoulders. The pain radiated from his wound down to his hips and up to the top of his skull. But he wasn't going to give up, and he wasn't going to faint. He was going to mount that damn horse if it killed him, and the way he felt now, it very well might.

"Need a leg up, Sheriff?" asked Judge Nourse.

Charles pulled himself into the saddle and hung on until the ground stopped reeling. He glanced at the old man who looked as fresh as if he'd had a full night's sleep and lost thirty years in the process. "How old did you say you were, Judge Nourse?"

The judge straightened his broad, bony shoulders. "I didn't. You know, Sheriff, if the law won't let me drive, I'll think I'll buy a horse. I can ride it down to the doughnut shop and have coffee every morning. I can tie it up to somebody's fender since there aren't any hitching posts anymore. What do you think?"

Charles kicked his horse and led his posse out. "I think you're crazy."

The judge chuckled. "Anybody who lives as long as I have is a little crazy, Sheriff. Except when you pass the seventy-five-year mark, you're eccentric, not crazy."

Charles took several deep breaths to clear his head. "Rodriquez, where should we start?"

The ranger was silent a moment, his eyes raking the horizon to the south of headquarters. "I think he'll be in the same general area. He's got to come back to the house if he's thinking of trying to escape. He needs money, identification, transportation. I think we should ride down the riverbed where there's cover, and have the helicopter try to chase him that way. If the rest of the deputies can make a loose circle to the west, he'll be caught between us and them."

Charles shook his head and fought the dizziness the motion caused. "He'll never take another shot at me, then. There'll be too many witnesses. Meenie, get on the walkie-talkie, and tell the deputies what the situation is. I don't want anybody shooting Johnny while we're trying to trap Reynolds. Tell them to start toward the river, but to stay back at least a mile or more. Reynolds can't know they're anywhere near. Tell the copter pilot to fly a random pattern on this side of the river. If he sees anybody, tell us, but don't let Reynolds knew he's been spotted."

"What if it ain't Reynolds?" asked Meenie. "What if it's Johnny?"

"Damn it! Just do what I tell you for a change, and stop arguing with me," Charles snapped.

Surprisingly Meenie did, and Charles realized the deputy knew he'd pushed far enough. Clutching the saddle horn, he listened to Meenie's voice giving instructions and was thankful J.T. had offered to carry his rifle. He had all he could do just staying on, much less balancing a rifle across the saddle. "When do we cut over to the river Rodriquez?"

The ranger turned his horse. "Now," he said. "Hang on. It's not really very steep here, but it'll seem like it to you. Riding down an incline on a horse isn't what I'd recommend for a wounded man."

"It can't be any worse than riding across a pasture,"

Charles said. A minute later he realized it was. Every step the mare took sent spasms of pain through his back. He hung on grimly, leaning back in the saddle to compensate for the forty-five-degree angle of his horse.

Finally the horse leveled out, and he let out his breath. It was cooler on the river, where giant cottonwoods provided shade. The only bad part was the swarms of gnats that seemed to pick him out to torment. He rode in a half-conscious state, time and distance seeming to blur together into one long, insect-ridden eternity. He jerked himself out of his stupor when the judge's voice broke the silence.

"Here it is, the Santiago Plaza. You were shot on the bluff just above."

Charles looked closely at the ruins of foundations that stretched to the edge of the river. Weeds and salt cedar softened the starkness of the flat, sandstone rocks that formed the walls of the plaza. Weathered logs, many of them still showing charred ends where they had burned through and collapsed, choked the interiors of what used to be rooms. There was something infinitely sad about the ruins, a brooding quality that pulled at his mind.

"It didn't used to be so close to the river," the judge said softly. "River's changed its course since then. In fact, the river's a whole lot different than it was when the Santiagos built the plaza, different even than when my dad first saw it. Used to be only about twenty feet wide most places, and deep. There was always water in it then, and lots of bushes growing along the bank. Some people claim the cattle grazed down the grass and killed the bushes, and that changed the river. I don't think that's true. God knows there were more buffalo grazing and drinking from the river than cattle for hundreds of years, and the river never changed. I think it was when all the beaver were trapped and their dams destroyed. The river could run where it pleased then. So now the Canadian is what you see: a broad, sandy river without much water excepting during flood stage.''

The judge reined in his horse and dismounted. He pointed toward the bluff. ''There was a spring back of the plaza for drinking water. Most of these old plazas were built near a spring. The Canadian used to be a springfed river. Most of the springs are gone now. Oh, you hear some of the ranchers talking about water leaking out of the sides of some of the bluffs, but only in spring when the snows are melting. Country's changing; the water's disappearing. I read one prediction that the Panhandles' got enough water to last about twenty years before we run out. If that happens, gonna be some desperate people around here. There's going to be towns, whole communities that look just like this plaza, just ruins where people used to live.''

The judge stared at the west end of the plaza. ''I'm glad I won't be around to see it, Sheriff.''

Charles dismounted, stumbling and falling to his knees. He wondered later if luck, instinct, or some uneasy ghost had been responsible for his not trying to retain his balance. Perhaps it was only his own weariness. Whatever it was, it saved his life. He stared numbly as his contrary little mare jerked and screamed when the bullet tore through her belly.

Rodriquez rode between Charles and the river, slipping sideways off his mount but managing to keep hold of the reins, forcing the horse to provide cover. He grabbed Charles around the waist and supported him as he pulled him along. ''Hang on, Sheriff. It's just a few yards to the old foundations. It's not much, but it's the only cover that really gives any protection.''

''Sheriff! Are you all right?'' screamed Meenie as he reined his horse in a tight circle, crouching low in the saddle to offer less of a target.

''I'm all right!'' shouted Charles, sweat half blinding him

as he stumbled along by Rodriquez. "Stay away from me, and get under cover."

The judge vaulted over the ruined foundation of the Santiago house with the ease of a much younger man. Charles thought a man never knew what physical feats he was capable of until someone was using him as a target. He rolled over the foundation, groaning as his shoulder hit the ground. He lifted his head and glanced around quickly. J.T. and Raul were hugging the foundation, J.T. with a rifle pointed toward the other side of the river. Meenie was crawling toward him, his revolver drawn, and a dangerous look on his face.

"You're bleedin', Sheriff. Did the bastard hit you again?"

Charles looked at his shoulder where blood was soaking through his shirt. "He must have, I guess. I don't feel anything."

Meenie pulled at Charles' shirt, freeing his shoulder. "Just nicked the top of your shoulder. It's not nearly as bad as your back, but it's bleeding pretty good. Let me tear off this sleeve and bind it up, stop the bleeding."

"I'm hard on shirts today," Charles joked, then groaned as the numbness of shock wore off and his new wound started to hurt. Amazing how such a small place could hurt so badly.

"Judge, put that horse out of its misery," yelled Meenie over the dying screams of Charles's mare.

"I'll do it," J.T. said, aiming his rifle at the thrashing mare. "I don't need someone else to do my dirty work for me."

The sound of the shot echoed off the surrounding bluffs, and Charles closed his eyes. In some indefinable way the mare's death seemed to underscore the savagery of the whole case. Opening his eyes, he glanced around the jagged remnants of the plaza. Once more it was a mute witness to violent death.

"Why doesn't he fire again?" J.T. asked, nervously sighting down his rifle.

"He may think he killed the sheriff this time," Raul answered. "Or he may be waiting for a better shot."

"He must have crossed the river to throw us off," said Judge Nourse. "Or he may be drifting toward Amarillo. It's about fifty or so miles southeast of here."

"So much for our plans," Charles said grimly. "The posse is on this side of the river. Meenie, radio that copter pilot and tell him to take a swing over. If he sees anybody, tell him to shoot. I'm not in the mood to be a target anymore, and I want him any way I can get him."

"Sheriff, that walkie-talkie's hanging on my saddle horn, and my horse took off down the river."

Charles cursed long, feverently, and imaginatively, until even Judge Nourse looked at him in awe. Pulling himself over to a wall, he rested his uninjured shoulder against it. "How much ammunition do we have?"

"You got any more than what you got in your belt?" Meenie asked Raul.

Silently Raul shook his head.

Charles shifted to look at J.T. "How much do we have for the rifles?"

J.T. reached in his pocket and pulled out a single box of shells. "This, plus what's already loaded in our guns. I never expected to have to stand off an attack."

"I didn't either, J.T.," Charles said. "Everybody fire a shot in the air. No, wait a minute. As long as we're shooting, we might as well make it count. Did anybody see where the shot came from?"

Rodriquez cautiously peered over the wall. "I think it came from that sand dune, the one by the clump of salt cedar. It's the best place I think. He can move down the river in either direction for fifty yards or more without being exposed. Of course, he may have decided not to hang around."

"No. Remember he still thinks we're after Johnny. He'll

stay there until I'm dead and Johnny can take the blame. Lay a line of fire along that dune.''

"Waste of ammunition, Sheriff," Meenie said. "We can't see anybody over there."

Charles leaned his head against the wall, his wounds beginning to make him feverish. "I know, Meenie, but the sound of gunfire may alert the helicopter. I don't have any wish to emulate the Santiagos by being pinned up here until we're all wounded or dead."

Meenie rested his revolver on the wall. "Everybody try to kick some sand. If that pilot can't hear the shots, maybe he can see them."

Charles held up his hand. "Wait until we hear the helicopter making his sweep on the top of the bluff."

Everyone was motionless as they listened for the approaching sound. "There it is," Charles whispered as a whirling sound became audible. "Now," he said, bringing his hand down.

The shots echoed and re-echoed along the river, and the resulting clouds of sand were lifted by the wind to curtain the dune. A bullet whined over the plaza, chipping one of the sandstone walls, as Reynolds returned their fire. Everyone grinned as they saw the helicopter swoop down toward the river.

"We'll see some action now," Meenie shouted, throwing his hat in the air.

Charles turned and peered through a clink in the wall. The helicopter was over the river down, dropping close to the ground. He could see the sun glint off a rifle barrel as the copilot leaned out. He didn't know if the deputy was actually able to fire or not, and as Reynolds snapped off two quick rounds, it didn't really matter. One bullet caught the rotor, while the other hit the pilot. Charles was unfamiliar with aircraft of any description, but he could imagine the panic inside the cockpit as the remaining deputy fought to avoid what was really inevitable.

He found he couldn't turn away, couldn't close his eyes, but was instead was frozen in place, watching in horror as the helicopter crashed in the middle of the Canadian, exploding in a brilliant flash of light. An oily cloud of smoke mushroomed from the wreck as the figure of a man struggled from the burning cockpit, turning back to drag a body from the inferno.

Charles crawled toward the judge and grabbed the spare rifle. "Shoot, damn it! Give them covering fire!"

"They're both hurt," Raul cried.

Rodriquez vaulted over the wall, firing his gun from the hip, running a zigzag course toward the river. The greasy cloud of smoke spread a gray, wavering screen between the plaza and the opposite bank. The ranger hit the shallow water of the river, sending geysers of spray into the air.

"Don't anyone miss and hit those men," shouted Charles for the ringing burst of gunfire. Bracing his rifle on the wall, he fired repeatedly, ignoring the spasm of pain as the recoil slammed into his wounded shoulder. Out of the corner of his eye he saw Raul leap over the wall to run crouched over to the edge of the bank.

"Hurry up, damn it!" shouted Charles as the slim figure of his deputy lifted the limp body of one man onto his shoulders in a classic fireman's carry.

A bullet ricocheted off one of the foundations just as Raul reached it. J.T. reached up to help with the wounded man while Rodriquez half dragged the other across the open plaza and into cover. The ranger fell to the ground, his breaths coming in heaving shudders. "Someone else take the next turn," he panted.

Charles crawled over to check the copilot. "Where are you hit?"

The man sat up holding one arm. "I think I broke my arm,

and I'm burned some, but I'll make it. Eddie is hurt bad. That bastard shot him.''

"Raul, J.T., how is the pilot?'' Charles asked, taking off his shirt.

Raul crossed himself. "He's dead, Sheriff. The bullet got him in the chest. I don't think he was alive when he hit the ground.''

The copilot sat quietly, tears making white furrows down his smoke-blackened cheeks. "Damn it to hell, Sheriff. He was my friend. We flew copters in 'Nam together, and never had a scratch, either one of us. Who is that bastard, Sheriff? What's he done?''

"He killed two men and tried to frame somebody else for the murders. And he wants to kill me.''

The copilot looked at the bandage around Charles's chest and the torn sleeve binding up his shoulder. "Well, he's sure as hell tryin', isn't he?''

Charles smiled reluctantly and ripped his shirts into strips. "I guess you might say that. Here, I'm going to make a sling for that arm to at least keep it immobile until we can get to back to the ranch.''

The man wiped at his eyes. "When's that going to be?''

Charles shrugged his shoulders. "Until the posse hears all the shooting and comes to investigate. Surely they'll have sense enough to cross the river and get behind him.''

"You know, Sheriff,'' the copilot said, supporting his arm while Charles made a sling. "I was just tellin' Eddie I was tired of flying around tryin' to catch speeders, that I joined the Department of Public Safety to do something more exciting than that.'' He was silent a moment. "I never wanted this much excitement.''

Charles shivered as the hot wind blew against his feverish body. That's all he needed: fever and chills. He jerked as the judge touched his arm.

"Sheriff, there has to be a way out of here. After all, Dolores escaped with the crucifix."

Charles glanced around the plaza, letting his memory of the sketches overlay his perception. The bluff rose behind the Santiago's home. A young, frightened woman carrying a baby and a heavy crucifix couldn't have scaled it. If she'd tried running along the base of the canyon wall, she would've been seen. But if she didn't leave, where could she have hidden, and why didn't she come out when help arrived? "Judge, what did these old plazas look like? How were they constructed. Were there tunnels, or hiding places in case of Indian attacks?"

The judge frowned. "They were all pretty much alike, dirt floors, cottonwood rafters with a layer of mud, then a layer of dirt on top that. This one had stone walls held together with a mortar made of adobe. Most of them were just plain adobe. If any of them had tunnels, I never heard of it. The Indians were on the reservation before these sheepherders ever came to the Panhandle, so these places weren't constructed for defense."

Charles's eyes focused on a thicker section of wall rising like a jagged tooth from the foundation. "Santiago and his son both tried to get Casados to help them. Why did they need help, and what did the priest mean when he said Dolores was safe and beyond Diego's reach?"

"What are you getting, at Sheriff?" Meenie asked.

Raul's soft voice answered. "To a priest, being safe meant Dolores was in God's hands."

Judge Nourse nodded. "And in God's hands meant she was dead."

"Exactly," Charles said. "Dolores never left the Santiago plaza that night. Her father and brother hid her, the baby, and the crucifix, but they didn't count on Casados setting fire to the plaza. And she couldn't come out when J.T.'s grandfather arrived with his cowboys because she was already dead.''

"But where?'' the judge burst out. "Casados searched the house and couldn't find her.''

Charles pointed toward the fireplace. "Dirt floors, Judge, and a huge fireplace. It's my guess they dug a hole, put Dolores and her baby with the crucifix in it, covered it up with a board and firewood, and prepared to sacrifice themselves to save her. But Diego burned them out instead. The smoke probably asphyxiated her. Of course, they might have hidden her somewhere else, but the fireplace would've been the best bet because they could hide the evidence of digging.''

"Then how did Willie find the crucifix?'' J.T. asked, staring with horrified fascination at the fireplace.

"His sketch was absolutely accurate as to size and location of the plaza. He probably spent a lot of time down here before he painted it, and found the crucifix by accident.''

"And Dolores and the baby? Why didn't he say anything about finding them?'' demanded the judge.

"He may have,'' Charles answered. "That may be why he had Dolores crouching by the fireplace and the priest holding up the crucifix for a final blessing.''

"That's a good idea, Sheriff,'' Meenie said, "but if we don't want to end up like the sheepherders, we better think up a way to get out of here.''

Charles took a handful of shells from the box and stuffed them in his pocket. "The only way out that I can see is for someone to climb the bluff, cross the river downstream, and come up behind Reynolds. Otherwise, he's going to circle around us and pick us off one at a time from the top of the bluff. I don't know where that posse is, but I'm not willing to wait for them to arrive in time for a burial detail.''

"I'll go up the bluff,'' Meenie said, "but I want a rifle. Don't want to get any closer than fifty yards to him, and this revolver just ain't the best gun for any long distance shootin'.

Everybody cover me, 'cause I'm gonna be a sittin' duck while I'm climbin'.''

Charles reloaded his rifle. "Judge, give him your gun. And Meenie, don't worry about being a target. He'll be too busy to shoot at you."

"What do you mean?" Meenie asked, his eyes narrowing suspiciously.

"Because he'll be shooting at me," Charles said as he rose and jumped over the low foundation.

"Damn it to hell, Sheriff!" screamed Meenie. "Get back here!"

Charles ignored him and ran toward a tall cottonwood, flattening himself against it. "Reynolds!" he called. "Reynolds, I'm coming after you."

Her jerked back as a bullet chipped off a piece of bark. "You missed, Reynolds. Your shot with the buffalo gun must have been blind luck."

Charles dropped to the ground. Lying on his stomach, he peered around the tree trunk toward the opposite bank. Thanking God he used to watch cowboy movies, he placed his hat over his rifle barrel, and raised his gun. A bullet knocked it spinning to the ground. Charles screamed, putting all the pain he felt into it. Still lying prone he examined the sand dune foot by foot. Something moved behind the screen of salt cedars, perhaps only the wind, perhaps not.

He sighted carefully, bracing himself with his elbows. He had to make this shot count. He didn't know if he had the strength to try again. Sight and sound were fading in and out, and chills were beginning to catch him without warning, rippling through his body and causing muscles to quiver uncontrollably. His finger began to tighten imperceptibly around the trigger when a flash of movement on the mesa behind his target distracted him. Thank God, the cavalry had arrived! The deputies were behind Reynolds. The killer was surrounded.

Charles lowered his gun to demand Reynolds's surrender when the figure on the mesa became distinct. Charles cursed and raised his gun again. Damn Johnny Brentwood for standing out in the open like some movie hero from a bad film. These guns had real bullets, and he wouldn't get up at the end of a scene if Reynolds shot him.

"Reynolds! Back here!" Johnny's words carried easily across the river, and the sound of Charles's shot was swallowed up as the two actors in the drama being played out on the opposite bank fired simultaneously.

Charles was up and staggering drunkenly toward the river before the echoes had died. He could see Reynolds's body sprawled limply in the middle of a salt cedar bush, but Johnny had fallen off the mesa and was hidden from view. "Don't move, Johnny; I'm coming!"

He heard footsteps behind him and felt Meenie steady him as he stumbled into the water. "I'm all right," he snapped, shrugging off his deputy's hand.

He seemed to be running in slow motion, the shallow water and sand sucking at his feet, holding him back. He fell to his knees, catching himself with his hands, and felt Meenie and Raul haul him to his feet. "Thanks," he panted, and kept going, out of the water, up over the sand dune to the bottom of the mesa, and the crumpled body of Johnny Brentwood.

He fell to his knees and turned Johnny over, his eyes going immediately to the obscene blossom of crimson sprouting from his chest. Helplessly he pressed his hand against the wound, trying to halt the bleeding. "Johnny, hang on. We'll get you to a doctor."

The hazel eyes so like Angie's opened. "Wasn't going to let him kill you. Angie needs you."

"Why did you stand up there like that? Why didn't you stay undercover? Why did you shoot him?"

Johnny drew a shallow breath. "I wasn't going to let him have the ranch."

"You damn stupid kid! Angie would get the ranch!"

Johnny coughed. Charles watched helplessly as the crimson thread of blood trickled from the corner of the his mouth. "Might kill Angie. Couldn't take the chance."

"But why did you stand up and make yourself a target?" demanded Charles. He saw J.T. grasp his son's hand and felt Meenie and Raul stir beside him.

Johnny looked at his father and the two deputies, then raised his eyes to see Rodriquez and the judge. Weakly he lifted a hand. "Go 'way. Want to talk to the sheriff." A spasm of coughing shook his body.

Charles looked at the other men. "Get out of here!" he snapped.

Johnny turned his head to watch as the men reluctantly left. He lifted his hand beckoning Charles closer. "Take care of Angie and the girls. And the ranch."

Charles squeezed Johnny's hand. "You're not going to die, damn you. I won't let you!"

"Not your choice, Sheriff."

Charles felt the tears wetting his cheeks. "Why, Johnny? Why did you do it? He might have killed you and still gotten away."

Johnny smiled. "I always hit what I aim at, Sheriff, and Kurt doesn't sometimes. Those are good odds."

"You're a lousy gambler, Johnny."

Johnny closed his eyes. "I always was, Sheriff." He opened his eyes to look at Charles. "This is better anyway. I never could stand jails."

"You wouldn't have gone to jail. We found the tally book, and we broke Reynolds's alibi. You're letting yourself die for nothing."

Johnny's eyes shifted toward the sky. "No, Sheriff, I'm

dying for something. I'm paying my debts and leaving the ranch free and clear.''

Charles cupped Johnny's chin. "It's all over! Don't you understand? We know how Reynolds killed Willie and Skinny. You're free. You won't go to jail or even stand trial. So hang on, damn it!"

Johnny smiled sadly. "I don't think so, Sheriff," he whispered. His body sagged as he lapsed into unconsciousness.

Charles looked up. "J.T., come hold him. Keep his head elevated so he can breath."

He stood up and clutched Meenie's arm for support. "Think those horses are close enough to catch?"

Meenie nodded toward the river. "Don't matter now. Damn posse finally decided to show up. He still alive?" he asked, jerking his head toward Johnny.

"Barely," Charles answered.

"What did he want to tell you?" Meenie asked.

Charles wiped his forehead and watched as a Potter County deputy helped J.T. put Johnny on a horse. "I don't know," he finally answered. "A lot of melodramatic nonsense about paying his debts."

Meenie looked at the bluffs lining the opposite side of the river, his eyes unfocused. "All the evidence still points to him. Is that why he let himself be shot? Did he owe a debt he figured was past due?"

Charles stared at his deputy as the meaning of his question became clear. "So help me, God, Meenie, I don't know."

EPILOGUE

CHARLES SCRATCHED HIS CHEST. THE WIDE BANDAGE itched abominably. Another week and it could come off, the doctor had promised, then had launched into a tirade about people who go rolling around dirty river bottoms and getting gunshot wounds infected instead getting proper treatment. The doctor had said the same thing every day of the week Charles had spent in the hospital, and he was heartily sick of the lecture.

Opening the door, Miss Poole balanced a tray of coffee and cups on one hip. "I saw you sneak in, Sheriff, and made some coffee."

She set the tray on his desk. "The doctor called a few minutes ago to tell me to see that you left early the next two weeks. You know, Sheriff, if you'd gone straight to the hospital for treatment instead of being a macho hero, you wouldn't have had that infection."

"Miss Poole," Charles roared, "I've already heard what a fool I am once this morning. I don't need it from you."

"You must be feeling better. You're yelling again."

"I'm not," Charles said in a lower tone of voice.

"Did you see the judge and Mr. Rodriquez off this morning?" Miss Poole asked, wisely changing the subject.

Charles nodded. "Yes, and it was a three-ring circus. All three national networks had camera crews there. Crawford County is famous."

"You missed the memorial service at the cemetery for Dolores Santiago and her baby," Miss Poole said.

Charles leaned cautiously back and put his feet on his desk. "She's not really there, you know."

Miss Poole blinked, totally disconcerted for the first time since he'd met her. "Well, my goodness, where is she?"

"She's buried next to her father and brother behind the ruins of the plaza. I think she'd rather be there than in a cemetery alone. J.T. pointed out the graves. He said his grandfather showed them to him. Another year and there'll be no trace of Dolores's grave, and she can have some peace."

Charles carefully lowered his feet to the floor and got up. Walking to the window, he looked down at the crowds still gathered on the courthouse steps. Most of the town had turned out to watch Judge Nourse and Rodriquez accept the crucifix this morning. He thought of the speech he'd made as he'd laid the crucifix in the judge's gnarled hands, a speech extolling truth, justice, repentance, and two men's determination to redress old wrongs, and felt his grief choke him.

He braced his hands on the windowsill and leaned his forehead against the cool glass. He could have said something else. He could have talked of paying one's debts, of laying down one's life in retribution for sins. But that would have sounded too much like a sermon, and he wouldn't have handled it well, anyway. The crowd would have sensed his hesitancy, his uncertainty, because, damn it, he was uncertain. Was Johnny a murderer or not? Had Reynolds used that guilt as a cover for his own attempt at murder?

"Sheriff, what's wrong? You're white as a sheet. You better sit down before you fall. In fact, you better go home. I'm calling Meenie in to take you."

Charles turned away from the window. "I'm fine, Miss Poole. I'll have a cup of coffee, and I'll sit down. You'd better get back to the radio. You've been in here five minutes already. The last time you left Slim alone that long, he took apart the radio with a screwdriver.''

Miss Poole looked smug. "I hid all the screwdrivers, Sheriff."

Charles sat down and poured himself a cup of coffee. "Very wise, Miss Poole." He took an infinitesimal sip of the brew and cleared his throat several times. Miss Poole had outdone herself. She must have used the whole can of coffee in one pot. He'd be willing to swear he'd lost half the lining of his esophagus with that one sip.

"Thanks for the coffee, Miss Poole. It's just what I needed." If he were interested in scrubbing out the drunk tank he thought silently.

Miss Poole blushed and walked to the door. "I hope so, Sheriff. You have more color in your face already." She waved her fingers and went out.

Charles fumbled in his desk drawer for antacid pills. Jalapeño peppers put color in your face, too, but he wouldn't recommend them any more than he would Miss Poole's coffee. "Come in," he mumbled through a mouthful of chalky white pills.

Angie hesitantly came in. "Charles, may I talk to you?"

He got up quickly. "Of course, Angie. Sit here," he said, pointing to his own chair.

She sat down, and nervously pleated her fingers together. Her left hand still looked bruised, but the swelling was gone. "Charles, Johnny's not responding to treatment. He wakes up, recognizes us, then is unconscious again. It's as if he wants to die. I don't know what to do anymore. When he was younger, I could always talk him out of these spells, but—"

"You mean he's acted this way before?"

Surprised, Angie looked up at him. "Of course. Everytime he felt guilty about something, he'd lock himself away in his room and refuse to talk to anyone. Dad always said being locked up alone was Johnny's way of punishing himself. But Charles, this time he could die!''

Charles turned away and walked to the window. Somehow he had to offer comfort, tell her it would be all right. But it wouldn't. This time Johnny had done something that demanded a punishment greater than merely locking himself away from people. Angie's voice interrupted his thoughts.

"I should have known he didn't kill Willie and Skinny when he didn't try to punish himself. But I was so wrapped up in my own problems and so angry with him for gambling, I never thought. Then the evidence was so strong, and I knew how much he loved the ranch, I just accepted his guilt. I should have known better. Johnny never killed anything in his life. He owns one of the most valuable gun collections in the Panhandle, and the only thing he's ever shot at is a target. He won't even go hunting. And when we butcher a steer, he always makes sure he has something else to do. That's why it's so incredible that he killed Reynolds."

Charles stalked across the room, and plucked Angie out of the chair. He kissed her exurberantly, grabbed his hat, and pulled her through the door with him. "Meenie, Raul, pull the report on Reynolds's autopsy and meet me at the hospital. And hurry, damn it!" He herded Angie past Miss Poole's desk and on to the stairs. Taking Angie's hand, he took the stairs two at a time. God, if after all this he were too late, he knew he could never forgive himself. He hit the front door at a run and almost pushed Angie into a patrol car. Flipping on his siren, he backed out and drove toward the hospital.

"Charles, what is this all about?"

"Later, Angie. Right now I have to talk to Johnny."

Angie grabbed the dashboard as Charles rounded a corner and into the hospital parking lot. "If you don't tell me what this is all about, I'm going to wring your neck, Charles Matthews."

"As soon as I've talked to Johnny, you're welcome to

try." He got out of the car, helped her out, and ran for the door. "However, I ought to warn you, any wrestling match with me might end differently than you intended."

He grinned at her shocked expression, grabbed her hand, and ran down the hospital corridor and into the Intensive Care Unit. Walking up to the bed, he put his hand on Johnny's shoulder. "Wake up, son."

A nurse whipped into the room, her double chin quivering with agitation. "Sheriff, leave that boy alone. He's very sick, and I won't have you bothering him."

Charles shook Johnny vigorously. "You're wrong, nurse. He's not a boy; he's a man. Aren't you, Johnny? And men don't run away and hide. Now wake up and listen to me."

"I'll call an orderly and have you thrown out, Sheriff," threatened the nurse.

Meenie and Raul came in, Meenie tipping his hat politely to the flustered nurse. "Excuse me, ma'am, I need to talk to the sheriff."

Charles stuck his hand out. "Did you bring it?"

Raul handed Charles a folder. "Yes, but it may be too late."

Charles slapped Johnny's face. "No, it's not. I won't let it be. Wake up, damn it!"

"Sheriff!" J.T. cried, rising from a chair in the corner. "What are you doing?"

"I don't know what he's doing, but I trust him. Please sit down," Angie said. She whirled on the nurse. "Don't you interfere, either."

Johnny's eyes opened. "You don't give up, do you, Sheriff?"

Charles knelt by the bed. "No, I don't, Johnny, because I'm a man. Even when I'm wrong, or when I commit some crime, I'm still a man. And a man accepts whatever self-loathing, or self-punishment his conscience deals out, and goes on. Are you a man, or a kid, Johnny?"

"My God, Sheriff! What are you tryin' to do to the kid? Let him go?"

"Shut up, Meenie!" Charles said savagely. "He's not a kid. He's a man. Aren't you, Johnny?"

Johnny turned his head to look at Charles. "I couldn't let him kill you."

Charles gripped the younger man's hand. "But you couldn't shoot even him without making it into a fair fight, could you?"

Johnny sighed. "No, Sheriff."

"You're a good man, Johnny Brentwood, perhaps a better man than anyone in this room. Now, are you going to get well?" Charles demanded.

"Yes," Johnny whispered.

"Good!" Charles said. "Now I'm going to take away your guilt. You never killed Kurt Reynolds. *I* did."

Johnny propped himself up on his elbow, confusion and hope clouding his eyes. "But I shot him, and I always hit what I aim for."

"You've never aimed at a man before, Johnny. Your conscience wouldn't let you kill him even when you wanted to. It was my bullet that killed him. I have the autopsy report right here if you want to see it."

Johnny fell back on the pillow, tears trickling from the corners of his eyes. "Thank you, Sheriff."

Charles rose and pressed Johnny's shoulder. "Go back to sleep, Johnny, and get well."

He leaned over and kissed Angie lightly. "I'll be back tonight."

Meenie and Raul followed him out of the room. "What would you've done if he looked at the autopsy report, Sheriff?" Raul asked.

Charles leaned against the wall, his strength suddenly deserting him. "I was gambling he wouldn't want to."

Meenie shifted his tobacco and aimed for a nearby spittoon. "I reckon there was more than one good man in that room just now."

Charles slapped his deputy on the shoulder. "No, just one slightly battered county sheriff that just occasionally does something right. Now, let's get back to the courthouse and have a cup of coffee."

Raul and Meenie looked stricken. "I think I need to check with the jailer, Sheriff," Raul said. "He's having trouble with a prisoner."

"I gotta help Raul, Sheriff. You never know when we might have a riot on our hands," Meenie said.

"We've got two drunks in jail, neither one of them under sixty. You just don't want to drink Miss Poole's coffee."

"I had a cup last week and my stomach's still burnin'," said Meenie.

"I was planning to use Judge Nourse's recipe," said Charles. "One part coffee to ten parts brandy. But, of course, if there's a riot . . ."

Meenie and Raul looked at each other. "What the hell, Sheriff," said Meenie. "Ain't nothin' the jailer can't handle himself." He grinned and aimed at the spittoon again.

ABOUT THE AUTHOR

Award-winning author D. R. MEREDITH has lent distinction to Ballantine's crime fiction list with her John Lloyd Branson series: MURDER BY IMPULSE, MURDER BY DECEPTION, MURDER BY MASQUERADE, and MURDER BY REFERENCE. Additionally, she had completed four installments in a cycle of novels featuring Sheriff Charles Matthews. The second novel in that series, THE SHERIFF AND THE BRANDING IRON MURDERS, is the sequel to THE SHERIFF AND THE PANHANDLE MURDERS. A former librarian and bookstore owner, Ms. Meredith lives in Amarillo, Texas, with her husband and their two children.